THE PRICE OF MURDER

ALAN MOODY

A CATHERINE FORRESTER MYSTERY

Copyright © 2025 Alan Moody
All rights reserved.

No part of this book may be reproduced, stored in a retrieval system, or transmitted in any form or by any means — electronic, mechanical, photocopying, recording, or otherwise — without the prior written permission of the publisher, except for brief quotations used in reviews or scholarly works.

This is a work of fiction. Names, characters, places, and events are either the product of the author's imagination or used fictitiously. Any resemblance to actual persons, living or dead, or actual events is purely coincidental.

First published in Great Britain by Alan Moody
Cover design by Alan Moody

For more books by Alan Moody, visit:
www.alanmoodymystery.com, alanmoody1234@gmail.com

To my Soph, my own personal Catherine Forrester.

If you enjoy this book, please head back to Amazon and put on a positive review, this will help me keep on writing.

Main Characters

Reginald Price- Head of the Price household in every way.

Marion Price- Reginald's wife.

Catherine Forrester- Reginald's and Marion's daughter.

Peter Price- Reginald's and Marion's son.

David Forrester- Catherines husband.

Philip Marsh- Reginald's business partner.

Inspector Tom Stowe- Inspector investigating the murder.

Debbie Stowe- Tom's wife

Detective Micheal Harris- Investigating murder.

Henshaw- The Butler.

Chapter 1: Catherine Forrester

The wind stirred gently along Elm Road that evening, rustling the bare branches of the sycamores and sending a low sigh through the quiet street. The air had that clean, brittle sharpness of early winter, the kind that nipped at cheeks, slipped beneath coat collars, and settled stubbornly into scarves. Porch lights glowed like distant beacons through a gauzy mist, casting long shadows onto pavements swept clean of anything interesting.

Television flickers blinked behind drawn curtains. Somewhere, the metallic bark of a dog echoed and faded. A fox, lean and pale, paused beneath a streetlamp, eyes glinting, before darting away into the hedges, unseen by all, save the night.

Elm Road was the kind of place where nothing ever happened. Where people mowed their lawns on Saturdays and asked after each other's children with mild sincerity. Where hedges were trimmed, bins were lined up like soldiers, and curtains were drawn more out of habit than secrecy. The kind of street where the most scandalous event of the past year was Mrs. Denning's cat being accidentally shut inside a wheelie bin for twelve hours, and even that had been smoothed over with tea and apology biscuits.

But inside the Price Mansion, warmth bloomed.

The Price house was old-fashioned in the best way: lived-in, not curated. Welcoming. The scent of polish clung faintly to the woodwork, mingling with pine smoke and something sweet, mulling spices, perhaps, or a recently extinguished candle. Firelight danced on the walls of the drawing room, casting shifting amber shadows over bookshelves, worn leather chairs, and portraits whose subjects hadn't been spoken of in years. A faded rug spread beneath the furniture like a memory trying not to be forgotten. Somewhere deeper in the house, the steady tick of the grandfather clock marked time like a calm heartbeat.

Catherine Forrester lounged in her chair like a cat in late afternoon sun, one arm draped lazily over the side, a glass of red wine held loosely in her other hand. Her dark hair, once neatly pinned, had begun to rebel, curling into soft, errant wisps around her face. Her legs were tucked beneath her, stocking feet just visible beneath the hem of her long knit dress. Her amusement, as always, hung in the air like perfume, light, unmistakable, and difficult to ignore.

"Nothing ever happens on this street," she declared with a sigh, eyes fixed on the fire. "It's all so desperately, aggressively dull."

Her younger brother, Peter, perched on the sofa across from her, sleeves rolled to the elbow, brow furrowed in concentration. A half-built model Spitfire lay before him on the coffee table, surrounded by glue tubes, tiny painted parts, and scraps of packaging. He didn't look up.

"That's rather the point, isn't it?" he replied. "Some of us prefer not living in a soap opera."

Catherine gave a languid smirk. "That's exactly what someone in a soap opera would say. Right before their kitchen explodes. Or they discover their husband is also their uncle."

Peter finally glanced up, the corner of his mouth twitching. "If our kitchen explodes, it'll be because you insisted on reheating mulled wine directly on the hob. Again."

"That was once. And it was barely a flame."

"It scorched the ceiling."

David Forrester chuckled from his armchair by the hearth, long legs stretched toward the fire, one hand absently rubbing the back of his neck. There was a tired affection in his eyes as he looked at his wife, half exasperated, half charmed. A softness lingered there that hadn't faded, despite everything.

"She'd be disappointed if anything *did* happen," he said. "She'd have nothing left to complain about."

"Don't be ridiculous," Catherine said, sipping her wine. "I'd thrive. I've been waiting years for a proper mystery. Something with stakes. A body, perhaps. Or a scandal. At the very least, a disappearance."

Peter snorted. "You sound like you're actively wishing for murder. I'm not sure that's healthy."

"I'm not *wishing* for it," she said, swirling the wine in her glass. "Just... prepared. Should the need arise."

David raised an eyebrow. "And what, exactly, would you do if a mystery did fall into your lap?"

"I'd solve it, obviously."

"Of course," Peter muttered. "Naturally."

"I'm serious," Catherine said, sitting upright now, a little flame of energy lighting behind her eyes. "I read all those detective novels growing up, Miss Marple, Poirot, Holmes. I know how it works. The truth's always in the details. People give themselves away if you know how to look."

David tilted his head. "And you think you know how to look?"

"I know how to listen," she replied. "That's the same thing."

A silence followed that, broken only by the slow crackling of the fire and the faint rattle of wind against the windows.

Peter leaned back and picked up a paintbrush. "Well, if something *is* going to happen, can it wait until after I finish this wing assembly?"

"No promises," Catherine said sweetly. "The universe works on its own schedule."

David laughed again, rubbing his eyes. "If something actually does happen on Elm Road, you'll be the first suspect. You sound far too eager."

"I'd be the last suspect," she said. "Too obvious. Everyone would assume I'm bluffing."

Peter shook his head. "That's not how murder works."

Catherine raised her glass in mock salute. "It is in the books."

Outside, the wind picked up, brushing the sycamores again, scattering the mist into threads. The fox returned to the edge of the garden, sat down on its haunches, and watched the house with unreadable eyes.

Inside, the fire snapped, a log settling deeper into the flames. Laughter faded into silence. Catherine swirled the last of her wine, lost in thought. The room glowed around her, quiet and contained.

"I'm just saying," she murmured, more to herself now, "still water runs deep. And this house, this street, it's been still far too long."

David glanced at her. "You're chasing ghosts, love."

Catherine smiled, the expression small and secretive. "Maybe. Or maybe I'm the only one who's been paying attention."

The grandfather clock struck nine, clear, deliberate. One chime for each hour past. It echoed faintly down the hall.

Catherine levelling a pointed look at Peter. "I was always three steps ahead of you in Cluedo."

"You were insufferable," he muttered, carefully adjusting the tiny wing of his model Spitfire without looking up.

"And undefeated," she added with a grin, raising her glass in mock salute. "You lot never stood a chance."

David shook his head, smiling in that half-exasperated, half-adoring way he reserved solely for his wife. "I remember that Christmas at Gran's. You made us all call you *Detective Forrester* for three straight days."

"Because I *earned* it," Catherine said triumphantly. "Not only did I solve the game in under ten minutes, I figured out who was sneaking off with the brandy."

She turned to the others with mock drama. "Spoiler: it was Gran. She was tipping it into her cocoa like a spy in a bad film."

Philip Marsh, leaning with practiced ease against the mantelpiece, swirled his brandy and let out a low, approving chuckle. "You had that look in your eye. Like you weren't playing a game, you were working a real case."

"I *was* working a case," Catherine said, her voice light but eyes bright. "Just fictional ones. For now."

Marion Price, sitting by the window with her knitting project untouched on her lap, sighed audibly. "Honestly, Catherine. Must everything be a performance?"

Catherine turned her smile toward her mother. It was dazzling, deliberate, and unapologetically cheeky. "Would you rather I took up baking?"

"I'd rather you sat still and stopped looking for corpses in the hydrangeas," Marion muttered, returning her gaze to the window.

"Only once," Catherine said under her breath, then grinned. "And in my defence, that hydrangea bush was suspiciously lumpy."

Laughter rippled around the room. Even Peter smirked behind the tailfin he was painting. The fire flared, sending a burst of sparks upward and casting the room briefly in shifting amber. The shadows flickered across the walls like dancers, stretching and retreating.

David reached for the wine bottle and refilled Catherine's glass without asking, an unspoken ritual between them, small but meaningful. His fingers brushed hers as he passed it back, and she didn't miss the way his touch lingered a half-second longer than it needed to.

"You know," he said, settling back into his chair, "sometimes I wonder if you *want* something terrible to happen. Just so you can dust off your imaginary magnifying glass and play Poirot."

She took the glass with a tilt of her head, not breaking eye contact. "If something terrible did happen, you'd all be glad I was here. I'd spot the killer before you even noticed someone was dead."

"I'd have the kettle on," David said.

"And I'd be dusting for fingerprints," she replied without missing a beat.

Peter gave a low whistle. "Morbid much?"

"It's a gift," Catherine said airily, sipping her wine.

"Delusional," Peter muttered, affection in the insult.

David was still watching her, his expression a little more thoughtful now. "You really believe that don't you? That you'd solve it?"

Catherine's eyes didn't waver. The grin softened just slightly, enough to show the steel beneath. "Yes. And so do you."

There was a beata moment that held more than anyone said. Then David shook his head, laughing. "You're impossible."

"And yet, you married me."

"I should have insisted on a background check."

She raised an eyebrow. "You'd never have passed mine."

From the mantel, Philip raised his glass. "Let's just hope Elm Road stays as boring as ever, then."

But Marion didn't laugh. She stared into the fire, her mouth a tight, unreadable line. When she spoke, it was soft, but the words landed like a dropped plate.

"Careful what you wish for."

The room stilled. The laughter didn't die, it withdrew. A heartbeat of silence followed, heavy enough to be felt in the chest.

Catherine tilted her head. "Was that... a threat, Mother?"

Marion didn't answer. She reached for her knitting instead, fingers clumsily finding the needles though she didn't cast on a stitch. Her eyes stayed on the flames.

To break the tension, Catherine flashed a grin. "Well, if something *does* happen, at least we'll have something new to talk about apart from Peter's airfix models."

Peter didn't even look up. He just lobbed a cushion at her. It missed by a full foot and thudded harmlessly against the fireplace.

"You know," David said, rubbing the bridge of his nose, "there's a small part of me that wonders how long it would take you to start suspecting *me* if anything ever went wrong."

Catherine's eyes lit up. "Three minutes."

He laughed. "That long?"

"I'd make tea first," she said. "You always confess after the second cup."

Their laughter returned, gentler this time. Warm. Familiar. Even Marion's mouth twitched into the ghost of a smile.

Outside, the wind pulled at the hedges again, a low moan curling down the street. A dog barked once, sharp and high. Somewhere down the lane, a torch flicked on, illuminating nothing but mist and fence posts. A shape moved near the road's edge. It lingered. Then slipped back into shadow.

Inside, no one noticed.

The fire crackled. The wine flowed. The clock ticked its slow rhythm. It was a moment held in amber, bright, burnished, and unknowing.

Outside, the fox vanished.

Inside, the wineglass emptied.

And Elm Road, for now, remained still.

Five years from now, in this very room, everything would be different.

A door would be locked.

A body would be found.

And Catherine Forrester, so quick to joke about death, so eager to play detective, would learn that real mysteries don't come with neat clues, perfect motives, or clever resolutions.

They come with grief.

And guilt.

And blood.

The game, when it finally arrived, would not be one she could win.

Chapter 2: Reginald's Rampage

Reginald Price was fifty but carried himself like someone who expected the world to answer when he called. His hair, once thick and dark, was now silvering at the temples in a way that suggested control rather than decay. He was tall, not imposing in stature but in presence, the kind of man whose voice rarely needed to rise to command a room. His suits were always well-cut, his cufflinks understated but expensive. He never fidgeted.

Reginald had the face of a man used to being listened to firm jaw, pale eyes that didn't wander, and a mouth that rarely smiled unless he was winning something. There was charm, when he wanted to use it, a sort of polished, practiced warmth but it slipped easily into coldness if someone disappointed him.

He'd built a company from nothing, or so he claimed, and treated it the way he treated most things: as something to be shaped, leveraged, or discarded when necessary. Family, business, reputation, they were all assets, in his view. Useful when aligned. Expendable when not.

Behind closed doors, Reginald was something else: secretive, calculating, restless. The study was his sanctuary. The silence, his armour. He trusted few, respected fewer, and forgave almost no one.

At fifty, Reginald Price was not a man in decline. He was a man planning his next move, one step ahead, as always. Or so he thought.

Reginald Price thundered through the grand halls of his mansion like a tempest barely contained.

Outside, the storm was in full cry, rain lashed the tall arched windows in staccato bursts, streaking down the glass like frantic brushstrokes. Wind howled through the gutters, and the distant boom of thunder underlined the mood inside like an ominous drumbeat.

But Reginald's rage outpaced even the weather.

His polished leather shoes struck the oak floor with punishing precision, crack, crack, crack, each step echoing off the high stone walls with the certainty of a man who had never once doubted his right to dominate. The house, a sprawling estate of cold grandeur and old money, felt smaller in his wake. Oppressive. Suffocating. As though the air itself braced when he entered a room.

He passed under the archway into the east wing, jaw clenched, breath sharp and uneven. His heavy wool coat flared as he walked, casting long, flapping shadows in the flickering gaslight.

"**Henshaw!**" he roared, his voice like a war horn splitting the hush.

The name crashed through the corridor, silencing everything.

From a side hallway, the elderly butler appeared as if conjured, already pale, already trembling. Henshaw had served the Price family for over three decades, and yet he still hadn't learned how to pre-empt Reginald's fury. No one had. It was unpredictable in the way lightning was, beautiful from a distance, deadly up close.

"Y-yes, sir?" Henshaw managed. His back was straight, but his hands were discreetly clasped behind him to hide their shaking.

Reginald didn't slow his pace. He stopped inches from the old man and extended his hand, holding a small silver teaspoon between two fingers as though it were something diseased. The light glinted off its tarnished surface.

"Are you *deliberately* trying to provoke me," he said slowly, dangerously, "or are you simply *staggeringly* incompetent?"

Henshaw blinked at the spoon. "Sir, I…I assure you, that piece was polished this morning"

"**Polished?**" Reginald's eyes flared, and his voice dropped to a low, venomous tone. "I can barely see my own reflection. This is filth. An insult to the house. An insult to *me*."

"I…I'll redo them all, sir. Of course. Immediately."

"I want every piece shining. I want them to gleam like they were *blessed by the sun itself.* Do you understand me?"

"Yes, sir," Henshaw whispered.

"And the study?" Reginald snapped before the man could retreat.

"The logs have been updated. The firewood was delivered. I've checked the door fittings, and the armchair has been reupholstered…"

"Poorly," Reginald cut in. "I sat in it for precisely two minutes before my back felt like it had been assaulted by church pews. Do you enjoy wasting my money?"

"No, sir…"

"Then stop acting like a saboteur and start behaving like a man who values his damn job."

Henshaw bowed slightly; eyes downcast. "I'll have it replaced by morning."

"You'll have it replaced *tonight*."

The butler bowed again, more deeply this time, and turned quickly, almost fleeing.

Reginald didn't watch him go.

He pivoted and stormed into the sitting room without knocking. The double doors slammed open so hard they bounced against the walls.

Marion Price let out a startled cry, the embroidery hoop sliding from her lap to the carpet. She clutched her chest, heart thudding beneath her cream blouse.

"Good heavens, Reginald!" she gasped.

Reginald's face curled into disgust. "Must you always act like a *terrified mouse?*"

Marion bent down to retrieve her stitching, fingers fumbling the thread. "You startled me, that's all."

He snorted. "Your constant timidity disgusts me. Honestly. You look like you're about to faint if the fire pops too loudly."

"I'm just nervous," she said quietly, eyes fixed on her lap.

"Of *what?* Me? Of this house? You walk around like a bloody guest instead of a wife."

Her chin lifted, but only barely. "I'm ill, Reginald. The doctor said…"

"I don't care what the doctor said. We all die eventually. That doesn't excuse you from holding yourself with *some* dignity. You're not an invalid. You're just lazy."

Marion said nothing. Her mouth pressed into a tight line, and her hands returned to her embroidery, though the thread trembled between her fingers.

Reginald turned toward the fire, took one look at the flames, and scowled.

"Too high. Wasteful. Does no one in this house know how to control anything anymore?"

He picked up the poker and jabbed at the logs with unnecessary force, sending sparks upward in a burst that made Marion flinch again. When he noticed, he laughed.

"See? Pathetic."

She didn't respond. He didn't wait for one.

Reginald turned and stormed from the room just as violently as he'd entered. The double doors slammed again, echoing down the corridor like a warning.

Back in the sitting room, Marion sat motionless, the warmth from the fire no longer touching her. She blinked down at her embroidery, thread tangled, fingers raw and quietly began to undo the last few stitches.

Across the hall, Henshaw stood at the foot of the stairs, silently catching his breath. He wiped his forehead with a handkerchief, then folded it with the precision of ritual, as if control over fabric could grant him control over anything else.

Reginald's storm rolled on.

And the house, ancient and proud, absorbed it like stone absorbs thunder, too stubborn to break, but never unchanged.

The library was next.

Peter sat hunched at the heavy mahogany desk, half-swallowed by ledgers, reports, and spreadsheets spread in a precise, hopeful pattern. He was chewing on the end of his pencil, eyes squinting at a column of numbers, jaw tight with the quiet intensity of someone trying, desperately, to prove himself.

The door exploded inward without warning.

Reginald didn't speak at first. He simply entered like a force of nature, the door slamming into the wall and making the overhead light shudder. Then, with a swift, violent motion, he swept an arm across the desk, sending papers fluttering to the floor like startled birds. A ceramic mug shattered against the hardwood with a sharp, final crack.

Peter jolted upright. "What the *hell...*"

"Still pretending to be useful?" Reginald snarled, towering over the desk.

Peter flushed, fists clenching at his sides. "I'm working..."

"On *what?* Your posture? Your delusions?" Reginald snapped, eyes scanning the scattered documents with theatrical disdain. "You've been 'working' for three months and haven't produced a single idea worth wiping off my boots."

"I've been handling the quarterly reports..."

"Incorrectly. I've seen them. A child could do better with a calculator and one functioning brain cell."

Peter's jaw tightened. He opened his mouth, then shut it again. His breathing was sharp. His eyes blazed but still, he didn't rise to it.

Reginald wasn't finished.

"You want to inherit something? Here..." He kicked a fallen folder toward Peter's feet. "Inherit that. Mediocrity in a branded folder."

Peter's voice shook as he spoke. "I'm trying to fix what you've broken."

Reginald chuckled darkly. "You don't fix legacies. You *earn* them. And you haven't earned so much as my contempt."

Peter's fists balled tighter. "Maybe if you'd treated me like a son instead of a liability"

"Spare me the whimpering," Reginald barked. "You've had everything handed to you: education, connections, name and still, you're the least promising man to ever wear a Price cufflink."

The silence that followed was louder than the outburst. Peter's face was stone, but his hands trembled.

Reginald turned, disgusted. "Get out of my sight. If I want incompetence, I'll read the morning markets."

He strode out without looking back, the door slamming behind him hard enough to make the chandelier sway.

Peter stood alone in the wreckage of his work, breathing hard. He didn't speak. Didn't cry. Just knelt down slowly and began to gather the scattered pages like a man stitching together what little he had left.

Reginald continued down the corridor, each step a punctuation of loathing.

Down the hall, Catherine heard him coming long before he reached her study. Not that he ever knocked. The door was flung open with theatrical disdain.

She didn't flinch.

She was seated at her desk, legs crossed, a fountain pen twirling between her fingers, flipping through a weathered copy of *Murder in the Vicarage*. Notes were scribbled across the margins in sharp, neat script. A single eyebrow lifted as she looked up calm, composed, and thoroughly unimpressed.

"Father," she said, evenly.

"I hear you've been playing detective again," Reginald said, his voice already sour.

"I enjoy logic and misdirection," she replied coolly. "It's refreshing, given how rarely either applies in this household."

He stepped inside, looming.

"You waste your intellect on fantasy," he snapped. "You could be working in politics, law, diplomacy, hell even finance. Instead, you're reading fiction and scribbling in the margins like a schoolgirl."

"I'm surviving," she said. "And honestly, I'd rather live among corpses on the page than the ones sitting at our dinner table."

Reginald's jaw tightened.

"You always were too clever for your own good."

"And you always mistook fear for respect," she said, standing now, chin lifted. "You bullied Peter into silence, Mother into submission, and the staff into shadows. But you can't bully me. Not anymore."

"You think you're brave?" Reginald growled, stepping closer. "You think this posture, this wit, this... attitude makes you immune?"

"I think," she said, voice steady as stone, "that your power is paper-thin. The more you shout, the more obvious it is that you've already lost it."

They locked eyes.

For a moment, just a moment, something like uncertainty flickered in Reginald's expression. Then it hardened again.

"You'll regret your mouth someday," he spat.

"Unlikely," Catherine said. "But you'll regret underestimating it."

A long silence stretched between them, thick with unfinished things.

Reginald's lip curled, but he said nothing more. He turned and stalked out, leaving the door wide open behind him.

Catherine exhaled, slow, measured. Then calmly walked to the door and closed it herself, gently, without drama. A final punctuation mark.

And somewhere deep in the house, in the storm's shadow, something cracked.

Not just glass or wood.

Something else.

Something vital.

Something final.

Chapter 3: Pressure Points

In the drawing room, Philip Marsh and David Forrester sat hunched over a low table strewn with financial reports, prospectuses, and thick manila folders. A brass reading lamp cast a warm pool of light over the mess, softening the sharp angles of concern etched into their faces. David's pen tapped softly against his knee, while Philip's fingers twitched at the edge of a page, eyes scanning figures for answers that refused to appear.

Outside, the storm still rolled across the hills, but it was the footsteps, steady, sharp, purposeful, that made both men freeze.

Then the door slammed open, hard enough to knock a framed painting askew.

"What idiocy are you two conspiring now?" Reginald Price's voice cracked through the room like a whip.

Philip's hand halted mid-page. David sat up straight, spine stiffening, jaw tightening.

"We're evaluating investment options," David said, voice level but controlled.

"*Investments*," Reginald repeated, already striding in like a man who owned not just the house but every breath inside it. "You mean *guesswork*, dressed in overpriced tailoring. Tossing money into a pit and praying it doesn't catch fire."

He reached the table, grabbed a stack of reports, and thumbed through them with visible disgust.

"This?" he snapped, holding up a page and shaking it in David's face. "This is your big idea. Mid-cap funds and Funding energy? I've seen children pitch more coherent ideas in school debates."

David didn't flinch. "It's a ten-year growth strategy. It's about long-term sustainability"

Reginald cut him off with a scoff so loud it drowned out the next clap of thunder.

"Spare me the brochure language," he snarled. "You don't build empires on buzzwords and hope. You build them with blood, grit, and a complete disregard for the whining of weak men. Something you've never understood."

His gaze pivoted to Philip, settling on him like a weight.

"And *you*," he said with deliberate venom. "You sit there nodding like a sidekick in a second-rate tragedy. What do you even do here? Pretend to advise? You think reading spreadsheets makes you strategic?"

Philip's face twitched. He opened his mouth but stopped himself. His fingers curled tight around the armrest, nails digging into the leather. The clock on the mantel ticked louder.

David glanced at him, subtle, supportive but Philip gave the smallest shake of his head. Not here. Not with him.

Reginald, emboldened by silence, leaned in over the table, one hand splayed across the reports as if smothering them.

"You talk like you understand legacy," he said, voice now low and cruel. "But you couldn't hold a legacy if I handed it to you with instructions. You're both liabilities, well-dressed liabilities."

He let that hang in the air, then dropped the reports to the floor with a flick of his wrist.

"Pick that up," he told Philip.

Philip stared at him.

"I said, pick it up."

Still, Philip didn't move.

Reginald smiled, cold and sharp. "Ah. *Some* spine after all. Shame it's about three decades too late."

David stood. Calmly. "That's enough."

Reginald turned, amused. "Or what? You'll quote ethics at me? Please. If this family had any backbone left, we wouldn't be buried in debt and hiding from press calls."

He looked between them both, contempt dripping from every syllable.

"You want to save this company?" he said. "Then get out of my way and let someone ruthless do the job. Otherwise, pour yourselves another drink and pretend you're men."

With that, he spun on his heel and stormed from the room, the door left yawning behind him. His footsteps echoed down the hall, fading only after the tension he left behind had rooted deep.

Philip slowly exhaled, dragging a hand down his face.

"I hate him," he said under his breath.

David didn't answer right away. He just leaned down, gathered the fallen reports, and set them back on the table with quiet precision.

Then, after a beat, he muttered, "Join the queue."

Inside, Catherine stood by the sideboard, arranging a fresh bouquet of roses in a tall, cut-glass vase. Her hands moved with care, slipping each stem into place with quiet precision. The scent of eucalyptus and petals perfumed the room, mingling with the soft clink of water and glass. The storm outside seemed to pause, caught in the breath between gusts.

Then came the sound that soured the air like curdled milk, **footsteps**, sharp and full of purpose. And contempt.

"**Roses again, Catherine?**" Reginald's voice slithered into the room behind her. "*Utterly predictable.* I expected better, even from you."

She didn't flinch. She turned slowly, keeping one hand resting on the rim of the vase. Her face remained calm, but her eyes, dark and still, flashed with something colder than ice.

"I chose roses deliberately," she said, voice even. "They're beautiful. But they bite. Much like this family."

Reginald stepped closer, invading her space with the entitlement of a man who believed the room like the people inside it, belonged to him.

"Poetic nonsense," he spat. "Do you think you're clever? Hiding your barbs in metaphors? You were always a disappointment, Catherine. A mind wasted on mood swings and melodrama."

She tilted her head, lips tightening into something just short of a smile. "And you've always mistaken bullying for leadership. I suppose we both have our blind spots."

His nostrils flared.

"Your husband's incompetence is bleeding this house dry," he growled. "If you had any sense, you'd rein him in before he drags us all into ruin."

Her gaze didn't waver. "He has more integrity than you ever did," she said. "And frankly, he doesn't need reigning in. *You* do."

Reginald's face flushed an ugly, mottled red. "You'd defend him to the end, wouldn't you? Even as he fails you. As he fails all of us. You sit here arranging flowers while the roof caves in."

"And you strut around shouting while the house burns," she said. "At least my hands are building something. Yours only ever tear down."

His hand twitched, barely noticeable, but it was there, the impulse to lash out in some way. But Catherine didn't move. She simply stared at him, unblinking, unbothered.

"I won't be spoken to like this," he snarled.

"You will," she replied. "And if not now, then soon. One day, you'll run out of people who flinch."

For a moment, the room held its breath. Then, with a noise somewhere between a growl and a scoff, Reginald turned on his heel and stormed out. The door slammed with enough force to make the chandelier tremble in its chain like a noose catching wind.

Silence followed. Not peace, never peace in this house. Just the echo of rage, retreating down the hall like a storm finally leaving the sky.

One by one, the members of the household emerged from wherever they'd scattered, each bearing the invisible bruises Reginald left behind like fingerprints.

In the drawing room, the fire had died to low embers, casting long, flickering shadows across the carpet. David Forrester stepped in quietly, glancing around until his eyes found Catherine, still standing at the sideboard, her fingers resting lightly on the vase. The roses remained untouched, their thorns catching the firelight like tiny daggers.

He moved toward her, his footsteps soft across the rug.

"You alright?" he asked, voice low, almost hesitant.

Catherine didn't look up immediately. Her fingers still circled the vase, the glass slick beneath her touch. When she did turn, her expression was composed but her eyes were tired. Tired in the way people are when their silence has become armour.

"I'm used to it," she said.

David frowned. "That doesn't mean you should be."

She gave a faint, crooked smile. "Someone in this house has to keep their feet. Even if they're planted in thorns."

He stepped closer. His hand brushed hers, brief, but deliberate. The warmth of the contact passed between them like a secret.

"You always speak your mind to him," David said.

"Would you rather I didn't?"

He shook his head. "No. I think it's the bravest thing I've ever seen."

She laughed softly wry, not bitter. "It's not bravery, David. It's survival. He doesn't know how to fight fair. So, I don't bother playing nice."

David looked at her a long moment. Then, gently, he reached for her hand again, this time fully, his fingers curling around hers.

"You're the only reason I haven't left this place," he said.

Her expression flickered. A softness behind the eyes. "And you're the only reason I believe it's still worth staying."

He leaned in, just enough for her to catch the faint scent of cedarwood and parchment.

"I hate what he says about you," he said. "About me. About all of us."

Her grip tightened slightly. "Then prove him wrong."

His brow furrowed. "How?"

"By building something he can't touch," she said. "Even if it's just between us."

Their eyes locked, the air suddenly fragile and weightless between them, like glass pulled thin. Catherine felt the heat of him, the steadiness. And something else. Something steadier than any vow spoken in that house.

David's voice dropped to a whisper. "I wish we could leave."

Catherine looked away, toward the roses. "One day," she said. "But not yet. Not while he's still the storm."

Footsteps echoed in the corridor, measured, familiar, oppressive. They both turned slightly, stepping apart on instinct, though their hands lingered a heartbeat longer before separating.

Catherine's voice was barely a murmur. "You keep me standing, David. Every day."

He nodded, and for once, said nothing.

Outside, the wind clawed at the windows. The storm showed no sign of leaving.

But inside, in the quiet aftermath, something remained.

Not rage. Not fear.

Something more dangerous.

Resolve.

And somewhere deep in Catherine's chest, past the roses and the ruin, a single ember refused to go out.

Chapter 4: Dinner

Elm Road was timeless in the worst possible way.

Catherine Forrester's eyes moved across the dining room like a scalpel, slicing through the genteel veneer with cold precision. She sat straight-backed in her chair, arms poised just so, a woman carved from granite rather than born of flesh. The rest of the country might have been groping its way toward modernity, cassette tapes, shoulder pads, political debates blaring from boxy televisions, but here, in this house, time was shackled. Stagnant. The year might as well have been 1885.

Everything was perfectly preserved. Neatly clipped hedges outside framed the windows like bars. Ivy, thick as rope, choked the exterior walls. Inside, the air was heavy with polish and obligation. Nothing breathed. Tradition had curdled into ritual. Respectability, like the house itself, was grand, dark, and slowly collapsing from within.

The dining room was designed to suppress dissent. Mahogany-panelled walls loomed with an oppressive, coffin-like weight. Faded ancestral portraits lined them, men in powdered wigs and severe coats, women in high collars, all long dead and long disapproving. The chandelier above flickered like gaslight; despite the electric wiring someone had hidden behind the ceiling roses. Its crystal ornaments jingled faintly in the silence, a sound, like, teeth chattering from the cold.

The long table stretched beneath it like an altar. Silver glinted from polished cutlery; the tablecloth was so starched it might've been armour. Silence hovered over the roast lamb like steam, thick and barely tolerable.

Catherine's gaze moved from face to face with clinical detachment, as if reviewing exhibits in a courtroom.

At the head sat Reginald Price, presiding like a judge whose verdict had already been decided. He carved the lamb with surgical precision, each slice cleaner than the last. There was something ritualistic about the way he held the knife, as though it had once been a scalpel. He said little. He didn't need to. His presence filled the room like smoke. Even in silence, he accused.

To his right, Philip Marsh seemed to shrink with every breath. His suit was too tight at the neck, the top button still fastened like a noose. His receding hair clung to his scalp in anxious strands. Every few seconds, his hand hovered toward his wine glass, but he never took a full sip, just held it, as if it might ward off whatever storm was brewing behind Reginald's eyes. A single bead of sweat crawled down his temple, but he didn't move to wipe it.

Across from him, Marion Price sat like a ghost in mourning. Her silver hair was pinned perfectly, her blouse pristine, her mouth locked into a polite, lifeless smile. She had once been a striking woman, people still said so, but decades of quiet suffering had softened the edges. Her hands, elegant and faintly trembling, rested in her lap. She picked at her food with the indifference of someone who no longer registered appetite. Her eyes, pale and distant, drifted to the clock on the wall every few minutes, as if waiting for the hour to release her.

Beside her, Peter slouched. His tie was nowhere in sight. His shirt was half-buttoned, his sleeves rolled, and his disdain practically steamed off his skin. He stabbed at his lamb like it had personally wronged him. The occasional clink of his fork against the plate sounded louder than it should have, like defiance echoing off marble.

Then there was David Forrester.

David, seated next to Catherine, looked like a man caught mid-exhale, too nervous to speak, too polite to flee. His suit was pressed, his cufflinks gleamed, but tension radiated from his every movement. He smiled when he was supposed to. He nodded when prompted. He folded his hands, then unfolded them. He toyed with his napkin, then set it back down in perfect alignment with the fork. Every few minutes, his eyes flicked toward Catherine, seeking reassurance, or perhaps simply proof that he wasn't losing his mind.

She gave it to him, just enough to keep him steady. A slight tilt of her head. A small glance. A curve of the lips that could be humour, or warning.

Now, Catherine leaned slightly toward David, her voice low and dry.

"Enjoying your evening?" she asked, arching a brow.

David breathed a small laugh. "Just as much as usual"

"You're holding up better than Philip," she said, her eyes sliding toward Reginald's business partner, who was visibly sweating beneath his collar. "He usually starts crying by dessert."

David's smile twisted into something grim. "Has it ever occurred to you," he whispered, "that maybe you're all characters in a very bleak play?"

"Oh, I'm aware," Catherine said. "But unlike the others, I didn't mistake this for a rehearsal."

Across the table, Reginald paused mid-slice. He didn't look up, but something in the air changed, like the oxygen had been sucked out of the room. The tension crept in, slow and surgical.

"You're quiet tonight, Catherine," Reginald said at last, his voice smooth as old steel. "Planning something?"

"Only my exit strategy," she replied lightly.

David stifled a cough. Catherine didn't look at him, but her lips twitched at the corner almost a smile.

Reginald's eyes finally lifted to meet hers, cold and flat. "Still wasting your time with cleverness?"

Catherine smiled slowly. "Someone in this house has to make conversation."

"Conversation?" Reginald snorted. "You call your verbal grenades 'conversation'? I call it attention-seeking in disguise. You've been clawing for relevance since the moment you walked through the doors."

"Well," she said, reaching for her wine with regal ease, "I'd rather claw than crawl. But we all make choices."

Philip cleared his throat, ever the pacifier. "If we could, perhaps, circle back to the estate figures…"

"No one asked you to speak, Philip," Reginald snapped, without so much as a glance in his direction. "I've heard enough of your cowardly bleating for one lifetime."

Philip recoiled as if slapped, shrinking into his seat like air leaving a balloon. His lips pressed into a hard, white line. Marion, seated beside him, flinched at the sound. Her fork slipped from her fingers and clattered onto her plate.

"I...I think he was just trying to help," she said quietly, barely audible.

Reginald turned on her with a glare. "Help? Philip couldn't help a drowning man out of a puddle."

A flicker of something sparked behind Marion's eyes, but she said nothing. She merely picked up her fork again, though her hand trembled faintly.

Peter didn't even blink. He just chewed, slow and silent, cutting his meat with mechanical precision. His jaw was tight, his posture tense, but he gave nothing away. Only his eyes, dark, distant, betrayed the storm behind them.

Reginald turned his attention to him next, ever hungry for the next weak link.

"And you, Peter," he said with a sneer. "I see you've mastered the art of doing nothing with style. Slouched there like a ghost in tailored wool."

Peter looked up; eyes flat. "I figured someone needed to balance the noise."

Reginald's laugh was humourless. "Careful. Your sarcasm might trick someone into thinking you have a personality."

"Better a personality than a complex," Peter muttered.

"What was that?"

"Nothing," Peter said, smiling with all the warmth of a closed door.

David's hand brushed lightly against Catherine's under the table. She didn't move it away.

The room seemed to shrink with every course. The air thickened. Conversation died. All that remained was the sound of cutlery on porcelain and wine being sipped as though it might sedate the nerves.

Catherine took another sip of wine and looked around the table, Philip, crushed into silence; Marion, breaking in small places; Peter, drifting in his own contempt; David, trying to stay upright beneath it all. A circus of bruised egos orbiting a tyrant.

"Such vibrant dinner conversation," she said aloud, slicing into her lamb with grace. "It's a wonder we don't dine together more often."

Reginald's fork paused mid-air. "You're one more remark away from eating with the staff."

"I'd prefer it," she said. "They seem less invested in passive-aggressive foreplay."

David nearly choked. Philip coughed. Marion blinked.

Reginald set down his utensils with theatrical care. "You're pushing it, Catherine."

"I've been pushed farther."

"You think you're some kind of martyr?" he snarled. "The misunderstood genius in pearls? You're a bored, bitter girl in a crumbling dress."

"No," she said, voice calm. "I'm the last one here still telling the truth. You're just angry I don't whisper it."

The room froze.

Reginald stood. Abruptly. His napkin hit the table like a gauntlet.

"I'll be in my study," he said, rising with the air of a man used to being obeyed. "Do try to keep the rest of the evening civil."

He stormed out, boots thudding down the hallway like war drums. The door swung closed in his wake with a heavy, final thud.

Silence reigned.

Philip stared into his untouched wine. Peter leaned back in his chair and exhaled through his nose like someone who'd been holding his breath for years.

Catherine didn't move.

David looked at her. Really looked. At the stillness in her jaw. The quiet fury in her eyes. The elegance, yes, but the armour too.

"You, okay?" he asked softly.

She turned to him, finally, and smiled. It wasn't kind. It was knowing.

"He thinks he's the house," she whispered. "But one day, this place will forget his name. And we'll still be standing."

She looked toward the candle in the centre of the table. The flame flickered gently.

And in Catherine's mind, the thought solidified, sharpened to a point.

If a house like this ever burned, it would take its time.

But it would burn.

And this time, she wouldn't just wait for the match.

She'd strike it.

Chapter 5: The Study

No one moved for a moment.

The dinner plates still sat untouched, wine glasses half-drained, but the conversation had curdled to silence. The tension that had hovered all evening finally settled with full weight, pressing down on every chest in the room.

Philip was the first to sag, shoulders dropping like a puppet with its strings cut. "Every dinner's a siege," he whispered, voice hollow. "I can't stand it."

"Then don't come," Peter snapped. "You're not chained here."

Philip bristled. "It's not that simple."

"No?" Peter's voice sharpened. "Feels pretty simple to me."

"You think running is bravery?" Philip muttered.

"I think staying here is self-pity in a velvet chair."

"None of us are chained," Marion said quietly, her gaze still locked on her plate. "And yet here we sit. Chosen prisoners. Locked in by loyalty... or cowardice."

Peter made a noise of disgust. "You always were good at poetic suffering."

Catherine's hand, beneath the table, brushed David's. More deliberately this time. Not comfort. Not distraction. A signal.

He didn't pull away.

Instead, he turned his palm to meet hers. A quiet answer in the middle of a battlefield.

Catherine stood. Her chair scraped back against the floor with finality. "I need air," she said, though her voice carried more iron than breath.

She strode from the room without looking back.

A heavy silence followed her.

The only sound was the grandfather clock in the hall as it struck ten, its chimes deep and sonorous, echoing through the house with funeral gravity.

Marion looked up, startled. "He should have returned by now," she said, voice thin, uncertain. "He always returns. Even if only to lecture."

"Maybe he's sulking," Peter offered, his tone half-joking, half-hopeless. He reached for his wine again, but his hand shook slightly.

"He doesn't sulk," Catherine's voice cut in as she re-entered the room, fast and focused. "He plots. He glares. But he never disappears. Not this long. Not without making it someone else's fault."

Peter blinked. "You think something's wrong?"

Catherine's eyes were already scanning the hallway beyond. "I think he doesn't get to manipulate us from the shadows. Not anymore."

"Catherine," David said, rising, "let's not..."

But she was already moving toward the corridor, her movements fluid and certain.

"He doesn't get to vanish and make us dance," she said over her shoulder. "Not this time."

David followed quickly, grabbing his jacket from the back of a chair. "You shouldn't go alone."

"I'm not afraid of him," she snapped, then glanced at him again. Softer. "But... come if you like."

Philip followed with slower steps, rubbing at his temples. Marion trailed behind; cardigan wrapped around her like armour. Peter brought up the rear, his pace uneven.

The house was darker in the corridor. Colder, somehow. The wallpaper, striped and slightly faded, seemed to press inward, as if the walls themselves were holding their breath.

At the door to the study, Catherine knocked. Firm. Measured. "Father."

No reply.

She didn't flinch. She knocked again, louder now. "Reginald."

Still silence.

Marion hovered behind them, twisting her wedding band on her finger. "Try the handle," she whispered, barely audible.

Catherine reached for the brass knob and twisted. It rattled.

"Locked," she said, voice flat. Not surprised.

Peter stepped beside her, rolling his shoulders like a man preparing for a bar fight. "Force it?"

Catherine nodded once. "On three."

They braced. On the count, they slammed into the door. It groaned. Again. The wood creaked under the strain.

On the third hit, the lock splintered, and the door flew inward with a sharp crack.

The room beyond was dim, lit only by the flicker of a desk lamp. The shadows danced across the shelves and books like silent witnesses. The air smelled of leather, old cigars, ink, and something sharper, something metallic.

Reginald Price was slumped over the desk.

His back was twisted unnaturally, a grotesque mimicry of rest. A silver-handled knife jutted from between his shoulder blades, stark and final. Blood soaked the fine wool of his jacket, dripping onto polished wood, staining paper, and pooling deep into the grain.

Marion screamed. The sound ripped through the hallway, raw and human.

Philip staggered backward and collapsed into the doorframe, his hand flying to his mouth as if he could shove the horror back inside.

Peter cursed, stepping back sharply and knocking over a small side table. A stack of leather-bound journals tumbled to the floor with a dull thud.

David froze, eyes wide. His breath caught in his throat like he'd swallowed ice.

Only Catherine stepped forward.

Her heels clicked against the hardwood, steady as a metronome. Her face remained calm, almost cold, but her eyes flicked from blood to blade to paper with the precision of someone taking inventory, not of grief, but of consequence.

She didn't look at the body.

She looked at what he had been working on.

She spoke without turning.

"Well," she said softly, almost conversational, "it finally happened."

David moved beside her. "You sound… unsurprised."

Catherine's gaze didn't lift from the desk. "I'm not."

"And you're not frightened?"

She turned to him now. Her expression unreadable, but her voice was ice under pressure. "Oh, I'm always frightened, David. But I've learned to carry it in my pockets, like a coin. You don't let fear lead. You let it remind you where the knife is."

Philip staggered to the window and pulled the curtain aside as if he could will the night to explain itself.

Marion dropped to a chair and covered her face with her hands, rocking slightly.

Peter said nothing. Just stared at the blade, his hands clenched at his sides.

Catherine stepped closer to the body. She examined the scattered papers, eyes narrowing slightly.

"Ledger entries," she murmured. "Two letters. One unfinished."

Peter finally spoke. "So, what now? We call the police and pretend we don't know what every one of us wanted?"

Catherine's head tilted; her voice razor-sharp. "No. We don't pretend. We cooperate. We answer what we're asked."

"And if they ask who had motive?" Philip said hoarsely.

Catherine looked at each of them in turn. "Then they'll have too many names and not enough facts."

David's voice was low. "And you? What will you say?"

She met his gaze. Her voice was quiet. Steady.

"I'll say the truth."

"Which is?"

"That he had it coming."

Then she turned back to the body, the light catching the edge of the knife like a glinting promise.

"Now," she said softly, "the real show begins."

Chapter 6: The Locked Room

The Price house had never known this kind of quiet.

Not the hush of polished manners, or the soft stillness of wealth wrapped in velvet and oak. This silence came after something *wrong*. Thick. Heavy. The kind that pressed in from the walls, humming in your ears and settling in your bones. It wasn't just absence of sound, it was presence. Something *had* happened. And nothing would quite go back to how it was.

Upstairs, a loose shutter caught the wind and let out a slow, screeching groan. The storm had mostly passed, but the rain still clung to the roof, dripping steadily in soft, stubborn taps. The moon fought behind thin clouds, casting a wan, ghost-coloured glow through the hallway glass.

In the drawing room, too perfectly arranged to ever feel *natural*, the fire had burned down to tired coals. The logs sagged inward, sending up a few dying sparks that faded before they reached the hearth. The warmth felt artificial now. Not comforting. Just something pretending to be.

The room had become a stage. And the script had gone dark.

Marion Price sat ramrod straight on the settee, like posture alone could hold her together. Her hands shook just slightly, pearls on her wrist clicking as she twisted her fingers over each other. Her eyes weren't focused, just trained somewhere past the fire, maybe on a memory she didn't want but couldn't stop replaying.

Peter stood by the fireplace; arms locked tight across his chest. He stared into the flames, unmoving. His jaw clenched and unclenched in slow rhythm, like his body was the only thing capable of showing tension. The fire lit half his face; the other half stayed hidden in shadow.

He hadn't spoken in twenty minutes. No one had.

Philip Marsh paced in a corner near the liquor cabinet, glass in hand, sweat blooming on the back of his shirt. His tie hung loose, collar wrinkled, and he kept muttering under his breath, flinching at every sudden sound. His eyes were rimmed in red, not from tears.

Panic. Like he was trying to edit the scene with his own version of events.

Catherine Forrester sat like a portrait in her high-backed chair near the window. Still. Elegant. Watching. A full glass of wine sat untouched beside her. Her hands rested calmly in her lap, but her eyes moved, fast and sharp. She was taking in everything: Marion's twitching fingers, Peter's locked jaw, Philip's shaky hands. It wasn't cruelty. It was calculation.

Her stillness was active. Deliberate.

David stood behind her, shifting from foot to foot like he couldn't find solid ground. His hands were buried in his pockets, and every few seconds his gaze would flick back to Catherine like he needed proof she was still there.

"I hate this," he muttered.

Catherine didn't look at him. "The room or the silence?"

"Yes," he said.

She allowed herself a small smile. "You get used to it. Or you figure out how to use it."

David scanned the room again. "No one's said anything."

"They're trying not to fall apart," she replied. "Guilt and fear sound the same in silence. Until someone names them."

A log snapped in the grate. Peter flinched. Marion winced. Philip drained his glass and poured another with hands that didn't want to hold still.

David leaned closer. "You don't think… he did it himself?"

Now Catherine turned her head. Slowly. Her voice was low, but cold.

"Reginald? Kill himself? That man would have buried spite in the garden just to outlive it. And what, stabbed himself in the back for good measure?"

David frowned. His voice was low, cautious. "You think someone here, did it?"

Catherine didn't look at him immediately. Her gaze remained fixed on the hallway beyond, where shadows pooled at the corners like secrets. "I think everyone here had a reason," she said at last. "Including me."

Her voice carried no drama, no flourish. Just fact, steady, sharp, unsettling.

David opened his mouth to reply, but the distant crunch of gravel cut through the tension like a blade. The unmistakable sound of tyres settling against the driveway stones reached their ears, followed by the soft whine of an engine winding down. Outside, a pair of headlights flared through the thinning mist, casting warped reflections across the hallway's old glass windows.

Chapter 7: The Arrival

A car door slammed. Then another.

Peter turned from his place at the fireplace, his expression unreadable. "That'll be them."

Catherine's hand tightened slightly around the back of her chair as she stood. Her movement was fluid, unhurried. Composed.

"The curtain's going up," she murmured.

David stepped forward. "Do we trust them?"

She glanced sideways at him, one brow lifting. "No. But we let them play their part. For now."

A moment later, the sound of a firm, deliberate knock echoed through the house. It was not hesitant. Not unsure. It announced.

Even Henshaw, the stoic butler of thirty years, startled slightly where he stood. He adjusted the cuffs of his jacket, looked once to Marion, still seated on the settee like a porcelain relic and waited.

She nodded once, stiffly, a mechanical motion.

Henshaw straightened and moved to the door; shoulders squared as though bracing for wind. With a click of the lock and a long creak of ancient hinges, the front door opened.

Two men stepped into the threshold.

The first was broad-shouldered, his coat dusted with rain, the collar turned slightly up. He removed his hat slowly, revealing a crown of silver-streaked hair and a weathered face carved with quiet authority. Inspector Thomas Stowe. His presence filled the space without noise, like a tide advancing.

The second followed close behind, Detective Sergeant Michael Harris. Lean, quick-eyed, younger. He already had his notebook in hand, pen uncapped and poised like a scalpel.

"Evenin'," Stowe said with a nod. His voice had the gravelly, thoughtful burr of the West Country, slow, deliberate, like someone who'd spent years letting silence do half the talking. "Inspector Thomas Stowe. This here's Sergeant Harris. Sorry for yer loss. We'll not take more of yer time than's necessary."

"Thank you," Marion said, her voice brittle as pressed flowers. "It's all been… very sudden."

"Aye," Stowe replied, not unkindly. "I'm sure it has." His eyes lingered on the set of her jaw, the way her hands clutched one another in her lap. "We'll need to see the scene, if that's all right."

Catherine moved before anyone else could rise. "This way," she said crisply, stepping into the hallway.

David trailed her, the others following more slowly, Peter with reluctant steps, Marion with whispered breath, Philip clutching the edges of his blazer as if for balance.

The hallway was dim, lit only by the flickering sconces along the walls. Their footsteps echoed against the black-and-white tile in rhythmic intervals, like the tick of a heavy clock. The deeper they went into the house, the quieter it became, the air cooling around them. Somewhere above, a floorboard creaked. The wind outside howled against the windowpanes in lonely protest.

David leaned closer to Catherine as they walked. "What's your take on this?"

She didn't look at him, just kept her eyes ahead. "He's not here to impress," she said softly. "That makes him more dangerous."

At the end of the corridor, the broken study door came into view, its frame splintered, hanging slightly askew. The light within flickered faintly, casting long, jagged shadows across the hallway floor like the fingers of something reaching.

Stowe paused, crouching beside the ruined threshold. His gloved fingers grazed the broken wood, eyes narrowing.

"Forced entry, was it?" he asked.

"Yes," Peter said from behind. "He locked it. Or someone did."

"Hmm." Stowe nodded and stepped inside, ducking slightly as he passed beneath the lintel.

Reginald Price was still there.

Slumped forward across the desk, arms limp, his shoulder blades forming a steep ridge beneath the fine cut of his jacket. The silver-handled knife protruded from his back like a flag planted in enemy ground. The blood had dried now, staining the edges of the polished desk and curling the corners of the papers beneath him. The scent of it, iron and finality, still lingered.

Harris crouched beside the body, examining the angle of the knife. "No sign of a struggle," he said, voice quiet. "Strike was clean. Deep. From behind. They knew exactly where to aim."

Catherine stood in the doorway; arms folded. "He trusted them," she said, softly.

"Or they were real quiet," Harris muttered.

Stowe moved slowly, methodically. He looked at the window, latched. Unbroken. Checked the grate, cold, unused. His fingers brushed over the clutter on the desk, careful not to disturb anything more than necessary. A matchbox. A pen. An envelope half-torn, contents missing.

"Locked from the inside," Harris said, rising. "Windows bolted. No tampering."

"Hmm." Stowe's eyes drifted toward the far bookcase, then to the corners of the ceiling. He didn't speak for a long moment.

"What about the key?" he asked at last.

Marion stepped forward "On the desk parallel with his pens, as usual"

Stowe straightened fully now, casting a long shadow across the desk. He looked at each face in turn, the grief etched into Marion's, the defensiveness in Peter's eyes, Philip's fatigue, Catherine's perfect stillness, David's wary concern.

Finally, the inspector exhaled, long and slow.

"Well then," he said, voice low and steady, "looks like we've got ourselves a proper locked-room mystery."

Catherine's mouth curled slightly. "And those always end badly."

"Not always," Stowe said.

"Only when someone gets away with it."

David looked between them, the tension finally finding voice. "So where do we start?"

Stowe's eyes swept the room again, this time slower. "Right here," he said. "With who had the means, the moment, and the mind to do it. The truth's in this house. Might be hidden. Might be whispered. But it never leaves."

"And you think the answer's in this room?" David asked.

Stowe's gaze was still. "Never left, if you ask me."

Outside, a roll of thunder echoed over the hills, low and distant.

Inside, the house held its breath.

And in the study, the shadows deepened, quiet and patient. Waiting.

Chapter 8: The Last Case

Outside, the rain had softened to a whisper, brushing the tall windows like a metronome marking the slow, deliberate passage of time. The storm had moved on, but the Price estate remained wrapped in its wake, damp, grey, and breathless. The trees beyond the glass stood motionless, black silhouettes against a pewter sky, like charcoal sketches never fully erased. Not a branch stirred. Not a leaf twitched.

Inside, the silence was heavier than it had been earlier. Not stunned, no, that moment had passed. This silence was tighter. More deliberate. It was the quiet that arrives after grief hardens into purpose. The kind of stillness that settles in when people stop mourning and start calculating.

In the drawing room, the once roaring fire had collapsed into a shallow bed of ash and glowing embers. It gave off a warmth that no longer reached the skin, only clung faintly to the air like the aftertaste of a memory. The room's grandeur, oil portraits in gilt frames, marble mantel, antique velvet chairs, felt theatrical now. Not comforting, but performative. Like a costume worn too long after the curtain call.

Inspector Thomas Stowe stood near the hearth, framed in the fire's fading glow. One thick, weather-beaten hand rested on the mantel, the other rubbing the stubble on his jaw. His coat hung damp around the hem, streaked with grit from the long gravel drive, and his boots had left small, muddy ghosts on the edge of the rug. But he hadn't noticed. Or didn't care.

His eyes, ringed with fatigue, remained alert. They moved slowly, carefully, scanning the lines of the room, the lingering shadows, as if the walls might whisper something useful if he stared long enough. He wasn't looking for spectacle. He was waiting for something quiet to give itself away.

Behind him, Detective Sergeant Michael Harris leaned against the tall cabinet in the corner, his arms folded loosely, notebook in hand, pen tapping a slow rhythm on the silver clip. Younger by two decades, leaner, sharper in both appearance and ambition, Harris wore his tailored coat like armour. But his eyes, quick and inquisitive, never stopped moving.

He was watching Stowe now.

"You meant it, didn't you?" Harris asked softly. "What you said earlier. About this being your last case."

Stowe didn't turn. His gaze remained fixed on a spot just above the fire, where the light curled like a question mark.

"Last case, last puzzle," he said, voice low, the words rolling out like smoke. "Last ghost."

Harris was quiet for a beat. Then, "You'll miss it."

Stowe exhaled through his nose. It could've been a sigh, or a laugh, or something stuck between.

"I'll miss what it *was*," he said. "Before it got so... polite."

He finally turned, the fire casting a ruddy sheen across the worn grooves of his face. His eyes still held the weight of a thousand crime scenes, but tonight they were softer. Not tired, just done.

"Used to be," he went on, "you'd walk into a murder and the truth would still be dripping from the walls. Raw. Messy. Ugly. You'd look someone in the eye, and they'd either fold or flare up. People didn't have practice yet. They hadn't watched a true-crime documentary or buried their guilt under five layers of learnt lying."

He gave a crooked smile, sardonic. "Now even murder wears a dinner jacket."

Harris smirked. "And a tie pin."

"Exactly," Stowe said, wagging a finger. "Everything's curated now. Even grief. These people? They're professionals. At lying. At grieving. At keeping the rot just under the wallpaper."

He jerked his chin slightly toward the hallway.

Harris followed his gaze. Beyond the door, the rest of the Price family waited, seated in stiff silence, grief folded into napkin shapes and balanced neatly beside their wine glasses. Pressed clothes, polite whispers, tearless eyes. A performance, down to the blinking.

And one of them, Stowe knew, had stood over Reginald Price as he bled out on that desk. Watched him die. Maybe even watched the last twitch, then smoothed their hair and walked away like they'd just left a meeting.

"You think they're all pretending?" Harris asked.

"I think," Stowe said, stepping away from the fire, "they've been pretending so long they don't remember what real looks like anymore."

He crossed to the window and tugged the curtain just enough to peer out. The gravel drive was empty now. No more police cars. No coroner's van. Just mist curling off the wet ground and the first dull streaks of twilight smudging the sky.

He stood there a moment longer, then added, almost to himself, "You remember the Darby case? '79?"

Harris let out a chuckle. "How could I forget? Guy tried to hide the body in his own septic tank. Left his bloody fingerprints on the wrench he used to tighten the lid."

"And tried to bribe us with a £20 Marks & Spencer voucher."

"Hey," Harris said, grinning. "That was my first free sandwich as a detective."

Stowe chuckled, the sound more gravel than mirth. "Back then it was desperation. Stupidity. Not... this." He gestured vaguely toward the opulence of the house. "This is arrogance. *Confidence.* These people don't panic, they delegate."

He turned back to Harris, face suddenly more serious.

"You know what the difference is? Back then, they tried to cover their tracks. Now? They plan the murder and the alibi in the same breath. Then they sit back and let people like us chase phantoms."

"You're saying we're too late."

"I'm saying we were never early enough." Stowe ran a hand through his hair. "And maybe I don't have the stomach for this version anymore. I liked it when guilt made people *sweat.* Now it just makes them call their solicitor."

Harris leaned against the mantel; arms crossed. "So, what'll you do, then? Retire? Sit on a beach somewhere, yelling at clouds?"

Stowe snorted. "God, no. Sand in my socks? Bloody sunburn? I'm thinking... a garden. Tomatoes, maybe. Something I can water and not interrogate."

Harris shook his head. "You'll last two weeks. Tops."

"Don't bet on it," Stowe said. "I already bought a bird feeder. That's stage one."

"Stage one of what?"

"Of getting boring," Stowe said, cracking a smile. "I've earned it."

Harris studied him a moment. "So, this is really it. You're done."

Stowe nodded slowly; his expression unreadable again. "After this one."

Harris tilted his head. "But you don't just want to solve it. You want to understand it."

Stowe didn't answer right away.

"I want to know *why* the knife went in," he said at last. "Not just who held it."

Harris scribbled something in his notebook, an absent line, more for rhythm than record than revelation. It curved off the page like a question no one wanted to ask directly.

"You think it was personal?" he asked.

Stowe's smile was brief and humourless. "A man like Reginald Price doesn't get murdered over *nothing*. He gets murdered because someone ran out of other options."

There was a pause. The grandfather clock in the hallway struck the half-hour with a dull, resonant chime that rippled through the house like a slow exhale.

Harris spoke again, quieter now. "So, what's your instinct say?"

Stowe turned back to the dying fire, the orange glow throwing shadows against his collar. "My instinct says this wasn't just about revenge. Or inheritance. Or secrets. It was about *power*. About finally taking it back."

He glanced at Harris, eyes narrowing slightly. "And that makes it dangerous. Because whoever did this…" he nodded toward the hallway, "they're not finished yet. They've tasted what it feels like to win. To get the better of him. And that… that can be addictive."

Harris's expression shifted, a flicker of discomfort flashing behind the practiced calm. "You think they'll do it again?"

"I think," Stowe said, voice like gravel and judgment, "if I press too hard, they might try to shut the book before I can finish the last page."

Silence fell again. But it wasn't empty now. It carried weight, like breath held too long.

Outside, the rain had fully stopped. The windows glistened with condensation, water beads distorting the trees into eerie, twisted silhouettes. The sky had dimmed further, sliding from pewter to slate, tugging night into the corners of the room like smoke curling under a door.

Stowe walked slowly back toward the hearth and picked up a coal poker, turning it slowly in one hand. He studied the embers, then gave them a single sharp jab.

"You know what makes a good murder case, Harris?"

The younger man looked up from his notes. "What's that?"

Stowe tapped the poker once against the edge of the grate. The metal rang softly.

"It's not the victim," he said. "It's the aftermath. How the people left behind deal with it. That's where the truth leaks out. Not in blood, but in silence. In what they try not to say."

Harris scratched behind his ear. "That sounds like something you stitched into a pillow in your past life."

"If I ever had a past life," Stowe muttered, "it probably involved more whiskey and fewer bodies."

"You still drink whiskey."

"Now it's medicinal."

"Right. Because threatening suspects on an empty stomach is doctor-recommended."

"Don't knock it," Stowe said, cracking the barest grin. "Better than caffeine. Puts hair on your instincts."

Harris chuckled, but it faded quickly. "And what about us?" he asked after a beat. "What do we leak?"

Stowe gave a long, tired smile, the kind that never quite reached the eyes. "We leak *time*. We leak *patience*. And then, eventually, we leak out of the job."

"Poetic."

"Morbidly accurate."

Harris snorted. "You know, when you retire, you will end up lecturing a postman about suspicious envelopes."

Stowe gave him a mock-thoughtful look. "Only if the envelope bleeds."

Then he looked around the room one last time, his eyes sweeping the shadows like they were waiting to whisper something back.

"Let's start with Catherine Forrester," he said finally.

Harris raised a brow. "Why her?"

Stowe paused at the door, one hand on the brass knob. "Because she's not scared," he said. "And everyone else is. That's either a strength… or a warning."

He pushed open the door. The hallway was colder now, the airtight with expectation.

They stepped into it together, toward the family, toward the silence, toward the mask of grief that someone wore just a little too well.

Behind them, the fire let out a final pop, one last ember snapping into ash.

"I'll say this for old Price," Stowe muttered as they walked, "he finally shut up."

Harris huffed. "It only took a knife."

Stowe shot him a look. "You're getting cynical, Harris."

"Learned from the best."

Stowe grinned faintly. "Then you'll survive."

The hallway stretched ahead, dark and heavy with secrets, the air thick like it was waiting to be stirred.

And behind them, the room went still.

Empty now. But not quiet. Not quite.

Chapter 9: A Shift in the Air

The parlour lay ahead, doors half-drawn like curtains before an act. They stepped inside.

The family was gathered, but not united. They were scattered like players waiting for direction. Peter stood stiffly with arms crossed, gaze pinned to the floor as though daring it to shift. Marion sat on the settee, dabbing at her eyes with a lace-edged handkerchief, though no tears fell. Philip paced near the windows, clutching a half-empty glass, the ice melting into nervous sweat on his palm. David stood near Catherine, not touching, but close, his posture taut, his mouth a grim line.

Catherine sat apart, still as sculpture. Her posture was impeccable, not rigid but practiced like someone who had long ago learned that stillness was its own kind of power. Her expression gave away nothing, but her eyes, sharp and ever moving, took everything in.

When the detectives entered, those eyes lifted. Curious, not alarmed. Catherine Price was never caught off guard, only interrupted.

"Mrs. Forrester," Harris said, stepping forward with quiet courtesy. "May we speak with you in private?"

She rose at once, fluid and calm. No protest. No hesitation. As she moved, she paused only to place a hand on David's forearm, just for a moment, just enough. He met her gaze and gave the barest nod, but his jaw clenched as she moved away. Worry hung behind his eyes like smoke behind glass.

She led them down the corridor without a word.

The morning room welcomed them like a painting from another century. Light filtered through fine lace curtains, turning everything into soft pastels. Dust motes drifted lazily in the air. A piano stood in the corner, its keys untouched, the lid slightly open as if expecting someone long gone to return. A delicate tea set sat on the side table, cups perfectly arranged, untouched, symbolic.

Catherine took the seat by the window, hands folding neatly in her lap. She didn't fidget. She didn't blink more than once. Her presence was as curated as the room around her, gentle, elegant, impenetrable.

Stowe remained standing, leaning slightly against the mantel, while Harris took the seat across from her, flipping open his notebook with a crisp snap.

"A real locked door mystery we have here" Stowe started.

"Mrs. Forrester," Harris began, voice professional but not unfriendly, "we'd like to know more about your father."

Catherine tilted her head slightly, as if they'd asked something quaint. "You'll have to be more specific. There were several versions of Reginald Price."

Stowe raised an eyebrow. "Let's start with yours."

She gave a faint smile. "My father was a man who considered empathy a design flaw. He valued control above kindness, obedience above dialogue. He prized strength, despised weakness, and kept his enemies close, not to forgive them, but to keep track."

"Did you admire him?" Harris asked.

"I outgrew him," she said simply. "And he resented that."

Harris scribbled a note, though his pen faltered a second longer than usual.

"Tell us about his relationship with Philip Marsh," he continued.

Catherine's gaze drifted to the window for a moment, as though watching something invisible. "Philip tried to bring the company into the twentieth century. My father preferred the nineteenth. Their meetings were… volatile. Shouting was the floor level. Sometimes furniture got involved."

"Did David get involved?" Harris asked.

Her head turned, just slightly. "David supported Philip. He believed in progress. Father never forgave him for it. Said he was disloyal. Weak. That was his favourite word."

Stowe stepped forward now, voice gravelly. "Sounds like motive. All around."

Catherine didn't blink. "Of course it is. Every single person in that parlour had motive. So, do I. But motive alone is meaningless. The real question is opportunity."

"Then let's talk about that," Harris said. "Did you leave the table during dinner?"

"Yes. Briefly. I went upstairs to powder my nose. Three minutes. Five at most."

"Did you see anyone?"

She hesitated, not like someone caught in a lie, but someone choosing her words. "No. But I didn't expect to. Everyone was avoiding each other by that point."

Stowe moved closer, his voice dropping. "Catherine, did you hate your father?"

For the first time, her composure cracked, just faintly. A flicker of something behind her eyes. Not sorrow. Something older. Harder.

"I hated what he did to the people I love," she said. "Does that count?"

Stowe met her gaze evenly. "Yes. It counts."

Silence fell like snowfall. Gentle. Suffocating.

Harris flipped a page. His voice was quieter now. "Did your mother know? What he was like?"

Catherine looked down briefly, then back up. "She knew. But denial was her gift. She built herself a little fantasy world, parties, shopping, surface smiles. She survived in the cracks."

"She didn't defend you?"

"She didn't defend anyone. She just… endured. Like wallpaper. Faded, but still clinging to the walls."

Stowe asked, "What about now? Could she have… snapped?"

Catherine's voice dropped to a near-whisper. "She doesn't have the strength. Or the clarity."

"Then who does?" Harris asked.

Catherine stood slowly, moving toward the window. The light traced the edges of her figure, making her look almost ethereal. But her voice was clear, measured. Controlled like a scalpel.

"You want me to name someone. But this wasn't a crime of passion. It wasn't an accident or a drunken argument. It was deliberate. Controlled. That narrows the field."

She turned back to them, her eyes sharp as glass. "You're asking the wrong question. It's not 'Who wanted him dead?' It's 'Who stopped being afraid of him?'"

Stowe nodded slowly, impressed despite himself. "And who would that be?"

Catherine stepped past them, paused at the door. Her hand rested lightly on the frame, her nails tapping once against the wood.

"Someone who realized," she said softly, "that the only way out was to kill him."

Stowe's voice followed her, more pointed now. "Is that what *you* realized?"

She looked back, not with fear or hesitation, but calm defiance. "If I had killed my father, Inspector, I wouldn't be standing here answering your questions."

She started to turn but stopped.

"Oh, and, did you *see* the knife?" she added, casually. "We have a set of those in the kitchen."

Stowe raised an eyebrow. "Identical?"

"Same handle. Same weight. Same shine when they catch the light." Her tone was flat. "He insisted on the best. Even when it came to carving flesh."

There was a flicker in Stowe's eyes, interest, calculation.

"You think someone took it from the kitchen?" Harris asked.

"I think someone knew where to find it," she replied. "And how to use it."

"And you?" Stowe asked. "How familiar are you with that set?"

Catherine smiled, slow and sharp. "I do some of the cooking. Father always said the staff never got the seasoning right."

"And did he get anything right?" Stowe asked.

There was a pause. Then:

"No," she said. "But he made sure we all paid the price for that."

"Any ideas on, how to solve the locked door problem?" Stowe stated, looking up, as he mulled over the problem once more.

"The problem with all locked doors start with the key."

She turned again. Her heels clicked twice on the floor before she stopped once more, just in the doorway.

"One more thing," she said, not looking back. "If you want to find the killer, stop asking who was angry."

Stowe stepped closer. "Then what do we ask?"

Her voice floated back like a razor wrapped in silk.

"Ask who finally realized they didn't need his permission to breathe."

Then she was gone.

Her footsteps echoed down the hall like punctuation marks, firm, final, unapologetic.

Harris let out a breath he hadn't realized he was holding. "She's not afraid of us at all."

"No," Stowe said, still staring at the door. "She's not afraid of *anything*. That's what worries me."

"You think she's hiding something?"

Stowe nodded. "Definitely."

"But not the murder?"

"No." He turned to Harris. "She doesn't feel guilty about *what* happened. She feels guilty about what she *didn't* do."

"To stop it?"

"To prevent it. Or maybe to welcome it."

Harris closed his notebook slowly. "You think she wanted him dead."

Stowe didn't blink. "I think *everyone* in this house did. But Catherine? Catherine might have made peace with it before it ever happened."

He looked around the room, its edges sharp with silence.

"Get Philip Marsh."

As they stepped into the corridor again, the house seemed to shift around them, just a little. The shadows darker. The floor creaked more than it had before. The kind of creak that sounds less like age and more like a house finally learning how to breathe without its master.

It wasn't grief in the walls now.

It was relief.

Chapter 10: Philip Marsh

The rain had stopped, leaving a fragile hush hanging over the estate like gauze stretched over a wound. The downpour had passed, but its memory lingered in every surface, wet leaves shimmered under the garden lamps, puddles mirrored the grey-black sky, and the mist that clung to the hedgerows hung heavy, like a breath not yet released.

Inside, the Price house had not exhaled. If anything, it seemed to be holding its breath tighter now, as though bracing for what might come next. The air was thick with things unspoken resentments, regrets, suspicion, all pressing in against the panelled walls.

Through the tall windows of the study, moonlight spilled in pale ribbons across the faded Persian rug, broken by the sharp-edged shadows of the mullioned glass. The chandeliers above had been dimmed to their lowest setting, casting a faint golden wash that did nothing to soften the room's edges. It was too quiet.

The fire had long since collapsed into dull, red smudges of heat. Thin curls of smoke rose lazily from the grate, drifting up and vanishing like old ghosts. The lingering scent of wax, charred wood, and old paper gave the room the feel of something just on the edge of being forgotten.

The armchairs near the hearth stood empty, but not unoccupied. The leather cushions held the shape of shoulders long tense, backs hunched with the weight of old arguments. In their silence, they whispered things no one dared repeat.

Inspector Thomas Stowe stood by the fireplace, unmoving. The firelight caught the silver at his temples, gleaming like frost. His large hands were clasped behind his back, and his jaw worked slowly, methodically, as though he were chewing on a truth not yet ready to be spoken aloud.

Behind him, Detective Sergeant Michael Harris leaned against the tall walnut cabinet that held a row of unread legal volumes. One foot tapped lightly against the polished floor. He held his notebook half-open in one hand, pen ready in the other, though he hadn't written anything for several minutes.

"He's taking a long time," Harris muttered, glancing toward the study door.

"He's gathering his story," Stowe replied without turning. "Or convincing himself he doesn't have one."

"You think he's hiding something?"

Stowe finally looked up, eyes narrowing. "They all are."

The door creaked open.

Philip Marsh stepped inside.

He looked every inch a man worn down by time, guilt, and something deeper, shame, perhaps. His suit, once tailored, now hung awkwardly on his frame. His tie was loosened to the point of irrelevance, and his jacket sagged from one shoulder as though it had given up trying to be presentable. His skin bore the waxy hue of someone who had skipped too many meals and too much sleep. His eyes were red-rimmed, tired, but still searching.

He stood in the doorway for a beat too long, as if unsure the room would let him in.

"Come in," Stowe said, his voice softer than usual. Not kind, just measured.

Philip shut the door behind him with care, as though afraid the latch might break beneath his fingers. He crossed the room slowly, each step cautious, and lowered himself into the armchair opposite the fireplace. He perched rather than relaxed, his shoulders tense, knees close together, hands folded too tightly in his lap.

Stowe turned to face him fully.

Harris, already flipping open his notebook with a crisp snap, kept his tone even. "Mr. Marsh, thank you for joining us."

Philip nodded. He didn't speak. He swallowed instead, a visible effort, his throat working once, twice.

Stowe sat as well, his weight settling into the armchair across from Philip like an anchor dropped into deep water. He didn't speak at first. Just watched.

Philip glanced up, met the stare, then quickly looked away. His eyes flicked toward the empty grate.

"I haven't been in this room since..." Philip's voice caught. He cleared it with a wince. "Since earlier. Since it happened."

"That makes sense," Stowe said, his tone low and even.

Philip rubbed the side of his jaw with trembling fingers. "Everything feels... warped now. Like the house is remembering things differently."

"Or maybe *you* are," Stowe said gently. "Memory does that. We shift the weight around. Grief helps it settle in strange places."

Philip gave a strained smile. "Is that what this is? Grief?"

"You tell me."

Philip looked down. His fingers picked at a loose thread on the knee of his trousers, the motion compulsive. "I don't know what it is. I feel... light-headed. Hollow. But also... heavy. Like I've been carrying something and just put it down."

"What were you carrying?" Harris asked, his voice soft.

Philip blinked, a breath escaping him like a confession. "Him."

The silence that followed wasn't awkward. It was dense, like wet wool, thick and clinging.

"He was your business partner," Stowe said. "Your friend, once."

Philip nodded slowly. "All of that. And more. And less."

Stowe stepped closer, folding his arms. "Tell us about your relationship in the last few years."

Philip gave a short, bitter laugh. "Strained. That's the polite version. We built something together, something real. But somewhere along the line, we stopped speaking the same language. I saw a future. He was married to the past. Every conversation turned into a tug-of-war. We didn't talk. We barked. Sometimes we just stared across the boardroom table, daring the other to blink."

"Did you hate him?" Harris asked.

Philip inhaled through his nose, sharp and shaky. "No. I hated what he became. But part of me... part of me never stopped seeing the man he used to be. And I think that's what made it worse. I kept waiting for *him* to come back. He never did."

Stowe nodded slowly. "Let's talk about dinner."

Philip hesitated, gaze flicking to the now-cold fireplace. "It was tense. The air was full of static. You could feel it. Like the house itself was waiting for someone to snap."

"Did you eat?"

"Barely." He laughed, short and without humour. "I moved food around my plate like it was a chessboard."

"Did you leave the table?" Stowe asked.

"Yes. Around eight. I remember because I checked my watch."

"Why?"

"Habit," Philip said. "Back in the day, I always tracked time during formal meetings. Conditioning. Pavlovian punctuality."

"Where did you go?" Harris prompted.

Philip frowned, as if trying to pull the memory from a thick fog. "I meant to go outside. Get air. But I ended up in the corridor. Just... pacing."

"Did anyone see you?" Stowe asked.

"I think Catherine did," he said after a moment. "She was on the stairs. She didn't say anything. Just... watched me. Then turned and went up."

"Did she look startled?"

"No. She looked... alert. Calm. Which is exactly why it rattled me."

"Did you see the door to the study?" Stowe asked, voice tighter now.

"Yes. It was closed."

"And that was unusual?"

"He never kept it closed unless he was furious. Or hiding something. If the door was shut, it meant you didn't belong inside. So, yes if he was inside, it was shut."

Stowe tilted his head. "And you didn't go in?"

"I wanted to," Philip said. "God, I wanted to walk in and scream at him one last time. But I didn't. Something held me back."

"Fear?" Harris asked.

"Exhaustion," Philip replied. "I was too tired to fight anymore. It didn't matter. None of it did."

Stowe looked at him for a long beat. "Did you hear anything?"

Philip swallowed. "Peter. On the phone. He was pacing just inside the drawing room. He said something about getting 'him out of the way.' I assumed he meant retirement. Or some corporate manoeuvring. But now... I don't know."

"We're not making accusations yet," Stowe said gently. "Just gathering threads."

Philip closed his eyes. "I didn't kill him. I didn't."

Stowe said nothing.

After a moment, Philip looked up at him, eyes red. "Do you believe me?"

Stowe paused, then nodded once. "I believe you didn't *want* him dead."

"But?"

"But that's not the same as not doing it."

Harris closed his notebook softly. "Mr. Marsh," he said, voice gentler now, "you had motive. You had opportunity. And now we've heard others implicate themselves. So, I have to ask: did you kill Reginald Price?"

Philip's hands trembled. He folded them tighter into his lap, trying to still them. "No," he whispered. "I didn't."

Stowe watched him closely. His expression didn't shift.

Then: "Do you think you know who did?"

Philip didn't answer right away. His gaze turned to the dying embers in the hearth. "I think everyone in this house wanted him dead," he said slowly. "But only one person finally stopped being afraid."

He stood, his knees cracking softly. "I wish I knew who that was. I really do."

"You may yet remember more," Stowe said calmly, rising as well. "People do. When they stop trying to forget."

Philip gave a slow nod, bitter, exhausted. "If I remember anything else... you'll be the first to know."

He walked to the door, paused with his hand on the knob, and added, "For what it's worth, I hope you catch them. Even if it's someone I care about."

He left without waiting for a response. The door clicked shut behind him, leaving only the soft hiss of the fire and the echo of a truth not quite confessed.

Harris turned to Stowe. "You believe him?"

Stowe stared at the chair Philip had just vacated.

"Yes."

"But you said earlier you don't trust him."

Stowe gave a faint, tired smile. "That's not a contradiction. That's just family logic."

He looked toward the hallway, the one leading back to the parlour, to the sitting room, to the phone Peter had used. The one that might've carried a voice saying, "get him out of the way."

And in the flickering firelight, Stowe turned to Harris.

"Two down. Three to go."

Outside, the mist clung to the windows like a secret not ready to leave.

Inside, the shadows listened, more eager now. More curious.

Stowe exhaled through his nose. "Bring in Peter," he said.

The game, he knew, was only just beginning. And someone in this house was starting to play for keeps.

Chapter 11: Catherine Takes the Case

The storm had passed, but the air inside the Price estate remained thick, charged, brittle. Not with weather now, but with tension. The kind of pressure that lingers after something has snapped. The kind that makes rooms feel smaller, walls closer. The kind that says something is coming, even if no one yet knows what.

Catherine stood by the tall bay window in the morning room, arms folded across her chest, her figure silhouetted against the faint moonlight. Her profile was etched in shadow and glass, sharp as a blade. The windowpane was flecked with raindrops, each droplet trailing downward in slow, quiet descent, like tears refusing to be seen. Outside, the garden glistened in the aftermath, hedges dripping, gravel shimmering. The gas lamps lining the drive gave everything a surreal glow, like the world had been painted over in soft watercolours.

Behind her, the hearth whispered and cracked. The low flames cast a warm but insufficient light. The scent of scorched wood mingled with old roses and lavender sachets tucked between cushions years ago by a housekeeper now long gone. Above the mantel hung the portrait of Reginald Price, imperious, lifeless, and watchful. His painted eyes, hard and grey, followed her movements with the same cold scrutiny he had exercised in life.

But Catherine didn't flinch. She didn't acknowledge the portrait at all. Her silence was its own rebellion.

From the hallway, voices wove in and out like drifting smoke, low, measured, clipped. Inspector Stowe's gravelled murmur came and went, occasionally joined by Harris's sharper, more exacting tone. Doors creaked open. Closed. A distant floorboard groaned. Somewhere down the corridor, someone sighed. The house had grown restless, its every noise loaded with expectation.

David sat in the velvet settee, one ankle resting across his knee, a glass of whisky cradled in his hand. The amber liquid shimmered in the firelight. He regarded her over the rim of the glass, eyes calm but watchful. Beneath his relaxed posture, there was tension in the line of his jaw. Like he was bracing for her next sentence.

"You've been staring out that window for ten minutes," David said quietly. "Are you planning to leap into the shrubbery and begin interrogating rose bushes?"

Catherine turned; her expression unreadable. A small, dry smile touched her lips. "Only if the roses start lying. Or refusing to testify."

David chuckled.

"Never trust a flower that blooms too early," she said, folding her arms. "Or anyone who speaks in riddles after a murder."

"You've got that look," he said, stepping closer. "The one that says you're about to do something clever and outrageous and possibly catastrophic."

She arched a brow. "You make it sound like I don't plan these things in advance."

"That's what worries me."

She walked to the fire, her heels whispering over the rug until they tapped against the polished wood in front of the hearth. She picked up the poker and prodded the coals, sending up a spatter of sparks like startled fireflies. The light caught in her eyes, but her focus was elsewhere.

"Would it be so outrageous," she said, still watching the fire, "to suggest that Stowe is completely wrong?"

David blinked, lowering his whisky. "About what? The murderer? Or the entire case?"

"Both."

She turned to face him fully. Her posture sharpened, like someone stepping onto a stage.

"He's treating this like a parlour mystery," she said. "Like if he waits long enough, someone will trip over their conscience and confess. He's searching for neat labels. The angry son. The bitter partner. The emotionally compromised daughter. But Reginald didn't die in fiction. He died in this house. With us."

David tilted his head. "So, you're saying... he's looking for story arcs, not suspects?"

"He's looking for a narrative that ties up neatly. But this, this is, chaos in a silk waistcoat. He's walking in with clean shoes trying to solve a crime committed in the mud."

David sighed and ran a hand through his hair. "I don't disagree. But Catherine, Stowe's not an idiot. He's slow, yes. But deliberate. Careful."

"Careful," she repeated, turning the word over like a stone in her mouth. "Careful is what people say when they're out of ideas but want to sound noble."

"You're being harsh."

"I'm being accurate. He's tired. I overheard him talking to Harris, this is his last case."

David's eyebrows lifted. "Retirement?"

She nodded. "More like surrender. He speaks about Reginald the way one speaks about an exorcism. He's not investigating anymore. He's mourning the idea of justice."

David crossed to the window where she'd stood minutes before. His reflection hovered beside hers in the glass, blurred by mist and rain. "Then what do we do?"

Catherine didn't respond immediately. She turned toward the tea table, picked up a porcelain cup, and set it back down again without drinking. Her fingers lingered on the edge of the saucer, searching for a flaw.

"I take the case," she said.

He turned. "What?"

"I'm the only one who can do this properly," she said, lifting her chin. "The only one who knows the players well enough to see where the truth fell out of the script."

"You're not a detective, Catherine."

She met his eyes, calm and clear. "No. But I'm the only person in this house who isn't pretending anymore. And that gives me an edge."

David sighed, scrubbing a hand down his face. "This is exactly how your schemes begin."

"And how most of them succeed," she added quickly.
"Except for the goat incident in Marrakesh."
"That was not my fault. That goat had issues."
"You bribed a customs officer with a bracelet and a croissant."
"And it worked."

David stared at her, half-exasperated, half-admiring. "You're terrifying, you know that?"

"I know," she said sweetly. "But I channel it toward justice."

He gave a quiet laugh. "And what happens if you find something you don't want to know?"

She didn't blink. "Then I'll know it. And I'll decide what to do with it."

"You think one of us did it."

She tilted her head. "Don't you?"

There was a long silence. The kind that builds between two people who have loved each other long enough to know every weakness and respected each other enough to leave most of them alone.

Finally, he nodded. "Where do you start?"

Catherine moved to the small desk in the corner and pulled open a drawer. Inside: old letters, scraps of invoices, a fountain pen, a pair of keys, and one slim leather-bound notebook. She lifted the notebook gently, as if it might whisper to her if handled correctly.

"I start by making a list," she said, thumbing through blank pages. "Of who had access, who had motive, and, most importantly, who changed after he died."

David moved beside her. "You think guilt leaves footprints?"

She sat down, opened the book to a fresh page. "No. But fear does. And fear always leaves a trail."

He sat beside her, lifting his glass again. "Do I make the list?"

She glanced at him sideways. "Oh, you're already on the list."

"Under what heading?"

"'Too kind. Too quiet. Probably hiding something.'"

"That's unfair."

"Is it?"

David grinned and raised his glass in mock salute. "Remind me not to cross you."

"Darling," she said, smiling as she wrote, "that reminder expired five years ago."

Outside, the mist thickened, curling through the hedgerows like smoke hunting for windows.

Inside, the fire flickered.

And beside the desk, Catherine wrote in silence, not chasing the truth, but stalking it.

Chapter 12: The Hidden Key

David sipped his drink, watching her over the rim. The fire cast soft amber light along the edges of his face, blurring the weariness that clung to his features and softening the concern in his eyes. He tilted his head slightly. "So, you think he's given up?"

Catherine didn't answer immediately. She paced slowly across the morning room, her fingers grazing the carved edge of an old armchair like a pianist dragging a hand across familiar keys. The firelight caught the gold thread in her blouse, making it shimmer like sparks trapped in fabric.

"No," she said at last, her tone not cold but precise, like someone cutting a thread with sharp scissors. "Not entirely. Not yet. But he's already written the first draft of the story in his head. And that's dangerous."

David raised an eyebrow, setting his glass down. "Dangerous how?"

She turned to face him, folding her arms. Her voice was low, but the conviction in it was razor-sharp. "Because he's not hunting for *truth* anymore. He's hunting for *confirmation.* And confirmation is always blind."

He leaned back in the chair, one arm resting along the edge of the cushion. "You make him sound like a priest hearing confessions he already thinks he understands."

She smiled faintly. "That's the problem. He doesn't *listen.* He just waits to be proven right."

David gave a small shrug. "It's a flaw. But it's also human."

Catherine walked to the window, not to look out, but to anchor her thoughts. The glass reflected her faintly, blurring her face with streaks of rain and branches tangled in the night.

"There's something he's missed," she said.

David stood, slowly. "What is it?"

She turned, her voice steady. "The door."

He blinked. "The locked study?"

She nodded. "The great theatrical mystery he's built the entire case around. As if Reginald staged his own death just to stump a detective on his way to retirement."

David gave her a wry look. "You don't think it was locked?"

"Oh, it was locked," Catherine replied, "but that's not the magic trick. The trick is that it could have been locked *after*."

David frowned. "Go on."

She walked slowly toward the mantel, the fire casting soft light across her face. "I've known that study since I was tall enough to reach the brass handles. It was Father's kingdom. No dust, no disorder. His pens aligned by colour and brand. His letters filed by year, sender, and level of threat. It wasn't just a workspace. It was a shrine to control."

"And you used to sneak in?"

She smiled at the memory. "When I was ten, it was my favourite game. I'd slip in when he wasn't home. Sit in his chair. Read his papers. I didn't want to *be* him, I just wanted to understand how he managed to hold a room with nothing but silence and a raised eyebrow."

David laughed quietly. "You've inherited that eyebrow, by the way."

"It's a family curse," she replied dryly. "The eyebrow of disapproval."

He stepped closer. "So, what happened?"

"One afternoon," she said, her voice softening, "I got caught. Not by him, almost. I heard him coming and panicked. In my scramble, I locked the door behind me."

"Locked it? From the outside?"

She nodded. "There's a hidden key. Behind the third wooden panel on the bookshelf. It slides out. I'd found it by accident one day. You wouldn't know it was there unless you were looking."

David blinked, the implications settling over him like dust. "So, the locked-room scenario... it's fake."

"It's stagecraft," she said. "A trick of perspective. Anyone who knew about that key could have killed him, exited quietly, locked the door behind them, and left the rest of us spinning conspiracy theories while sipping brandy."

"And Stowe doesn't know?"

She shook her head. "Not yet."

"Why not tell him?"

Catherine's gaze met his with cool deliberation. "Because I want to see who tries to use the locked door as an alibi. I want to see who acts like they *couldn't* have done it. Because when people think they're in the clear, they start getting sloppy."

David studied her for a long moment. Admiration flickered through him, tempered by unease. "You're planning something."

"I'm planning *everything*," she said, stepping toward him. "This house is a maze of masks. People here lie like they breathe. But I know them. I *see* them. I know who flinches when Reginald's name is mentioned. I know who hesitates before speaking. That's where the real clues are."

He smiled, but it was tempered by concern. "You terrify me sometimes."

"You married me."

"I know. I just thought I'd grow immune."

"You haven't?"

"Not even a little," he said, stepping close enough that their arms brushed. "Which is exactly why I'm worried."

She reached up and straightened the collar of his shirt, casually precise. "I'll be fine."

"You always say that."

"And I'm usually right."

He let out a sigh. "So, what now? You take this mystery into your own hands while Stowe ambles around like a Victorian relic?"

"Something like that," she said. "He's waiting for a reveal. I'm going to *trigger* one."

David moved to the fire, lifting his glass again. "You should have been a queen in another life."

"I am," she said with a grin. "Just stuck in the wrong century."

He laughed, leaning back against the mantel. "Then let's hope your loyal court doesn't turn on you."

Catherine picked up the notebook she'd started in the study. "They can try."

She sat, uncapping her pen with a quiet snap. "But if I'm going to war, I want to know who's behind me... and who's sharpening knives."

David approached her slowly, his voice gentler than she was used to hearing. "And what if," he asked, "it turns out to be someone you care about?"

Catherine didn't flinch. She met his gaze without hesitation, her expression still and certain. "Then I'll follow the truth," she said. "Wherever it leads. That's the price of clarity."

There was a pause. Not silence, because the house never truly fell silent. The old bones of it whispered constantly: wind rattling faintly against the eaves, a branch dragging its claws across the windowpanes, some distant door creaking open just far enough to suggest presence without proof.

Inside the room, though, the world felt slowed, like breath held too long.

David studied her for a moment, his features lit only by the fire and the low glow of a wall sconce. There was something in his eyes, half worry, half wonder. "You never cease to terrify me," he said.

Catherine's grin was quick and unapologetic. "That's why you married me."

He stepped closer, close enough that she could feel the warmth from his body before his hand reached out, resting gently against her arm. "That's part of it," he said. "The rest was, well, mostly cheekbones and sarcasm."

"And here I thought it was my obsession with knives and family drama."

"That too." He smiled, but his thumb brushed her sleeve with the softness of someone memorizing the moment. "But I worry, Catherine."

"Good," she said, smoothing the lapel of his jacket. "It means you're still thinking."

"I mean it," he said, quieter now. "If this turns bad, if it turns inward, you don't have to do it alone."

She tilted her head. "I've never done it alone. Even when I told myself I had."

"I know." He hesitated. "That's what makes this harder."

Catherine softened, just a shade. She leaned in, pressing her forehead lightly against his for a brief second, just long enough to pass something between them without needing to name it. Then she stepped back and walked to the side table.

She grabbed the leather notebook, the one she'd used to start her own investigation, and slipped it into her coat pocket. The sound of it sliding against the fabric was barely audible, but to her, it might as well have been the weight of a sword being sheathed.

Her boots clicked against the polished wooden floor as she crossed to the door. She reached for the handle, then paused.

"David," she said, not turning around.

"Yes?"

Her voice was soft but cut with steel. "Watch everyone. Closely. Especially the quiet ones. It's not always the loudest who do the damage."

"I know," he said. "But it's the quiet ones who break your heart."

She turned her head slightly, just enough for him to catch her profile in the firelight. "Then we brace for heartbreak."

David swallowed and nodded, though she didn't see it. "Just come back to me in one piece."

She smiled. "No promises."

Then she opened the door and stepped out into the corridor, which stretched dim and hushed before her. The sconces flickered along the walls, casting long shadows that leaned and curled like secrets waiting to be translated.

To Catherine, it no longer felt dark.

It felt like a map.

And she, at last, had chosen to follow it, not just for answers, not just for justice, but because she needed to understand the shape of the fear that had shaped them all.

Behind her, David stood still, watching the empty space she'd left behind. His hand rested lightly on the table where her notebook had been. His expression was calm, but his fingers tapped, once, twice, against the wood, as if trying to anchor himself.

He whispered to no one, "Please don't let me be on that list."

Outside, the wind pressed harder against the windows.

Inside, the house listened.

And Catherine, for the first time in her life, was no longer just surviving it.

She was hunting.

Chapter 13: Peter Speaks

The study had grown colder as night folded in fully around the house. The storm had moved on, but it had left something behind, a damp residue that clung to the walls, the curtains, the bones of the place. A chill crept in through unseen cracks, curling into corners, slipping beneath the doors, coiling like smoke around the heavy furniture. The embers in the hearth still glowed, low and stubborn, but they no longer pushed back the cold, just painted it in gold and orange.

Faint firelight flickered across the dark wood-panelled walls, catching the spines of dusty books and the brass arms of wall sconces. The shadows danced slowly, like spectres performing a funeral rite they had practiced for years. Everything in the room felt half-alive, as though waiting for someone to command it back to purpose.

Inspector Thomas Stowe sat with a kind of heavy precision in Reginald Price's favourite leather armchair. The chair was well worn creased along the seat edges, polished smooth at the headrest by decades of brooding and dominance. The weight of its former occupant still seemed to press into the leather. Stowe leaned back with a quiet exhale, rubbing his temple with one calloused thumb. His eyes, though bloodshot and rimmed with exhaustion, remained alert, two patient, weathered instruments tuned to human dissonance.

Across from him, Peter Price slouched in a smaller, less distinguished chair. It looked like it had been dragged in from another room, more functional than dignified. He sat awkwardly, as though the furniture resented him. His legs jittered, one heel bouncing against the rug. His arms were crossed tightly, and his posture oscillated between defiant and defensive. A small muscle in his jaw jumped every few seconds, like something trying to speak before he was ready.

Detective Sergeant Michael Harris stood near the fireplace, unmoving. His eyes remained locked on Peter, not aggressive, just unwavering. His pen, for now, was still hovering above his notepad like a question mark waiting for form.

The room was thick with unspoken things. Resentments, guilt, dread. The silence, long and pressing, grew heavier with each passing second, until it was no longer simply quiet it was judgment.

"Thank you for joining us, Peter," Stowe said finally. His voice was gravel, rough but deliberate, shaped like every word had been chewed before being offered. "I know this isn't easy."

Peter scoffed, glancing toward the fire like it had insulted him. His lips twisted into something that resembled a smirk, though it didn't reach his eyes. "I doubt anything about this house was ever *meant* to be easy."

Stowe didn't rise to the bait. Instead, he leaned forward, elbows on his knees, his voice low. "Tell me about your father. Not the man in the paper. The man behind the walls."

Peter exhaled through his nose a half-laugh, half-sigh. "You mean the man who gave lectures on loyalty while playing family members off each other like chess pieces? The man who once locked me out of my room for losing a cufflink, but let Philip misplace a million-pound investment and called it a learning opportunity?"

Stowe said nothing.

Peter's voice grew sharper. "He taught me about fiscal responsibility by berating me for buying a second-hand guitar, while spending thousands on Bordeaux he never drank and art he never understood. The man was a tyrant with taste."

Harris shifted slightly in his chair. Peter noticed. He kept going.

"He told me he loved me exactly once. I was seven. I'd fallen down the stairs, split my chin open. I was sobbing so hard I couldn't breathe. He picked me up, just once, and said it. Then never again. Guess he figured he'd ticked that box."

There was a long beat of silence.

"Did you love him?" Stowe asked, his tone not sympathetic, but not cruel either.

Peter's eyes flickered. "I tried to. For years, I tried. But he made love feel like a performance. If you didn't follow his script, it didn't count."

Harris leaned forward. "Let's talk about dinner. The night he died. What was the mood?"

Peter gave a brittle laugh. "Dinner with Reginald was always a bit like watching a knife juggler. You don't know when it's going to fall, but you know someone's going to bleed."

Stowe allowed himself a small grunt of acknowledgment. "Who seemed the most on edge?"

Peter thought for a moment, counting on his fingers like he was sorting suspects in his head. "Philip was twitchy, Catherine was... Catherine. Cool as ever. Too cool. Marion was quiet, which usually means she was overwhelmed or halfway through dissociating. And David was doing his best impression of a human buffer. He's always trying to mediate something that can't be mediated."

"And you?" Harris asked.

Peter smirked, but it cracked at the edges. "I was ready to walk out before the starter. But I didn't. I sat there like the dutiful son. Let him pour vinegar into every open wound he could find."

"Did you speak to him after dinner?" Stowe asked.

"No," Peter said. "He left the table first. Said something about needing to go to the study. Which is code for sulking or plotting. The moment he walked out, the oxygen came back into the room."

"Where did you go?" Harris asked.

"The sitting room. Took a call."

Stowe glanced up. "Business?"

Peter nodded. "Sort of. It started as venting. Then drifted into damage control."

"Let's rewind," Stowe said. "He refused to support your business proposal. Was that a surprise?"

Peter laughed under his breath. "Not at all. It was just confirmation. He always saw me as the liability. The wildcard. The bad son, waiting to happen. I could have brought him the next Micro-PC and he'd still call it reckless."

"What was the proposal?"

Peter's voice changed, just slightly. Firmer. Cleaner. "A software platform. Enterprise data management. I had a working prototype.

Demo-ready. Investors lined up for first-round meetings. All I needed was capital to make it through initial deployment."

"And he said no."

Peter nodded once; jaw tight. "He didn't just say no. He laughed. Called it a toy. Said I should stop chasing dreams and find a desk job that wouldn't embarrass the family name."

Stowe leaned forward. "And that made you angry."

"Of course it did," Peter snapped. "Wouldn't it make you angry?"

"I'm not your father," Stowe said.

Peter looked away. "No. You're listening, which already puts you ahead."

Harris flipped a page in his notebook. "Philip Marsh told us he overheard you on the phone. You said you needed to 'get your father out of the way.'"

Peter's eyes sharpened. "That's not what I meant," he said quickly. "It was just a phrase. An expression."

"Words matter," Stowe said, voice like gravel smoothed by rain.

Peter shifted, recrossing his legs. "It was business language. Frustration, not intent. I meant I wanted him removed from the equation. Not from existence."

"Who were you speaking to?"

"Marcus Westbrook," Peter said. "Friend from university. He's one of my partners now."

"Would he confirm the call?" Harris asked.

Peter nodded. "Yes. And he'll confirm what I meant. We talked about possible legal workarounds. A forced retirement. Pressure from the board. A buyout. We were looking for clean solutions. I wasn't plotting a murder. I was plotting leverage."

"But you said he had to be 'out of the picture.'"

Peter's voice cracked slightly. "Yes. I said it. But I meant boardroom exile. Not a body on a desk."

Stowe studied him. "And if someone misunderstood that call, if someone took it literally?"

Peter's face paled. "Then I gave them language to hide behind. But I didn't hand them a knife."

Silence. Dense, suffocating.

Stowe stood slowly. Walked toward the fireplace. "You used sharp words in a house already full of blades."

Peter swallowed. "Is that an accusation?"

"No," Stowe said, eyes on the dying fire. "It's a reminder."

Harris closed his notebook. "We may need to speak with Mr. Westbrook."

Peter stood. "Of course. He'll back me up."

"Let's hope so," Stowe murmured.

Peter turned to leave but paused at the door.

"For what it's worth," he said, voice quieter, "I hated the man. But I never wanted him dead. I just wanted him *gone*. There's a difference."

Stowe looked up. "And sometimes," he said, "not a big enough one."

Stowe leaned back in his chair, fingers laced across his stomach, voice low and calm. "You didn't mean to kill him. But you did mean to get rid of him."

Peter looked away, the flicker of firelight catching in his eyes but doing nothing to soften them.

"And what about David Forrester?" Harris asked, flipping his notebook with deliberate slowness.

Peter scoffed, crossing his arms. "He's a fraud. Built from charm and borrowed polish. He talks like a statesman and thinks like a salesman. All surface, no spine."

"Reginald didn't trust him?" Stowe asked.

"Despised him," Peter said, with a hiss of disdain. "Told me just last week he was planning to cut David off entirely. Said he was sick of watching Catherine prop up a man who didn't have the guts to stand on his own. Said she needed to open her eyes before the rot spread."

"Did you tell Catherine?" Stowe asked.

Peter hesitated. Then shook his head. "No."

"Why not?" Harris pressed.

Peter let out a breath through his nose. "Because she'd defend him. Like always. Catherine's many things, but blind to David's flaws? That's her one weakness. She believes in his potential like it's a religion."

Stowe tilted his head, curious. "And that bothers you."

Peter's eyes flashed. "No. What bothers me is that David gets the benefit of the doubt while the rest of us get dissected."

There was a pause.

"You jealous of him?" Stowe asked bluntly.

Peter gave a short, bitter laugh. "Jealous? No. I pity him. At least I know exactly what my father thought of me. David's still pretending there was affection buried somewhere under the contempt."

Stowe and Harris exchanged a look.

"So," Stowe said, ticking off on his fingers. "David had motive. Catherine had motive. Philip had motive."

Peter's smile was tight and cruel. "Everyone in this house did, Inspector. That's the Price legacy. We weren't a family. We were a firing squad, aimed inward."

Stowe leaned forward slightly, voice softening. "What do *you* think happened?"

Peter stared into the fire; jaw clenched. "I think someone finally stopped pretending that Reginald couldn't be touched. Someone got tired of waiting for karma. Someone dreamed about it, and then did it."

"But not you?" Harris asked.

Peter rose slowly, brushing invisible lint from his sleeve. "I'm angry. I'm bitter. But I'm not a killer. I know how to destroy someone *legally*. That's the one thing my father actually taught me."

He turned, walked to the door. His hand rested on the knob, but he didn't open it yet.

"You know what he feared more than death?" Peter said without looking back. "Irrelevance. Losing control. Being talked over."

Stowe folded his arms. "And yet, here we are. Talking about him. Obsessing over him. Still playing his game."

Peter chuckled, but it was hollow. "Exactly. Even dead, he's winning. That's why I couldn't have done it. Killing him would have set him free. And I wanted him to live long enough to see himself lose."

He paused, then added, voice lower now, darker, "You're digging in the right place. But you're looking at the wrong clues."

Stowe's eyes narrowed. "Which clues should we be looking at?"

Peter hesitated. His hand tightened on the knob.

"Ask Catherine," he said.

And with that, he stepped out, the door closing with a soft but deliberate click behind him.

For a long moment, neither man moved.

The room held its breath.

Finally, Harris leaned back, letting out a slow sigh. "That was almost a confession."

Stowe stared at the closed door. "Or a carefully rehearsed performance."

"You think he's lying?"

"I think Peter Price has been waiting to be heard for a very long time," Stowe said quietly. "And now that someone's listening, he's trying to edit the truth into something he can live with."

Harris scribbled a final note. "Self-pity makes a decent mask. But it's a poor shield."

Stowe stood, stretching his back as he walked toward the fire. The flames were low now, licking at the last few coals. "And it always cracks under pressure."

"What about Catherine?" Harris asked.

Stowe didn't answer right away. He bent down, picked up the fire poker, and stirred the embers gently. Sparks flickered up like secrets trying to escape.

"She's the one everyone defers to," he said finally. "Even Peter, in his own backhanded way. That tells me something."

"What does it tell you?"

Stowe turned toward the window, where rain whispered against the glass in long diagonal streaks. "That she knows more than she's said. Maybe everything. Maybe just enough."

Harris was quiet.

Stowe looked back at him. "The question isn't whether Catherine is involved. It's whether she's *protecting* the killer or preparing to expose them."

The fire popped. The shadows danced along the panelled walls, flickering like figures trying to speak.

"Either way," Stowe said, "she's not afraid. And that makes her the most dangerous person in the house."

Upstairs, in a room dim with memory and sharpened with silence, Catherine stood still in the dark listening.

She hadn't moved in ten minutes.

She didn't need to.

Because the next move, she knew, wouldn't be hers.

It would be theirs.

And that was when the real game would begin.

Chapter 14 : The Clue Outside

She was already halfway down the hall before David grabbed his coat and followed.

Outside, the night greeted them with a sharp, wet chill. The scent of soaked earth and the loamy decay of autumn leaves still hung thick in the air, rich and raw. A thin mist hovered close to the ground, curling around their ankles as they stepped onto the slick gravel path. Every step was a soft crunch, a whisper swallowed quickly by the night. The garden was still, holding its breath.

The estate loomed behind them, dark and monolithic, a cold stone relic watching over the grounds like a sentinel. Its upper windows were unlit, blank and watchful. Only the faint flicker of lamplight behind one curtain suggested any life inside.

Catherine moved with purpose across the damp lawn, her coat flaring around her legs. She didn't bother to look back. David quickened his pace to match hers.

"Where exactly are we going again?" he asked under his breath.

"The study window," she replied. Her tone was clipped, each word tightly wound with tension. "If the door was a distraction, the answer might be here."

The hedgerow rose up ahead of them like a shadow wall, the leaves slick with moisture, their edges trembling in the breeze. Beyond it, the eastern wing of the house crouched low against the sky. The window to Reginald's study sat above a narrow flower bed, its glass reflecting the moonlight in slanted shards.

David followed her, his brow furrowed, his jaw tight. "You think someone broke in?"

"I think we've all been looking in the wrong direction," she said, yanking the coat around her shoulders. "Everyone's obsessed with the locked door. The impossible room. But what if it wasn't impossible? What if someone did get in from the outside and we never thought to check properly?"

"It's not a leap," she replied sharply. "It's the only avenue no one's questioned. Everyone's too ready to believe the killer was one of us. It makes it personal. Contained. Easier to handle."

She turned, eyes dark and bright. "But what if it isn't easier? What if it's worse?"

"At the very least," he muttered, "this'll look great if someone sees us creeping around the garden like we're casing the place."

The stone steps glistened, slick with rainwater. Catherine's boots skidded slightly, but she regained her footing without missing a step.

David moved up beside her, flashlight sweeping ahead. "Let me go first. You always forget how to walk like a civilian."

She grinned without humour. "Remind me later how thrilling you found that on our honeymoon."

He gave a short laugh, but it faded quickly in the cold. Everything out here felt like it belonged to another world, silver and shadow, glinting and half-erased. The garden hedges curled along the path like walls of a forgotten maze.

"I hate this part of the house," David muttered. "Always felt... hollow."

"It is," Catherine said. "Father kept it because the land added value, not charm."

They rounded the far corner where the study jutted out into a narrow alcove, its mullioned window framed in ivy and rusted iron. From here, the study looked less like a room and more like a vault.

Catherine crouched by the stone ledge. "Careful," David murmured. "The ground's soft."

"Exactly," she whispered, already sifting through the wet soil. Her breath floated in front of her.

Then "There," she said, her voice tightening.

David leaned in, angling the light.

The beam landed on a clear boot print. Deep. Broad. Sharp at the heel. The tread clean, distinct.

"That's not one of ours," he said.

"No," Catherine replied, standing slowly. Her pulse surged in her neck. "And it shouldn't be there if the room was sealed from the inside."

They stared at the footprint in silence. The wind stirred through the trees. The air swirled around their feet.

"Whoever left that tried to be careful," David said. "But they didn't count on the rain."

Catherine nodded. "And they didn't count on me."

She stepped up to the window, brushing fingers across the lower frame. "The wood's soft. Rotted in spots. If you knew where to press, you could pry it open without much force."

"Think Stowe missed it?"

"He didn't miss it," she said. "He dismissed it. He's chasing logic, not instinct."

She pulled a handkerchief from her pocket and gently pressed it into the print, then folded it with care.

"We'll need this," she murmured.

David gave her a look, half admiration, half disbelief. "You're really doing this. Turning detective."

She softened slightly. "My father's dead. Everyone's treating it like a parlour game. I want answers. Real ones."

David stepped closer. "Then I'm with you. Even if it's mad. Even if it's messy."

Their eyes met. For a moment, the cold faded. Then she nodded. "Let's go."

Back inside, the house was warm but not inviting. The weight of the place clung to them like wet wool. They peeled off coats and scarves. Neither spoke.

In the drawing room, Philip Marsh sat hunched in an armchair, one leg crossed over the other. A glass dangled from his fingers, nearly empty. The ice had melted into watery defiance.

He looked up slowly as they entered. "You two look like grave robbers."

Catherine smiled faintly. "Depends on who's buried."

David coughed, hiding a smirk.

Philip gestured toward the hearth. "Want a drink?"

Catherine shook her head. "No. I want to know what you were doing an hour before Reginald died."

Philip blinked. "Why?"

"Because" she said, stepping forward, "I just found proof someone entered from the outside. And if that someone, isn't you, then it's someone else we haven't accounted for."

David remained by the doorway, watching them both. He didn't speak. He didn't have to.

Catherine had just shifted the board. And they were all back in play.

Philip's brow furrowed. He shifted in his chair, placing his glass down with more care than necessary. "You look remarkably determined," he said, his voice dry.

"I am," Catherine replied.

He raised an eyebrow. "Should I be worried?"

Catherine tilted her head, her voice calm and cutting. "Did you stab my father in the back, Philip?"

Philip coughed mid-sip, eyes wide. "Excuse me?"

"You heard me," she said. "There's a footprint outside the study. Someone made it look like the room was sealed. But someone got in."

David took a step closer, arms crossed. His presence grounded her.

Philip ran a hand through his hair, voice dry. "That's ridiculous."

"Is it?" Catherine pressed. "You argued with him. You knew the room. And you had just as much reason as anyone."

Philip's mouth tightened. "I hated the man, sure. But so did you. So did half the guests that night. Doesn't make me the one holding the knife."

"Then help me prove it," she said. "Help me find who did."

He studied her for a long moment. "You're serious."

"Deadly."

"And what do you want from me?"

"A timeline. The truth. No edits."

Philip exhaled and leaned back. "Fine. I last saw Reginald around eight. He was in one of his moods. We had words. He left. Door slammed. After that, I bumped into Peter. By quarter past, we were back at the table."

"Anything unusual?"

"Around nine, I heard footsteps. I thought it was Marion, but I never saw who."

"Did you see David?"

Philip looked at him. "No. Why?"

David answered calmly. "I was outside. Clearing my head."

Catherine turned back to Philip. "If anything, else comes back, you tell me. Not Stowe."

Philip smirked. "What are you, now? Detective Forrester?"

She straightened. "Exactly."

She turned on her heel. David followed without hesitation.

At the base of the stairs, he caught her arm gently. "You were brilliant."

She smiled, soft but confident. "You are too."

His voice lowered. "Do you think we'll find the killer before Stowe does?"

Her eyes gleamed. "I think we already found the first thread. And that's how it always starts."

David chuckled, but it held nerves beneath. "You horrify me sometimes."

"Good," she whispered, kissing his cheek. "Let's stay sharp."

And together, they climbed the stairs. Their hands brushed as they walked, just briefly, but neither pulled away.

The house loomed above them, a shell of elegance and secrets. And somewhere inside its walls, the next truth was waiting to be unearthed.

Chapter 15: Marion's Tears

The night had stretched long, shadows growing deeper in the corners of the grand house. The once lively hum of conversation and the clinking of glasses had faded into an uneasy silence, punctuated only by the occasional creak of the old floorboards. The great chandelier overhead swayed ever so slightly in a draft that whispered through the corridors, casting flickering shapes against the ornate wallpaper. The clock in the hall struck midnight, a solemn chime that echoed through the vast space, but Inspector Stowe showed no sign of leaving.

He sighed, rubbing his temple as he looked over his notes. The weight of the evening pressed heavily upon him. His usually steady hand wavered slightly as he flipped back a page. "I know it's getting late, but I think we need to question Marion and David before we call it a night."

Detective Harris, standing near the unlit fireplace, nodded, his arms crossed. His reflection in the cold, darkened glass of the window was as stern as his expression. "Agreed. When I went to get Peter earlier, I noticed that Marion was still up lost in thought, but very much awake. She's in no state to sleep, so we might as well start with her."

Stowe grunted his approval. "Let's bring her in."

Marion Price entered the drawing room with slow, hesitant steps, her heeled shoes barely making a sound against the thick Persian rug. The heavy fabric of her evening gown rustled softly; a remnant of the grand dinner now long past. Though still clad in elegance, there was an unmistakable disarray to her appearance, her hair, once carefully pinned, had loosened, and a few stray curls fell across her pale cheeks. Dark smudges beneath her eyes spoke of exhaustion, of grief, and perhaps something more. Her hands, trembling slightly, clutched a crumpled handkerchief, its embroidered initials damp with tears.

She hesitated near the doorway for a moment, her eyes flicking between the two men. The weight of the room seemed oppressive, the tall bookshelves and dark-panelled walls pressing inward. A fire had once crackled in the hearth, but now only cold embers remained. She finally moved forward and sank into the chair opposite Stowe, drawing in a shuddering breath.

"I... I don't know how much help I can be," she whispered, her voice thick with emotion. Her gaze darted between the two men, wary yet weary, as though bracing herself for what was to come.

Harris moved closer, his tone gentler than usual. "Just tell us what you remember, Mrs. Price." He sat beside her, rather than across from her, offering a presence that felt less interrogative and more comforting. He leaned forward slightly, his notepad resting on his knee, his pen poised but unthreatening.

She dabbed at her eyes and sniffed softly, her fingers twisting the delicate lace of the handkerchief. "I... I'm going to miss him greatly." Her voice wavered, and she let out a sharp, shuddering breath. "He was my husband for so many years."

Stowe didn't respond immediately. He watched her with measured calm, then shifted in his seat, his voice low and even. "And yet, you must have known what people said about him. Reginald wasn't an easy man to live with."

Marion let out a brittle, humourless laugh, a short, bitter sound. "No, he wasn't." Her fingers stilled their nervous movements, and she looked away, blinking rapidly. "But he provided for me." She sighed, her voice suddenly hollow, her hands gripping the handkerchief tighter. "And now... where am I going to get the money I need?"

Harris's eyebrows lifted slightly. "Was he in financial trouble?"

Marion hesitated, her posture stiffening just a fraction. A flicker of something, guilt? Worry? crossed her face before she shook her head. "Not exactly. But he controlled everything. I never had to think about money before. I just... spent what I wanted, and he handled it." A thin, wavering smile touched her lips, but it lacked any real warmth. "Now, I don't know what's left for me."

Stowe leaned in slightly, not aggressively, but with a new attentiveness. "You say he controlled everything. Did he ever make you feel... trapped?"

She gave a hollow laugh. "All the time. But I suppose I got used to it. You'd be amazed what becomes normal after thirty years."

"You sound as if you were afraid of him," Stowe said, watching her carefully.

Marion met his gaze, eyes narrowing slightly. "I wasn't afraid. Not exactly." She paused, then added, "But I never crossed him."

She glanced toward the cold fireplace, as if trying to draw strength from the memory of its earlier warmth. "You may think I'm a fool," she continued, "but that house, his house, was my whole world. And now it's full of ghosts."

Stowe tapped his pen against his notebook, his gaze unwavering. "Tell us about last night. Did you leave the dinner table at any point?"

Marion nodded wearily. "Yes, I went to the toilet at nine o'clock. These meals are such long, drawn-out affairs." She waved a hand vaguely, as if dismissing the rigid structure of their dinner gatherings. "Too much wine, I suppose." Her lips twitched, but there was no mirth in her expression.

Stowe's eyes narrowed slightly. "And did you pass by Reginald's office?"

Her brow furrowed as she thought. The question seemed simple, but the way Stowe watched her made her hesitate. "Yes. The door was shut. I remember that clearly."

Harris, notebook in hand, scribbled something down. "Was he alone?"

Marion stilled, her fingers tightening around the handkerchief. A muscle twitched in her jaw. "I…I don't think so."

Stowe shifted forward. "What makes you say that?"

She swallowed hard, her throat bobbing with the effort. When she spoke, her voice had dropped to a near whisper. "I could hear his raised voice. He was arguing with someone inside."

Stowe exchanged a glance with Harris before gently steering her back. "Just Reginald's voice?"

"Yes," she said quickly, then hesitated. "At least… I think so. I only caught a few seconds, but he sounded furious."

Stowe leaned in; his voice now quieter, more intimate. "Marion, I need you to focus. You say it was just his voice, but could the other person have been quieter? Was there any indication at all of someone else?"

She faltered. "I... I don't know. Maybe a murmur. A shape behind the glass, but I couldn't see clearly. The light was on, but the curtains were drawn." She paused. "It didn't feel right. That's what I remember most. It didn't feel right."

Stowe's tone softened even further. "And the voice you heard, was it different in any way? Louder, softer, more... frantic?"

She hesitated, pressing the handkerchief to her lips. "It was sharper. Panicked, maybe. He sounded desperate, like he was losing control of something. That wasn't like him."

"Could he have been on the telephone?" Stowe asked.

"I can't explain it, it just felt like someone else was in the room." Marion replied.

A log in the fireplace settled with a dull crack, startling her. She flinched slightly, the tension in her shoulders tightening as her hands clenched the handkerchief into a knot. Harris exchanged a glance with Stowe, the unspoken understanding passing between them there was no doubt now. Someone had been inside that office with Reginald Price before his murder.

Stowe's voice dropped. "Marion, think carefully. Was there anything else? A sound? A shadow? Something you couldn't explain?"

She hesitated again, her gaze darting towards the dimly lit hallway beyond. Her breath quickened slightly, as though a realization was just beyond her grasp. "I... I don't know," she murmured. "I didn't stop. I should have."

Harris leaned closer, his tone low and steady. "Did Reginald seem particularly on edge earlier in the day?"

Marion closed her eyes for a moment. "He was agitated. He'd received a letter that morning. I never saw it, but after reading it, he paced for hours. Snapped at everyone. Even the staff."

"A letter?" Stowe asked, instantly alert. "Do you know what it was about?"

She shook her head. "No. But he put it in his inside jacket pocket. It upset him more than anything I'd seen in years."

Stowe's tone shifted again softer, but urgent. "Did he say anything to you about it? Anything at all?"

She nodded slowly. "He told me once that everything he'd built could collapse from within. That the real danger always came from inside the walls. I thought it was just his usual melodrama."

Stowe scribbled a note, then looked back up. "Marion," he said gently, "you've lived in this house a long time. Have you ever seen anything or anyone you couldn't explain? Any locked doors that weren't usually locked? Any spaces that felt... different?"

She was quiet for a long moment. Then, in a voice barely audible: "There's a room on the third floor. It's always been locked. Reginald said it was for storage. But I never saw what was inside."

Stowe and Harris exchanged another glance. The tension between them now was thick enough to cut.

Marion slowly stood but paused near the fireplace, her eyes flicking toward a faded family portrait hanging crookedly on the wall. Her voice trembled. "This house... I used to know every inch of it. But tonight, it feels like a stranger."

Stowe stood with her. "Thank you, Mrs. Price," he said. "You've been very helpful."

She nodded, her hand shaking slightly. Before leaving, she turned back to Stowe.

"I don't know who did this," she whispered, voice cracking. "But someone in this house knows. They must."

And with that, she disappeared down the hallway, her footsteps fading, leaving behind a silence even deeper than before.

"Harris, we need to get on to those telephone people, did a call from this study come in or out. We also need to look at that letter. Marion was very helpful. More clues mean we are moving on the right track. Now for David."

Chapter 16: The Wrong Puzzle

The house was steeped in a deep, brooding silence, thick and pressing like the hush before a storm. Catherine Forrester moved through it like a restless spirit, her thoughts spinning with precision even as the night pressed close against the tall windows. Outside, the rain continued to fall, persistent, rhythmic, soft as secrets. Each droplet tapped against the glass as though seeking entry, whispering reminders of what had been lost.

The library was her sanctuary, and tonight, her war room.

Warm lamplight spilled over the rich wood panelling and lined bookshelves, casting flickering shadows that swayed like watchful figures in the periphery. The scent of leather-bound volumes, ink, and old paper clung to the air. The fire crackled low in the hearth, giving off more light than warmth, and casting amber hues across the disarray she had wrought in her search for truth.

Catherine sat at the long mahogany desk, its surface hidden beneath a fortress of documents, household ledgers, guest lists, scraps of correspondence both typed and handwritten, and fading copies of the estate's financial records. Teacups, some drained, others forgotten halfway through, sat perched precariously on corners and shelves, remnants of long hours spent in frenzied concentration. Open notebooks spilled across the floor at her feet, their pages a chaotic mixture of elegant cursive and frantic scrawl. Diagrams and sketches, timelines with colour-coded annotations, and a hand-drawn floor plan of the house marked with bold arrows and red ink surrounded her like a cocoon of deduction.

Catherine rubbed her temples, her eyes burning with exhaustion, but her thoughts refused to still. She flipped open another ledger, scanning a series of notations in her father's handwriting. A column of unexplained withdrawals caught her attention. Her pen hovered over the page.

The door creaked open behind her. She didn't startle. Her instincts told her who it would be.

David.

He stepped inside slowly, carefully, as if unsure whether to interrupt her storm of thought. His footsteps were nearly silent against the thick Persian rug. He wore the same shirt from earlier, now rumpled and open at the collar. His face was pale, drawn, the flickering firelight carving shadows into the lines of weariness around his mouth and eyes.

Catherine didn't look up immediately. Her pen tapped against the margin of the ledger with a soft, steady rhythm, a clock counting down to something only she could see.

"You look determined," David said after a beat, his voice low and tinged with fatigue. There was admiration there, too, though it sat hidden beneath the weariness."

Finally, Catherine lifted her gaze. Her eyes were sharp, fever-bright with clarity, her mind ablaze with some invisible calculus. "Because I am."

David walked to the hearth, letting the fire's glow wash over him. He turned to face her, arms folded loosely. "Stowe's been at it all night. He's spoken to everyone, twice, in some cases. Are you trying to race him?"

Catherine offered a thin smile, one that didn't reach her eyes. "Outrun him," she corrected. "I intend to be at the finish line before he even realises the racecourse curves in a different direction."

David gave a soft, rueful chuckle. "That sounds like something your father would have said."

She tensed at that, but only briefly. "Yes, well. He didn't win his race, did he?"

He didn't answer. There was no good answer to that. Silence bloomed between them, thick with shared grief and unspoken doubts. Catherine turned back to her notes, flipping a page, her fingers leaving faint smudges where the ink had not quite dried.

"I found something," she said, almost to herself. "Something odd in the ledgers."

David stepped closer, peering over her shoulder. She tapped a figure on the page.

"Large sums. Withdrawn regularly. In cash. No paper trail. No explanation."

He frowned. "Maybe he was paying someone off?"

"Or being blackmailed," she said grimly. "It would explain his agitation that day."

She stood abruptly and began pacing the length of the library, the hem of her coat trailing behind her like a cape, her boots tapping sharply against the oak floor. Her hands moved as she spoke, slicing the air like a conductor orchestrating a symphony of tension and suspicion. The fire crackled behind her, casting long shadows against the shelves lined with brittle, leather-bound books.

"He's obsessed with the locked room," Catherine said, voice clipped, frustrated. "It's the wrong puzzle."

David sat in one of the high-backed armchairs by the hearth, arms folded across his chest. He studied her for a moment, his brow furrowed in concern. "So, what should we be looking at instead?"

Catherine spun to face him, eyes bright with revelation, her pupils wide with adrenaline. "Marion. It was a good job we spoke to her before she went into the interview with Stowe"

David blinked. "Marion?"

She crossed the room in three strides and pointed to the long scroll of paper unfurled across the writing desk, a timeline meticulously inked with names, times, and short phrases like *Powder Room?* and *Study locked.* The ink glistened faintly under the lamplight.

He exhaled through his nose, rubbing the back of his neck. "This is madness. None of this makes sense."

"It does," she said, eyes alight. "It *will*. You must stop thinking of this house as a home. It's a stage. Every room, every line spoken, every shadow scripted."

David gave her a searching look. "You've changed, Catherine."

She arched a brow. "Changed how?"

"You're fiercer. Sharper. It's like… like you've stepped into his shoes, only you've laced them tighter."

Catherine looked away, down at the timeline again. "Someone has to."

A beat of silence stretched between them.

He nodded, and silence returned, but it was different now. Not the silence of grief, or tension, but a kind of pact. A shared resolve.

She picked up a photograph from the desk, one of the whole family on the back lawn, years ago. Reginald, in his crisp linen suit. Marion, shielding her eyes from the sun. David with his arm around her, both laughing at something Peter had said off-camera.

Catherine stared at it, then set it down gently. "He thought he was untouchable. But something rattled him. Someone got close enough to make him panic."

David crossed his arms. "Then that's who we find."

She jabbed a finger toward a mark on the timeline. "Philip left the table at eight. Peter stepped out for his little call around the same time. I left for ten minutes at most. But if Reginald was still alive at nine, none of those matters. The murder couldn't have happened until later."

David rubbed the back of his neck, visibly processing. "And Marion claims she passed by the study, heard his voice, but didn't see anyone?"

Catherine nodded sharply. "Only his voice. No reply. Either the person he argued with wasn't talking... or they didn't want to be heard. Maybe it was the telephone, but she is convinced someone else was in the room."

David rose from the chair and moved to the desk, scanning her notes. His fingertips brushed the edge of a page covered in cross-referenced times and small annotations in the margin. "You think she's lying?"

Catherine scoffed. "I think everyone in this house is lying about something. But Marion... yes. I think she's hiding more than grief."

David turned toward her slowly. "And what about me?"

She met his gaze without flinching. "You left at nine. Just like she did."

David sighed and looked toward the window, the storm pressing against the glass in sheets of rain. "So now I'm a suspect?"

"If I were Stowe, yes," she said. "But I'm not. I know you, David. You couldn't kill a spider without apologizing to it. But you were unaccounted for. Which means Stowe will circle back to you. We need to be ahead of him."

He pulled the curtain aside and stared into the drenched garden, the mist clinging to the ground like smoke. "So, what do you think happened?"

Catherine joined him at the window, her voice low and taut. "I think someone was in that study with him. Marion only heard Reginald. That means the other person was either silent... or already gone."

She turned abruptly and pointed at the sketch pinned beside the fireplace. "Then there's this. Size ten boot, outside the window. Fresh in the wet soil. Either it's a staged break-in, or someone really was there."

David studied her face, lit by the fire's glow. "And if no one broke in?"

Catherine's eyes darkened. "Then it was one of us."

Her hands trembled slightly as she braced herself on the desk. David crossed the room and covered her fingers with his. "You're pushing yourself too hard."

She gave a faint smile. "There's no other way. We're all in the dark, but someone in this house is pretending they're not."

"I just don't want to see you burn out."

She looked at him then, really looked. "I won't burn out, David. I'll burn through."

He chuckled softly despite the tension. "Spoken like a true Price."

The moment lingered. Then she looked down again at the tangle of notes. "Philip gave me most of the times," she said. "He swears Peter never left the drawing room after eight. But Peter is impulsive, secretive. He could've slipped away."

David nodded, glancing at the clock on the mantel. "He was on the phone, wasn't he? Didn't Philip mention that?"

"Yes! He overheard Peter say something about 'finally getting his father out of the way.' That isn't coincidence."

"But he meant it metaphorically, didn't he? Like stepping away from Reginald's control?"

"Maybe," Catherine murmured. "Or maybe he meant it literally."

David frowned, eyes narrowing. "You always used to give Peter the benefit of the doubt."

"Not anymore," she said flatly. "He was never as clever as he thought he was."

Silence settled over them like dust. The fire hissed and popped, trying in vain to warm the corners of the vast room. The wind keened through the eaves.

Catherine stood again, resuming her pacing, her hands clasped behind her back. "Marion said she heard yelling but didn't linger. That's strange. She never ignored a dramatic scene, especially not with Reginald."

"And the locked door?"

"A misdirect," she said. "It could've been locked from the outside. As I said, I used the special key as a child."

David nodded, his expression darkening. "Is it missing now?"

She moved to the bookcase and tugged at a volume of classic poetry, revealing a small compartment behind it. Empty.

"There are hiding spots everywhere," she said. "This house was built to conceal."

David exhaled. "You're scaring me a little, you know that?"

She laughed softly, a brittle sound. "Good. Means I'm getting close."

She resumed her pacing, slower now, fingers trailing along the spines of ancient tomes. "Then there's the letter. Marion said Reginald got something that shook him."

"A threat?"

"Or a confession. Or leverage. Whatever it was, it's part of this. If we find it, we find the motive."

David crossed to the sideboard and poured two glasses of brandy. He handed her one.

"You're vibrating," he said. "You need to slow down."

She stared at the glass for a moment, then set it down untouched. Her eyes burned with purpose. "Not yet."

He looked at her, brows furrowed. "Catherine... can I ask you something?"

She tilted her head. "Go on."

"All this, what you're doing, how you're thinking, it's impressive. It's brilliant, even. But is it just about justice? Or is this about proving something?"

She blinked, caught off guard. "What are you saying?"

"I'm saying… I know how hard it was for you after he cut you out of the business. You want the truth. But do you also want revenge?"

Her jaw tightened, but she didn't look away. "I want the truth. And if that truth burns down everything he built, so, be it."

David nodded slowly. "Then let it be truth. Not vengeance."

She looked down at her hands. "Sometimes they're the same thing."

David didn't reply. Instead, he stepped closer, brushing a lock of hair from her forehead. "Whatever happens, I'm with you."

Her voice was quiet. "Even if it leads back to someone we love?"

He hesitated, but only for a second. "Even then."

She gave the faintest nod, then returned to her notes, the fire's glow painting her silhouette against the bookshelves. The rain intensified, thunder rolling overhead like a warning.

"Tomorrow," she said, more to herself than him. "I talk to Peter. Alone."

David raised an eyebrow. "Should I be worried for him?"

"He should be," Catherine replied.

She lifted her gaze once more to the timeline, eyes flitting across names and arrows and questions yet unanswered.

The truth was closing in, and Catherine intended to meet it head-on.

And when the house finally gave up its secrets, she would be ready to strike the final match.

Chapter 17: David's Interview

The fire had dwindled to a sullen glow. No longer warming, it now resembled something closer to a wound an open, pulsing gash of ember and ash beneath the iron grate. The smoke curled upward lazily; its ghostly tendrils swallowed by the chimney. Shadows gathered thickly in the corners of the drawing room, no longer dancing, but watching. The heavy velvet curtains were drawn tight, but the wind still found its way in, insinuating itself under doors and around window frames with long, whining sighs. The glass shuddered in its casements, fragile as a lie.

Inspector Thomas Stowe stood motionless in the gloom, framed against the fire like a figure carved from dark stone. His overcoat was still buttoned up to the neck, despite the flickering warmth. He had not sat since entering. He rarely did. His presence solid, silent, unswerving was the very weight pressing down on the room.

David Forrester sat opposite him, his posture formal, hands clenched around the carved armrests of the old chair, as if he might hold himself together by sheer will. The lamplight struck his face at a harsh angle, throwing one eye into shadow and lighting the tension in his jaw. His gaze flicked restlessly around the room as if the right answer might be hiding in the moulding, in the tapestries, in the fire itself.

He cleared his throat, then spoke, voice low but edged with the faintest crack. "I assume this is the part where you tell me I'm not a suspect, but..."

Stowe cut across him without raising his voice. "No. This is the part where you talk."

David exhaled slowly, as though trying to let go of something he'd been gripping too tightly. "Alright," he said. "Ask your questions."

Detective Harris stepped forward from his station by the fireplace, notebook in hand. His pen tapped once against the page before he spoke. "Let's begin with last night. What time did you leave the dining room?"

David didn't answer immediately. He glanced toward the clock on the mantel, as if replaying the scene in his mind. "Just after nine," he said. "The conversation had... deteriorated."

"How so?" Harris asked.

David gave a brief, humourless laugh. "The usual. Reginald ridiculing every opinion I had, treating my proposals like child's play. He called my handling of the trust 'amateurish'. Right in front of everyone."

"You were embarrassed," Stowe said.

"No," David replied, eyes flashing. "I was furious."

"Reginald left before eight. I vented and went into an internal spiral, then I got up at about nine."

Stowe nodded slowly, filing away the emotion. "So, you got up. Then what?"

David looked down at his hands, unclenched them slowly. "I walked. Just… walked. Down the hall. Out through the side door."

"Into the garden?"

He nodded. "It was raining lightly. Misty. I didn't care. I needed air. Space."

"And you didn't see anyone?" Harris's voice was neutral, but sharp around the edges.

David hesitated. "No one. It was quiet. Too quiet."

Harris jotted something down. "Did you pass the study?"

Another pause. "Yes. The curtains were drawn. Light was on. I remember thinking how odd that was. Reginald usually worked in the dark like a crypt keeper."

"Did you hear anything?"

David shook his head. "No. No shouting. No footsteps. Just... stillness."

Stowe took a step forward, his voice soft but firm. "Did you enter the study?"

David looked up sharply. "No."

"Why not?"

A long pause. "Because I was afraid, I might say something I couldn't take back."

Harris shifted his weight. "So, you admit you were angry enough to lash out?"

David's mouth twisted. "Lash out verbally, yes. Physically? No. That's not who I am."

Stowe studied him. The fire cast long shadows across David's face, making him look older. More worn. More human.

"You loved Catherine," Harris said, changing tack. "Still do. Reginald never approved. Did you ever feel trapped?"

David chuckled bitterly. "Feel? Inspector, I was trapped. This house... this family... it's a net. And Reginald wove every thread."

Harris tilted his head. "That's a poetic way to describe resentment."

"It's a truthful one."

"Did you want him gone?" Stowe asked quietly.

David leaned back, rubbing his eyes. "Yes. Not dead. Just... gone. Out of our lives. Out of Catherine's life."

Stowe's voice was calm, steady. "You said 'our' lives."

David met his gaze. "She's, my wife. Everything I did, I did for her."

Stowe was silent for a beat. Then, in a tone just short of gentle: "If you're covering for her, now would be the time to say so."

David blinked. "I'm not."

"But you'd protect her if you had to."

David didn't flinch. "Yes."

The room settled into silence again, heavy and still. Outside, the wind scraped across the windows like fingernails against glass.

Stowe broke the quiet with a slight change in rhythm. "Tell me more about that walk. How long were you outside?"

"I don't know. Ten minutes. Maybe fifteen."

"You left angry," Harris said. "And you came back... calmer?"

David nodded. "I'd cooled off. I knew if I stayed in that room any longer, I'd say something I couldn't take back. Reginald knew exactly how to provoke people. And I'd let him do it again."

"Did you rejoin the others?"

"No. I came in through the back and went upstairs. I wanted to be alone. I had a drink. Then I went back to join the others."

Stowe raised an eyebrow. "And no one can confirm that?"

David gave a humourless smile. "That's correct."

Harris scribbled again, then paused, looking up. "You said you saw light in the study. Was the door closed?"

"Yes. I think so."

"Think?"

David shifted, irritation beginning to surface. "I didn't try the handle, if that's what you're asking."

"You thought Reginald was in there?" Stowe pressed.

"I assumed," David said. "He always worked late, especially after stirring up drama. He fed off it."

Stowe nodded slowly. "You ever see anyone else use that study?"

David hesitated. "No. He didn't allow anyone in. Not even Marion. All the files and cabinets were always locked, the key only locked on the inside."

"And the key?"

"Reginald kept it on his desk."

Stowe tilted his head slightly. "Always?"

"Always. That study was his sanctuary."

Harris tapped his pen again, then looked up. "You ever see Marion with that key?"

David frowned. "No, never. She wasn't allowed in his sanctuaries."

More silence. Then, unexpectedly, Stowe took a softer tone. "David... do you believe Catherine is capable of violence?"

David blinked. "Absolutely not."

"But you said you'd protect her."

"I said I'd protect her from injustice," David snapped. "Not from truth."

Stowe didn't react to the outburst. "And if the truth points to her?"

David's voice dropped. "Then I'll help her face it. But I won't let you build a lie around her because it's convenient."

There was a pause, and then Harris asked, "What do you think happened, David?"

He ran a hand through his hair, clearly weary. "I think Reginald pushed someone too far. Someone close. Someone desperate."

"Who?"

David looked between them; his expression unreadable. "I don't know. But I know what guilt looks like, Inspector. And someone in this house is carrying it around like a second skin."

Stowe stepped back, folding his arms. "Then help us peel it away."

David gave a bitter smile. "That's what I'm trying to do."

Another pause.

"Catherine showed me something earlier. Footprints. In the flowerbed beneath Reginald's study window. Size ten. Deep impressions. Someone was out there."

Stowe's head tilted slightly. "When did she show you?"

"Just now."

David's jaw tightened. "We weren't sure what we were seeing at first. The soil was wet, the impressions still sharp. Catherine spotted them through the rain-streaked glass. We didn't want to contaminate the scene."

"Besides you?" Harris said.

David's back straightened. "I wasn't near the study window. I smoked by the side wall, near the ivy."

"Still outside," Stowe said. The tone was mild but loaded.

David stepped forward, his voice rising with his temper. "Are you accusing me, or just trying to trap me in my own words?"

"We didn't touch anything," David snapped. "Catherine insisted we leave them alone. She thought they could be important thought you'd want to see them undisturbed."

Stowe's brow arched slightly. "'We' again. You and Catherine are working together?"

David hesitated. "She's... looking for answers. So am I."

"Do you trust her judgment?" Harris asked, voice calm but pointed.

David looked away. "Most of the time."

"And this time?"

He turned back; eyes narrowed. "Yes. She's sharper than all of us right now."

"Sharper," Stowe repeated. "Or more desperate?"

David didn't answer.

Stowe unfolded his arms and stepped closer to the map on the wall. He tapped it once, near the rough sketch of the study's rear elevation. "The flowerbed's soft. It wouldn't take much to leave a mark. But it would also be easy to fake."

David's jaw clenched. "You think we planted them?"

"I think it's curious," Stowe said, "that the one person who keeps trying to outpace this investigation is the same one suddenly discovering key evidence after dark."

David didn't bite. "She's trying to find the truth. You should be thanking her."

"I will," Stowe said, "if what she finds leads us closer to it."

Harris interjected, flipping back a page in his notebook. "Do you think someone came in through the study window?"

David nodded. "I think it's possible. Reginald rarely locked it. He hated feeling shut in."

"Yet you heard nothing," Stowe said.

"I've said that already."

"No creaking wood, no wet shoes squelching down the hall?"

David shook his head. "Just the rain. The wind. I was alone."

Stowe folded his arms again, watching him. "And you never spoke to Reginald again. After dinner."

David looked tired now, worn down. "No."

"Not even to make peace?"

His lips parted, then closed again. He looked toward the fire as if it might offer clarity. Then he shook his head. "No. There was nothing left to say."

"What would you have said?" Harris asked softly.

David blinked. The question surprised him. "I... I don't know. That I deserved a seat at the table. That I wasn't some errand boy. That Catherine saw something in me he never bothered to."

"Would it have made a difference?"

David's smile was bitter. "With Reginald? Probably not. But maybe with me."

Stowe nodded, slowly. "And now he's dead."

David rose to his feet. "I didn't kill him. Whatever you think, I didn't."

The silence afterward stretched too long. The fire popped, releasing a single spark that vanished before it could reach the hearth.

"You can go," Stowe said at last.

David paused, his hand on the doorknob. "Someone in this house knows more than they're saying. I hope you find them, Inspector. I really do."

Then he was gone.

The door clicked shut behind him with a sound too final.

Harris watched it for a moment, then turned back to Stowe. "He's not telling the whole story."

"No," Stowe murmured, moving to the window. He peeled back the curtain just enough to peer into the dark.

"What do you think he's holding back?"

"Something Catherine told him not to say. Or something he's afraid of discovering himself."

"You believe him? That he didn't do it?"

Stowe didn't answer right away. His eyes were focused on the blackened silhouette of the east garden. "He's angry. Cornered. He left the dinner table when Reginald was still alive"

"And Catherine?"

Stowe let the curtain fall back into place. "She's hunting ghosts. The question is whether one of them turns out to be real."

Outside, the wind surged again, rattling the shutters and moaning across the slate roof tiles like a voice lost in the rafters. Down in the east garden, the flowerbed remained undisturbed, dark, wet, and waiting.

And within the room, the fire gave one final hiss and slumped into ash.

The shadows watched.

And Stowe remained, thinking.

Always thinking.

Chapter 18: Redrawing the Map

The silence in the garden was thick and sodden, wrapped around the house like a second skin. Fog clung to every hedge and eave, transforming the landscape into a smudged charcoal sketch. A droplet slid from the edge of the study's window frame, falling in a slow arc before landing with a dull splat in the mud beside the sharp-edged footprint.

A light gust stirred the ivy on the brick wall, rustling it like whispered secrets. The lantern above flickered, casting tremulous golden light that shimmered across the glossy leaves and slick stone, making everything seem alive in an eerie, expectant way.

Inspector Stowe stood with his hands deep in his pockets, gaze fixed on the footprint below. The print looked darker now, more ominous, as though it had deepened with meaning overnight. He could feel the house at his back, watching, waiting.

"We need to redraw the timeline," he said at last, his voice barely more than gravel. He stepped back from the window, boots crunching in the grit. "Dinner ended at 8. Reginald's study door was closed not long after. Marion claims she heard raised voices at 9. David says he didn't."

"And then he went for a walk," Harris added, crouched near the edge of the flowerbed. His breath puffed faintly in the chilled air. "Smoked a cigarette, just happened to be outside. Close enough to this footprint."

Stowe turned slowly toward him. His eyes narrowed against the lantern's glow. "Which means he could've made that print. Or seen it. Or stepped in it before it formed."

Harris rose, brushing damp soil from his gloves. "No one's off the hook."

They began walking the edge of the flowerbed, the ground soft beneath their feet, their boots squelching slightly with each step. The path wrapped like a question mark around the side of the house, and every darkened window above seemed to peer down on them like disapproving ancestors.

"We need everyone's movements pinned to the minute," Stowe muttered. "No more vague guesses. I want clocks. Chimes. Eyewitnesses. Where they were, when, and who they were with. Down to the second if possible."

"We'll need the staff's statements too," Harris said. "They might've seen something without realizing it."

Stowe gave a grunt of agreement. "And no more of these drawing-room interviews. We knock on doors. No warning. Catch them raw. Force the truth through the cracks."

"They'll hate it."

"Good," Stowe replied. "They've been rehearsing too long."

They paused beneath the study window again. The glass was dark and blank now, its curtains drawn tight. The house loomed above them in silence, the mist hugging its walls like breath held too long.

"They're not grieving," Harris said, almost to himself.

Stowe glanced sideways. "You noticed it too."

Harris nodded. "No mourning. Just strategy. Careful words, hollow eyes. No one's cried for that man. Not really."

Stowe exhaled slowly, a cloud of mist escaping into the air. "They're grieving the change. Not the death. The balance of power just shifted, and every one of them is doing the maths."

Harris flipped open his notebook and skimmed down a page. "Marion inherits most of it, doesn't she? The house. The land. If the will's standard."

"Unless Reginald rewrote it recently," Stowe said. "He was the kind of man who'd make last-minute edits just to spite someone."

"And if she's next to go?" Harris asked.

Stowe didn't answer. He just stared at the footprint for a moment longer, the mud around it glistening under the lantern light like congealed blood.

"That's the shadow behind the curtains," he murmured. "That's the shape behind everything. Fear and ambition. They don't always walk hand in hand, but they always share a destination."

The breeze picked up again, this time sharper. The mist coiled around their legs, crawling along the ground like it wanted to listen in.

"You think it's about money?" Harris asked.

Stowe's reply came slower. "It's always about something. Money. Control. Revenge. With families like this, the lines blur." He looked up toward the east-facing windows. "But yes. Money's the root that feeds every poison in this place."

A pause. Then Stowe added, "We need to check Reginald's financial records. All of them. If someone's been bleeding him dry, it won't be in the tea gossip. It'll be in the ledgers."

"I'll get started on that first thing," Harris said. "We'll need access to his study, or wherever he kept the business files."

"And the kitchen," Stowe said, turning slightly. "Check the knives. Every one of them. Count the blades, inspect for signs of cleaning, sharpening, wiping."

Harris nodded. "You think the murder weapon came from the house?"

"I think it was close. Familiar. Easy to reach. Something someone knew wouldn't be missed until it mattered."

The lantern above them flickered once more, then steadied. Its brief dimming threw a ripple across the glass, a flash of movement that made both men instinctively glance upward.

"Feels like the house is holding its breath," Harris whispered.

Stowe nodded. "Or waiting to see if we'll flinch."

They stood in silence a moment longer, the garden around them swallowed in soundless fog.

Then Stowe sighed. "My pastie'll be stone cold by now. Wife'll have drafted a missing person's report."

Harris gave a brief, startled laugh. "You? Missing? Unthinkable."

"I'm terrified of my wife," Stowe deadpanned. "It's what keeps me honest."

The humour faded slowly, but it left something warmer behind, shared, unspoken understanding. Trust earned, not just assigned.

"You ever think about walking away from all this?" Harris asked suddenly, his voice low. "The mess. The lies. The cold footprints that go nowhere."

Stowe looked at him for a moment, then offered a faint smile. "Every morning. And by nightfall, I remember why I can't."

"Because of people like this?"

"Because someone always lies. And someone else always bleeds for it."

They began walking back toward the front of the house. Their boots thudded softly on the gravel path, and their shadows trailed behind them, long and bent by the mist.

"Eleven sharp?" Harris asked as they reached the front steps.

"Bring strong tea and sharper questions," Stowe replied.

Before stepping through the door, they turned once more toward the side of the house. The footprint remained, clear and solitary, like a signature carved in earth.

An echo of whoever had stood there. An echo waiting for a name.

And above it all, the house watched, silent and waiting.

Chapter 19: Stowe Goes Home

The road away from the Price estate wound like a ribbon of ink through the sleeping countryside, slick with rain and ghosted with mist. Inspector Thomas Stowe drove with the window slightly cracked, letting the cold air sting his face. It helped him stay sharp, or at least that's what he told himself. The dashboard clock glowed dimly in the gloom, 2:03 a.m.

The heater clicked softly, doing little against the creeping damp in his bones. He hadn't taken off his overcoat since dinner. The scent of woodsmoke clung to the fabric, mingling with the familiar trace of tobacco he'd long given up. His shoulders ached. His head throbbed. But more than anything, his mind would not be still.

Catherine Forrester. David. Marion. Philip. Peter. The names circled each other like wolves in the dark, each baring a sliver of truth, each concealing something behind their eyes. Stowe had been a policeman too long to trust first impressions. Or second. Or third..

He couldn't shake that footprint. The way it sat in the mud, so deliberate. Not careless. Not frantic. Whoever had been there had taken their time.

He passed a gatepost shrouded in ivy, the stone slick with years of weather and moss. In his rearview mirror, the Price house receded into the mist like a ship in fog. It looked almost peaceful from a distance. Almost innocent.

Ten minutes later, Stowe pulled into the gravel drive of a modest cottage nestled in a hollow by the woods. It wasn't much, but it was quiet. The porch light flickered as he stepped out, the front garden scattered with fallen branches from the earlier storm.

Inside, the hallway was dim and smelled faintly of mint tea and old paper. Stowe hung his coat with practiced ease and tossed his notebook on the kitchen table.

The soft murmur of the radio drifted from the living room, mixed with the faint clink of china. As Inspector Thomas Stowe stepped through the doorway, he found Debbie curled in her armchair, a knitted cardigan pulled tight around her shoulders, a steaming cup of tea resting in her hands. She looked up, her eyes lighting with quiet relief.

"There you are," she murmured. "You look like you've been fighting ghosts."

He let out a low chuckle as he pulled off his coat and draped it over the chair. "Feels that way."

"Sit down," she said, already pouring him a fresh cup.

Stowe lowered himself into his usual chair with a quiet groan, his body sinking into the familiar cushions. The warmth of the fire licked at his tired limbs as he took the cup from her, letting its heat seep into his fingers.

"New case?" she asked gently.

"Last case," he sighed. "A locked room. Strange details. Family acting like their dead relative is just a minor inconvenience."

Debbie tilted her head, considering. "Maybe it was."

Stowe frowned. "What do you mean?"

She shrugged, setting her cup down. "Maybe his death was just an inconvenience to them. Maybe they'd already come to terms with it before it happened."

He stared at her a moment, something shifting, though the thought stayed just out of reach. "I don't know. Something's off. I just can't see what it is yet."

Debbie smiled knowingly. "You will."

Stowe gave a soft grunt, neither agreement nor denial. He took a sip of tea, letting the warmth settle in his chest. "They're all liars. Smooth ones, too. Like they've been trained. Every word is weighed. Every glance rehearsed."

"Sounds exhausting," she said, tucking her feet beneath her on the sofa.

"It is. But it's also the most alive I've felt in weeks. That's the part I don't like admitting."

She gave him a look, half fond, half exasperated. "You're addicted to the puzzle, Tom. You always have been."

He gave a tired chuckle. "I thought I was slowing down."

"You say that every winter."

"This one's colder."

He sighed, leaned his head back, eyes closing. "One month."

Debbie raised an eyebrow. "One month until what?"

He rubbed his temple with a smirk. "Until we finally go on that bloody cruise."

Her face softened. She sighed, stretching her legs beneath the blanket. "I can't wait. Lazy mornings, fresh coffee on the deck. No crime, no late nights, no worrying if some locked door is a clue or just a broken latch." She opened her eyes and gave a playful smirk. "What will you do without a murder to solve?"

"Probably drive you mad."

"You already do."

They both laughed quietly. It didn't last long, but it lingered in the air, like the scent of something comforting.

Stowe's smile stayed, but his gaze drifted toward the mantelpiece. The familiar photograph stood in its place beside the clock.

Susan.

Even now, nearly two years later, the loss sat heavy in his chest. Some days it was dull, woven into the routine. Other days, it cut sharp. Tonight, was somewhere in between.

Debbie followed his gaze. "She'd be proud of you, Tom."

His throat tightened. "Aye. I hope so."

They sat for a while in the flickering firelight, the hush between them steadying.

Then Debbie leaned forward slightly, resting her hand on the arm of his chair. "What's really bothering you?"

He was quiet for a moment. "It's not just the lies. It's the way they *fit*. All the gaps filled too cleanly. Like someone painted over the mess instead of cleaning it up."

"You think someone's setting the stage."

"I think someone already has."

Debbie gave a small nod. "So, you dig deeper. Pull away the paint."

He sighed again. "Tomorrow, we start checking the kitchen. Knives, drawers, everything. And the ledgers, Reginald's business books. If there's a paper trail, we'll follow it."

"Sounds like Harris'll be busy."

Stowe smiled faintly. "He's sharp. Steady. Not afraid to disagree with me when it counts."

Debbie smiled. "That's why you keep him close."

He gave a soft grunt of agreement. "Everyone else is performing. Harris? He's listening."

A pause. Then: "He reminds me of you. Back when we started. You were the one who noticed the details I missed."

Debbie chuckled. "And you were the one who always made sure we followed them."

Their eyes met. Something unspoken passed between them. Familiarity. Gratitude. Something warmer.

"I don't say it enough," Stowe murmured.

"You don't need to," she replied, just as softly. "I'm still here."

He leaned back again, and for the first time that day, the tension in his shoulders eased.

The fire cracked softly. Outside, the wind tapped gently at the window, as though asking to be let in.

Inside, there was calm. Temporary, but real.

Stowe closed his eyes. "Just one more piece. That's all I need."

Debbie's voice was quiet. "And then what?"

His lips curved faintly. "Then I pull the whole thread."

Until headlights swept across the front window.

Stowe tensed. The light moved slowly, paused, then disappeared. A moment later, came the knock. Not urgent, but firm.

He stood, wary but curious. Debbie set down her tea and tilted her head.

"Expecting someone?"

"No," Stowe said.

When he opened the door, Harris stood on the porch, coat dripping, hair plastered to his forehead. He looked like he'd run through the storm itself.

"Thought you were headed home," Stowe said, stepping aside.

"I was," Harris replied, shaking water from his collar. "Made it halfway down the lane, then remembered something you said. About someone watching."

"Come in," Stowe said, ushering him through. "You'll drown out there."

Debbie appeared in the doorway, arms crossed, one eyebrow raised. She had a towel already in her hand.

"Of course it's you," she said, handing it to Harris with a small smile. "Teas on. You want a cup?"

Harris nodded gratefully. "God, yes. If it's strong."

"Always is," she said, disappearing back toward the kitchen.

Stowe moved to the kettle, already warming again on the hob. "What brought you back?" he asked, not looking up.

Harris reached into his coat and pulled out a small envelope, sealed in dark blue wax. He held it carefully, like it might bite. "Found this in the post box at the gate. Addressed to you. No return address."

Stowe took it. Turned it over in his hands.

The seal was unmistakable, the Price family crest, embossed and sharp against the wax. A lion flanked by two crows.

His stomach sank.

He didn't open it. Not yet. Instead, he placed it on the table beside his notebook. Debbie entered quietly, setting down three cups of tea on the small table. Her eyes flicked to the envelope, then to Stowe. She didn't say a word.

They all stood around it for a second, as though expecting it to do something.

The room was still. The only sounds were the tick of the mantel clock and the hiss of wind beyond the window.

"Go on, then," Harris said softly. "Open it."

Stowe shook his head. "It can wait."

Harris raised an eyebrow. "You're sure?"

"One more hour," Stowe said. "Until the water boils. Until the steam rises." He glanced back at the letter. "Until the final game begins."

Harris pulled off his coat and dropped into the opposite armchair, glancing at Debbie's book on the side table. "You ever wonder what kind of person sends a sealed letter in a storm instead of just slipping it under a door?"

"Someone who wants to be noticed," Debbie said, curling back into her seat with her tea. "Or someone who wants you to hesitate."

"Mission accomplished," Harris muttered.

Stowe took a slow sip. "No. I'm not hesitating. I'm waiting."

He sank deeper into his chair. The fire crackled. The smell of damp wool and bergamot filled the room.

"They all know something," he said suddenly. "Every one of them. Even the ones pretending to be clueless. The footprint outside the window wasn't the only thing out of place. It was the silence. Too perfect. Too aligned."

"They rehearsed it," Harris said. "I felt that too."

"They've been living with this possibility," Stowe said. "Not the event, maybe. But the idea. That Reginald might not wake up one day and the world might actually be better for it."

"Then someone made sure of it," Debbie said quietly.

Stowe didn't answer. He didn't need to.

His eyes drifted back to the envelope. The wax glinted dully in the firelight.

"You think it's a warning?" Harris asked.

"Or a confession," Stowe said. "Or an invitation."

"To what?"

He let out a breath. "To the final act."

They sat together in the hush, the three of them, the weary inspector, the steadfast partner, and the curious detective, watching the sealed letter like it might crack itself open and spill its secrets.

Stowe didn't know who had killed Reginald Price, not yet. But the truth was circling closer now. The air had shifted. The stage was set. And something in his gut told him by morning, the mask would crack.

And when it
 did, he'd be ready.

Ready to name it. To catch the lie that started it all.

And end the performance once and for all.

Chapter 20: Catherine's Conversation with Marion

The house held its breath.

It was well past two in the morning, but the silence that filled Elm Road was not the stillness of sleep. It was something heavier. Denser. The kind of silence that listens. That watches. That waits for someone to break it.

Catherine moved slowly along the upstairs corridor, her hand trailing the wall, fingertips grazing over the grooves in the wallpaper like reading a language only memory could translate. The flickering oil lamps cast long shadows that swayed with every creak of the floorboards, making the hallway feel like a tunnel narrowing with every step. A cold draft slipped from under the doorframes and bit at her ankles.

She descended the staircase without a sound, the old wood groaning under her weight like it remembered her childhood. At the base, she paused. The sitting room door was ajar. A faint orange glow bled into the hallway, pulsing gently like the dying breath of something once warm.

She pushed the door open slowly.

Marion was there, as Catherine had guessed she would be, seated low in the armchair by the hearth, a thick shawl wrapped tightly around her slight frame. Her body was curled in on itself, her shoulders hunched as she stared into the fire as though it might speak. The embers hissed quietly, the fire having long since settled into a soft, irregular glow.

The room smelled of lavender, faint woodsmoke, and the dusty edges of old fabric. The same scent that had always clung to the curtains and cushions. Familiar, but now strange, like something belonging to another time.

Catherine stood in the doorway for a moment before speaking.

"Mother?"

Marion turned slowly; her eyes slightly wide as she surfaced from thought. Her gaze settled on Catherine's face with a mixture of recognition and weariness.

"You're still up?" she asked, her voice soft and cracked at the edges.

Catherine stepped into the room, letting the door close behind her. "I couldn't sleep."

Marion offered a smile, small and fragile. "That makes two of us."

Catherine crossed the room and lowered herself into the armchair opposite, curling her legs beneath her, hugging a cushion tightly to her chest. "I had a feeling I'd find you down here."

Marion looked back at the fire. "This room used to soothe me. Now it just reminds me how quiet the house is without him."

Catherine nodded, watching her mother. "It's not just quiet, though. It's... different."

Marion exhaled slowly. "I know. Like something's shifted and won't shift back."

There was a pause. The fire popped, a log collapsing slightly into itself.

"You've been remembering things," Catherine said softly.

"Not dreams," Marion replied. "Waking memories. Things I thought I'd packed away."

Catherine leaned in slightly. "About Father?"

Marion hesitated, then gave a single, almost imperceptible nod. "About everything. The early years. The tension before the children came. The silence we wrapped around ourselves to stay married."

"Why did you stay?" Catherine asked, not with accusation, but with genuine curiosity.

Marion's fingers tightened on her shawl. "Because leaving felt harder than staying. Because I thought if I endured long enough, something would change. But nothing ever did."

The firelight flickered over her face, highlighting the lines drawn by decades of silence.

"He frightened you," Catherine said.

"Yes. Not with fists. With his voice. His expectations. He made kindness feel like a currency he controlled."

"Did you see anything unusual that day? Anything out of place?"

Marion didn't answer for a long moment. Then she said, "There was a letter. One he wouldn't show me."

Catherine's eyes sharpened. "Do you remember who it was from?"

"The envelope was plain. The paper thick. Expensive. But the signature... no. I never saw it."

"Do you know what happened to it?"

Marion shook her head. "He put it in the inside jacket pocket."

"Do you think it upset him?"

"It unmoored him," Marion said, her voice shaking. "He was pacing like a man with ghosts snapping at his heels."

Catherine sat forward; her tone urgent. "If we find that letter, we may find the motive."

Marion looked up at her daughter, tears glinting in the firelight. "And if it leads to one of us?"

Catherine reached out, placing her hand over Marion's. "Then we face that truth. Together."

Marion's fingers tightened around hers.

"I sometimes wondered," she whispered, "what kind of woman I might've become if I hadn't married him. I think... I think I lost parts of myself before you were even born."

"You didn't lose them," Catherine said. "They were buried. You're still here."

Marion gave a small, unsteady laugh. "You sound like your father. But kinder."

Catherine smiled faintly. "He taught me what not to become."

They sat in silence again, but it was different now. Not the heavy, stifling quiet of the past, but the stillness of something slowly beginning to heal.

"I found an old letter once," Catherine said. "Years ago. Tucked inside one of his ledgers. It was addressed to someone called 'G' just the initial. I didn't understand it at the time. But he wrote about trust. About how he was 'running out of time to fix things.'"

Marion blinked slowly. "That wasn't his style."

"No," Catherine agreed. "Which is why it stuck with me."

Marion stared into the fire, eyes distant. "I think he knew something was coming. Maybe not the murder, but the reckoning. He felt it closing in."

"Then we need to open every drawer, every journal," Catherine said. "We need to find what he was afraid of."

Marion gave a small nod, her voice barely audible. "Be careful, Catherine. Secrets buried too long don't always want to be found."

"I'm not afraid of secrets anymore," Catherine said.

"For your sake," Marion murmured, "I hope that's true."

For the first time that evening, Marion's face softened into something close to peace. She closed her eyes.

"He built this house to last," she said softly. "But he never made it safe."

Catherine nodded, her voice low. "Now it's our turn."

Catherine's voice dropped to a murmur. "Can I ask you something odd?"

Marion looked up, her eyes glassy but alert. "Of course."

"You remember how Father always complained about the study being too hot? Even in winter?"

Marion's brow furrowed slightly as she nodded. "Yes. He'd fling the windows open at the slightest warmth. I used to scold him about catching a chill." Her voice trembled with the ghost of routine arguments and old affections.

Catherine hesitated. "Then why were the windows bolted shut when they found him?"

Marion's expression changed instantly, her body stiffening, her lips parting slightly. She leaned forward, as though trying to better understand the words.

"They were locked?"

Catherine nodded. "Stowe mentioned it. Shut. Latched from the inside."

Marion's eyes drifted back to the fire, her face shadowed and drawn. "That… that's not right. He never left them closed. Not at night. Not ever. Even the cold didn't stop him."

Catherine leaned forward; the cushion gripped tightly in her lap. "Which means someone else shut them. After."

Marion's hand trembled where it rested on her knee. "Why would they do that?"

"To make it look like no one came in or out," Catherine said softly. "Like it was all self-contained. Like he died alone."

Marion shook her head slowly. "I...I can't make sense of that."

"I can," Catherine said quietly. "It means whoever did it... knew him. Knew the room. Knew what needed to be staged."

Marion's lips parted. Her eyes shone with sudden, welling tears. "No. You can't believe that. Not someone in the house."

Catherine looked down. "I don't want to. But everything we've seen says otherwise."

She looked back up and met her mother's gaze, her voice firmer now. "This wasn't a stranger, Mother."

Marion flinched as if struck.

"This was someone close. Someone he let in. Someone who knew the layout. The habits. The timing."

"No," Marion whispered. "We can't"

"We have to," Catherine interrupted, gently but insistently. "If we don't face it, we'll never know the truth."

The silence stretched again. Marion stared into the fire as if hoping it would burn the thought away. Her face was pale, her lips pressed into a tight line.

"I need you to think," Catherine said gently. "The night he died. You said you heard him arguing."

Marion nodded slowly. "Yes... I didn't mean to eavesdrop. I was coming up the hall. The door was closed, but his voice—it was loud. Sharp."

"Just him?"

Marion's eyes flickered. "I thought so. I didn't hear anyone else. But he was furious. It was like he'd been pushed too far."

"Do you remember what he said?"

"I... I think... he said, 'I told you this was finished. We are not doing this again.'"

Catherine stilled. "The Madison deal."

Marion blinked, surprised. "Yes. That was it."

Catherine sat back, her grip tightening around the cushion. "Why would anyone bring that up now?"

Marion shook her head, her brow furrowing. "It nearly destroyed him once. We weren't supposed to speak of it again."

"If someone brought it up," Catherine said slowly, "they wanted something. Or they wanted it hidden. For good."

Marion's voice was barely a whisper. "You think that's why he was killed."

"I think it's connected. And if someone was desperate enough to reopen that, they may be desperate enough to do worse."

Marion looked at her daughter really looked and the fear in her eyes was stark. Her voice trembled. "Be careful. If you're right… this goes deeper than we thought."

"I know," Catherine said. "And that's why I have to keep going."

She reached out and took her mother's hand, holding it tightly. Marion's fingers closed over hers like a lifeline.

"I want to check the study again tomorrow," Catherine said. "Carefully. There's something we missed."

Marion nodded slowly. "Don't go alone."

"I'll be careful."

"Promise me."

Catherine squeezed her hand. "I promise."

But inside, she wasn't sure it was a promise she could keep.

The fire sighed low. Outside, the wind rattled the windowpanes like knuckles on a coffin lid. The walls of the house creaked, old bones settling or protesting. In the shadows above them, the house held its secrets tightly, unwilling to give them up without a fight.

The house was not at peace. And neither were they.

Chapter 21: Rattling the Cage

The frost clung to everything that morning, silvery and sharp-edged, turning hedges into sculptures and rooftops into brittle planes of white. Even the telephone wires sagged under a fine crust, humming faintly in the wind. It wasn't snowing, not quite, but the sky had that heavy, gunmetal look, like it was holding something back.

The cold wasn't just outdoors. It wormed its way under doorframes and behind plaster walls, sank into boots and cuffs, and deeper still, into thoughts a man might have managed to bury on a warmer day.

Inside Inspector Stowe's cramped kitchen, the weak heat from the old boiler caused a tired clank every few minutes, like it, too, resented being awake. The tile floor was cold as stone, and the corners of the room remained in shadow, untouched by the narrow beam of early light slipping through the gap in the curtain.

His tea had gone cold ten minutes ago. The steam had long vanished from the chipped ceramic mug, an ugly thing, pale blue with a faded logo, the chip a reminder of a careless elbow last spring. Stowe sat hunched, elbows planted on the table, both hands wrapped loosely around the mug as if memory alone might warm it.

His face was slack, the way it got when his mind drifted into long corridors, unlit, quiet, full of things better not disturbed too quickly. His eyes weren't on the curtain dead in front of him, not really. They were somewhere else. Somewhere behind yesterday's interview.

The ticking of the wall clock counted each second like a nudge. Then, finally, he blinked. Once. Slowly.

He reached for the telephone.

The rotary dial turned beneath his thick fingers with a mechanical patience. Each click of the returning dial was deliberate. Old muscle memory, half-forgotten. But this wasn't instinct anymore. This was method. Calculation. The patience of a man who'd waited before.

The line rang.

Once.

Twice.

There was a shuffle on the other end. Sheets, maybe. A muttered curse, and then Harris's voice, rough with sleep and the mild panic of being called too early. "Morning, sir. Everything alright?"

"No," Stowe said, flat and certain. "But it will be."

That pulled Harris into the present. The pause stretched, Stowe could hear the slow grind of him waking up, a bed creaking, the dull thump of feet hitting the floorboards. A sigh, followed by the soft click of a light switch.

"What happened?"

"Not over the phone," Stowe said. "Not yet. Just listen."

"All right," Harris muttered. Stowe could hear him moving, probably pulling on yesterday's jumper, the kind he kept at the foot of the bed. The man was slow in the mornings, but smart. Stowe didn't need him fast. He needed him precise.

"I want you at David Forrester's office. Today. This morning. Quietly. I want you in his books, deep. Dig through everything. Accounts, partnerships, debt trails, shady donors. Anything Reginald might've stonewalled or conveniently ignored."

Harris hesitated. "You think this thing goes deeper?"

"I think money always runs underneath. People lie. Numbers don't, unless someone's taught them how."

There was a rustling on the other end, papers being pulled from a drawer, the edge of a pen cap snapping off.

"I think anyone close enough to Reginald is worth a second look."

Another pause. Harris was writing something now, jotting notes by hand like he always did when something felt real. "You think he's desperate?"

"I think desperation makes people clever. But it wears thin fast. Then comes the sloppiness."

Harris grunted. "How far do you want me to go?"

"All the way," Stowe said. "Start with the surface. The public stuff. But don't stop there. I want everything. Especially the pieces they'd rather bury."

"Hidden accounts?"

"If they exist, I want them."

"Backdated transfers?"

"Same."

"Shell companies?"

"Yes, find out who's fronting them. Follow names. Don't stop at initials."

There was a shift in Harris's tone now, more awake, more grounded. "You got something already?"

"Bits. Fragments. Enough to smell rot." Stowe hesitated. "The letter. We'll talk about that later. Not over the phone."

The line was quiet.

"What was in it?"

"I said later."

A breath. Harris didn't push, which is why Stowe trusted him.

"You think they're listening?"

"I think they're smarter than we gave them credit for."

"Copy that," Harris said. "I'll start with the donor reports. If Forrester's been cooking something, he left grease somewhere."

Stowe nodded, though Harris couldn't see it. "Don't trust clean desks. Or sudden silence."

"I'll keep my head low."

"I know you will."

Harris paused, voice softer. "You all right, sir?"

Stowe didn't answer right away. His gaze flicked to the window, frost blooming in crooked lines across the glass. "I don't know yet."

"I'll ring you soon as I've got something."

"Good." Then, almost an afterthought: "And Harris, watch your back."

Click.

The line went dead, but the silence stayed.

Stowe sat with it a moment. The receiver still warm in his hand. He placed it back on the cradle gently, like it might break. Then he rose, slowly. His knees cracked in protest. He reached for his coat, the grey wool one with the stitched elbow, the one softened with time and habit and slung it over his shoulders like armour.

He paused at the door, fingers raking through thinning hair, catching at the stubborn crown that refused to lie flat.

The house felt still. Too still. Even the boiler had gone quiet. Outside, the hum of winter hung in the air like breath held too long.

Something had shifted. He'd felt it yesterday, barely noticeable, like a wrong note in a familiar tune. A hesitation mid-sentence. A glance that lingered just long enough to matter.

Now the air was different. The quiet had weight.

His own cage was rattling.

And if the cracks had started here, in the small things, a chipped mug, a cold boiler, a late-night call, then it was time to see how far they'd spread.

And who else had felt the tremor. Who else was listening in the quiet.

Chapter 22 : Inspector arrives

The Forrester estate looked no different than it had the morning after the murder, but it *felt* different. Something under the skin had shifted. The hedges were clipped to their usual geometric precision, the gravel drive was still raked in perfect symmetry, but the air had thickened. The place no longer merely *stood* in its solitude, it *waited*. Like something watching. Like something remembering.

Stowe stepped from the car, the crunch of gravel beneath his shoes unnervingly loud in the brittle morning quiet. Each step echoed. The stones popped like joints. Like bone. The windows stared back at him, not blankly, but knowingly. Observant. Judging. Somewhere above, he imagined a curtain twitching, a ghost of motion behind frost-laced glass.

The front door opened before he could knock.

Henshaw.

Immaculate, as ever, grey suit without a speck, not a single strand of hair out of place. If the house were to collapse into ash, Stowe suspected Henshaw would still be there in the ruins, offering tea with an unshaken calm.

"Inspector," the butler said, his tone politely devoid of emotion. He stepped aside with the precision of a clock striking the hour. "You're expected."

Stowe raised an eyebrow but said nothing. *Expected,* were he? That wasn't supposed to mean anything, but it did. It always did, in a house like this, words chosen like weapons, never without weight.

He stepped into the entry hall, and warmth wrapped around him like a quiet warning. The air was thick with layered scents; the waxy glow of furniture polish, the ghost of toast and marmalade from a breakfast no one had truly tasted, and beneath it all, the dry must of old paper. The smell of history clinging to walls too proud to admit decay.

He shrugged off his coat, slow and deliberate, eyes scanning the familiar hallway. The side table still bore its usual fan of post, arranged like display pieces. Not a single envelope out of line.

And there it was.

The envelope.

County Hospital. Half-hidden, but not well enough. The stark blandness of it stood out like a bruise. Addressed to *Mrs. M. Price*. He could just make out the subject line, tucked beneath another envelope: *Follow-up re: cancer diagnosis*.

Stowe stared.

Marion. Always composed. Always cold, like a blade laid flat. But this wasn't the kind of thing one carried easily. It explained the weight in her eyes, the tired precision in her voice. Grief, yes. But something more private too. A quiet kind of fear, the kind that stays folded up in coat pockets and medicine drawers.

He didn't touch the letter.

He didn't need to.

Footsteps behind him. Measured, purposeful.

"Back so soon, Inspector?" Her voice floated down like perfume through a vent, cool, effortless, but laced with edge.

Catherine Forrester.

She stood halfway down the staircase, one hand resting lightly on the rail, the other cradling her shawl. Dove-grey, not quite mourning. Not quite not.

Stowe turned to face her, letting the silence hang for a beat. "Morning, Mrs. Forrester."

She descended slowly, her movements fluid. "Can't stay away, can you? We're beginning to consider giving you a guest room."

Stowe didn't smile. "You'd be surprised how much comes loose when you shake something long enough."

Her eyes sparkled with interest. "I'm beginning to think that's what you enjoy most."

"I enjoy the truth," he said. "Even when it doesn't flatter anyone."

She stopped just short of him, eyebrow raised. "Especially then, I'd wager."

They began walking together down the corridor, steps slow, sound muffled by thick carpet and tension.

"I'll admit," she said, quickening her pace slightly, "I wasn't expecting you back so soon. We thought we'd earned at least a morning's peace."

"I was in the kitchen," he said simply. "Curiosity's a habit of mine."

"Dangerous habit," she murmured.

"I have just been to the kitchen," he repeated, slower this time, letting the sentence land. "It would seem you are correct. They are missing a carving knife."

That stopped her, half a step, a breath, but she masked it well. "Is that so? Bit rustic for a house like this."

"Rust works like anything else," he replied. "Just takes the right pressure."

"And you think someone used it?"

"I think it's not where it should be."

"Well," she said, with a light shrug, "I'm sure it'll turn up. Things do. Eventually."

"I don't like things that vanish."

"Neither do I. But sometimes they must. To make room for something worse."

They walked in silence for a moment, their rhythm mismatched her steps light and fast, his slow and planted.

"You should know," she said at last, "the study door can be locked from both sides."

Stowe stopped.

"What?"

She didn't blink. "I found the key as a child. Hidden away."

He stared. The weight of it landed fully now, rearranging what he thought he knew. "That wasn't in the reports."

"It wouldn't be," she said smoothly. "No one thought to ask."

"That means it wasn't sealed."

"Not truly."

"And someone inside the house had the key. The one I used as a child, hidden in the library, it's gone missing."

Her lips parted slightly, then pressed shut again.

Stowe's eyes narrowed. "What's David hiding?"

Catherine's gaze flicked to the banister, then back. "Look at his investments, some are not doing as well as we thought"

"You're giving me puzzle pieces."

"I like puzzles," she said. "Especially watching someone else try to solve them with shaking hands."

He moved past her, heading for the sitting room. But her voice came after him, quieter now, more dangerous for it. "Careful, Inspector," she said, just loud enough for the walls to remember. "You're not the only one who knows how to shake a cage."

Chapter 23: The Interrogation

The sitting room of the Price estate had always carried an air of quiet dignity, carved oak, velvet drapes, inherited portraits that watched without blinking. It was the kind of room where voices rarely rose, and secrets were meant to settle into the upholstery. But this morning, that dignity hung limp, like curtains after a storm.

The fire in the hearth whispered low, its glow less warmth than warning, flickering like the final breath of something that once believed itself untouchable. A faint scent of burnt pine clung to the air, brittle, sharp, almost medicinal. The logs hissed quietly, a background to the larger silence no one quite dared to break.

Outside, rain tapped steadily at the tall sash windows, streaking the glass in watery veils and turning the garden beyond into a watercolour of grey and green. The branches of the yew trees bent in the wind, their silhouettes shifting like figures turning away. The steady patter of rain became its own clock, ticking down toward whatever would happen next.

Inspector Thomas Stowe stood at the centre of the room, a still point around which everything else seemed to waver. He was neither relaxed nor aggressive, just *present*, with a gravity that couldn't be ignored. His boots rested just inside the edge of the Persian rug, his coat damp from the walk, but he hadn't removed it. He didn't need to. His authority didn't come from how he dressed, or the badge in his pocket. It came from what he knew and what he was about to do.

Detective Harris stood a pace behind, a man-shaped shadow of anticipation. A thick folder in his hand, thumb tapping its spine in a steady rhythm. His eyes moved from face to face, not nervously, but precisely. Expecting something. A denial. A shout. A confession. He didn't care which.

David Forrester sat on the edge of the settee; shoulders hunched like someone bracing for a blow. His elbows were pressed to his knees, fingers steepled in front of his lips as if praying or suppressing a scream. The sharp line of his jaw had gone slack with fatigue. His eyes were hollow, his skin pale beneath the dim firelight. He wasn't trembling, but his whole frame was tight, a spring wound too far, a truth curled around his spine like wire.

Catherine sat beside him. Not close enough to touch, though she could have. Her hand had hovered once near his, fingers twitching in instinct before pulling back. Her face was unreadable, sculpted in that way some women learn, when to show concern, when to show nothing. Her gaze wasn't on him, but on the rug beneath their feet. The pattern there intricate and blood-red held her attention like a lifeline.

Peter stood by the window, arms folded, back like a plank of wood. His silhouette blurred by the streaked glass behind him. His mouth was a hard, bitter line. His foot tapped once, twice, against the skirting board in a silent rhythm of nerves or judgment maybe both.

And Marion. Wrapped in that pale shawl she always wore now, like armour. She sat in her usual chair near the fire, hands resting in her lap like porcelain gloves. Her gaze didn't shift. It was fixed on nothing and everything the kind of gaze that's done mourning and moved on to watching. There was something in her expression that hadn't been there before. An age. A quiet verdict already rendered in her mind.

Stowe let the silence thicken. Let it settle into their lungs, make them breathe harder. Then he gave a slight nod.

Harris cleared his throat. Not nervous, just ceremonial. He opened the folder, the pages inside hissing like a match being struck.

"We've completed our financial investigation into Mr. Forrester's business affairs," Harris said. "The findings are extensive."

He looked up from the folder in his lap, voice steady, but not without weight.

"Significant losses. Failed investments going back at least eighteen months. Loans acquired through intermediaries who are, let's say not known for transparency. Several accounts tucked under shell entities. Two of those trace back to international banks in jurisdictions that specialize in turning a blind eye."

There was a silence that stretched just long enough to be uncomfortable.

David's head dipped. Just barely. A fraction of an inch. Enough to register, if you were watching for it. Not quite guilt, but something in the same family.

"Two international creditors are preparing legal action," Harris continued. "There's evidence Reginald Forrester discovered at least one of these accounts three days before his death. There's correspondence suggesting he planned to take it to legal counsel. He had a meeting pencilled in. He just didn't make it."

No one spoke. The room seemed to hold its breath.

Then Catherine's voice came, soft but clean. "Is that true?"

She didn't look at David when she asked. She didn't need to.

David didn't answer right away. His eyes were on the floor, jaw set.

"Yes," he said finally. Barely audible. "It's true."

Peter scoffed, a bitter, barked sound that seemed to ricochet off the fireplace. He shifted his stance, arms crossing, then uncrossing, then folding again. His glare could've blistered wood.

"You didn't think to mention that, David? Before now?"

David looked up. And something had shifted in his face, shame twisted into defiance. "What good would it have done?"

"Honesty?" Peter shot back. "Might've been a decent place to start."

David's voice cracked sharp across the room. "Would it? Or would it have just confirmed everything you already think of me?"

Peter opened his mouth to reply but stopped. Something in him teetered at the edge of anger and disappointment. His lips parted, then closed. His jaw clenched tight.

The fire popped in the hearth. A small, spiteful sound.

Stowe stepped forward, slow and steady. His eyes didn't leave David. "You weren't just desperate. You were cornered. You stacked one lie on top of another, and Reginald finally saw it for what it was. He was ready to blow it open."

David didn't deny it. But he didn't confirm it either. His hands, clenched between his knees, were trembling now.

"I didn't kill him," he said quietly. "I swear I didn't."

Stowe voice dropped, heavy with implication. "You were there. You lied about your financial situation."

David shook his head once, almost involuntarily. "I was scared."

"You should be," said Marion.

Her voice wasn't loud. It didn't need to be. It moved through the room like a blade, clean and final.

Everyone turned toward her. She sat straight-backed in her chair, hands folded neatly in her lap, eyes fixed on the fire. Her tone was perfectly level. No tremor. No emotion. Just judgment.

"You shamed this family," she said. "You made Reginald carry your failures in silence. And when he finally gathered the strength to confront them, you let him."

David's whole body recoiled, like she'd slapped him.

"I didn't let him die," he said quickly. "I didn't…"

But no one responded. No one moved.

Stowe studied Marion's profile, the way her expression didn't falter, the stillness in her hands. This wasn't grief speaking. It was something colder. Older. The voice of a woman who'd seen rot long before anyone else noticed the smell.

"Did you confront him?" Stowe asked David, eyes narrowing. "Before he could speak to the lawyers?"

David hesitated. Then nodded once. "We argued. Yes."

"About the money?"

"And other things," David said, his voice hollow.

Peter snorted again. "How convenient."

David snapped toward him. "You think I haven't paid for this already? Every bloody day since…"

"Not enough," Marion said.

That shut him up.

Catherine rose slowly from her place by the window. "So that's it, then. Financial ruin in a nice suit. Buried under a rug and lit on fire."

"No," Stowe said. "Not quite it. There's still the matter of where you were at nine last night. The telephone people got back to us. Luckily for us Reginald had his own line, different from the rest of the house. No phone calls came in or out from that number between 8:30 and 9:30 that night. Meaning there must have been someone in the study with Reginald just after 9."

David looked down again.

"And the knife," Stowe added.

That made David blink. "What knife?"

Stowe took a long breath. "The carving knife. Missing from the kitchen."

A long, quiet beat.

"I didn't touch it," David said.

"But someone did," Catherine murmured. "Didn't they, Inspector?"

Stowe didn't answer right away. His gaze swept the room, weighing silences.

"Yes," he said. "Someone did."

And again, the fire popped, small, steady, and watching.

Chapter 24: The Arrest

David gave a short, bitter laugh, more air than sound. "This is ridiculous," he said, voice tight. "Being in debt doesn't make me a murderer."

"No," Stowe replied, pacing slowly, each step deliberate, as though walking out the shape of David's story. His eyes never left him. "But being cornered? Frightened? Out of options? That has a way of turning people into someone they don't recognize. That kind of fear opens certain doors."

He stopped; gaze sharpened. "Or in this case closes them. From the outside."

The words fell like a stone through the room. Final. Unmistakable. The fire behind them hissed in protest, and the wind tapped against the windowpanes like it was listening in or waiting to be let out.

His gaze stayed fixed on the edge of the fireplace. "I didn't go in," he said, jaw tight. "I didn't even knock."

Stowe arched a brow, arms folding across his chest. "About the Madison deal?"

David blinked. Just once. A subtle flinch, but unmistakable. "Yes" he admitted. The word left his mouth like it cost him. "but that was last year"

"You didn't just lose money," Harris cut in, stepping forward. His voice was firmer now, no longer the neutral investigator but the man laying bricks of evidence, one by one. "Reginald knew. He'd written to his solicitor. Dated two days before his death. He was cutting you out of his business."

David exhaled sharply, as if trying to shake it off, but the air caught in his throat. His hand dragged through his hair, leaving it sticking up at awkward angles. His gaze dropped to the patterned rug, eyes scanning it like the answer might be stitched between the threads.

Across from him, Catherine's voice cut through the tension, thin and brittle. "Why didn't you tell me?"

David looked at her then. Really looked. His voice was softer now, pleading. "Because I didn't want to lose you."

She turned her face toward the fire, away from him. Away from all of them. Her lips pressed into a line. Her throat moved as she swallowed hard, but she didn't respond.

Stowe allowed the silence to stretch just enough to let the pressure build. Then he turned to Marion.

She sat like a sculpture, unmoving, with one hand resting gently on the armrest, the other clutching the edge of her shawl as though it anchored her to something perhaps dignity, perhaps truth. Her eyes were distant but not detached.

"You heard Reginald arguing that night," Stowe said. "Do you remember anything more? A voice? A phrase?"

Marion didn't answer at once. Her fingers twitched slightly; the movement barely noticeable except to those who were watching closely.

"Just his voice," she said at last, each word crisp. "Angry. Not irritated not scolding. It was fury. The kind that comes when someone you trust turns on you. It was betrayal."

Stowe tilted his head. "Could David have been in there?"

Marion hesitated. Her eyes flicked toward David, just briefly.

Then, with a quiet, weighted sigh: "He could have."

The words fell like a blade through linen. Clean. Precise. And undeniable.

Catherine stood abruptly. Her voice came out louder than she meant it to, but steady. "No. No, this is all wrong." She shook her head. "He wouldn't hurt my father. No matter what passed between them. He wouldn't. He *couldn't*."

David stood too, almost reflexively. "I didn't kill him," he said, turning to her. "I swear to you, Catherine, I didn't. I didn't even touch the door."

Stowe took a step closer. His voice lowered, but the force of it didn't fade. "You were unaccounted for. In the window when Reginald died, no one saw you. No one heard you. Everyone else has an alibi. You were gone nearly twenty minutes."

David's jaw clenched. "I took a phone call."

"From whom?" Harris asked, eyes narrowing.

David hesitated.

Too long.

"A client," he said finally. "In Hong Kong."

"What's their name?" Stowe asked, pressing forward.

David glanced around the room, searching for backup. But there was none. Not from Catherine, who stood rigid beside the fireplace. Not from Peter, arms crossed like a wall. Not from Marion, who stared at him now with something like pity and something colder.

He swallowed, hard. "You wouldn't know them. It's not important."

"Try me," Harris said. His voice had gone flat. Heavy.

David's mouth moved, but no sound came out.

"I'll get the number later," he muttered.

"No," Stowe said. "You'll give it now."

The room contracted around them. Even the rain outside had taken on a rhythm, a slow, deliberate tapping against the windows. Like time, running out.

David opened his mouth again. But still, nothing came. No name. No number.

Only silence.

Even Catherine didn't defend him.

David shifted his weight, like he'd just realized, maybe for the first time, that something in the room had turned against him. Not just the mood. Something deeper. Something final.

"I'll give you the number at the station," he said quietly.

Stowe didn't speak right away. He just nodded, slow and solemn, as though he'd just placed the final piece in a long, grim puzzle.

"David Forrester," Stowe said, voice clear, even, and with the kind of calm that comes only from grim certainty. "I am arresting you on suspicion of the murder of Reginald Price. You do not have to say anything…"

There was a soft gasp, half shock, half protest from Catherine. It broke through the air like a glass cracking under pressure.

"...but anything you do say may be used in evidence against you."

The room changed in that instant.

Something shifted, subtle but seismic. The weight of the accusation wasn't just on David now. It pressed down on everyone. A moment suspended in time; breath held by walls that had heard too much already.

Harris stepped forward. He didn't rush, but there was purpose in his movement. From his coat, he withdrew the handcuffs. The dull, metallic *click* as they opened was louder than it should have been. It sliced through the stillness like a scalpel.

"Please place your hands in front of you," he said, voice firm but not cruel.

David didn't move at first. His eyes went to Catherine. Searching. Desperate, but restrained. His mouth opened maybe to speak, to explain, to plead but no words came. Just breath, tight in his throat.

Catherine stood frozen. Her hands were clasped near her collarbone, knuckles white. Her lips parted slightly, like she wanted to say something, anything, but didn't trust her voice to carry it.

David blinked. Then, slowly, as if each motion had to be wrestled from a deeper part of him, he extended his arms. Palms forward. Resigned.

The cuffs snapped closed with a crisp *snick*. A sound of finality.

Catherine sank down onto the edge of the settee, her knees folding beneath her like someone had pulled the string that held her upright. One hand went to her mouth. She didn't cry, not yet, but her shoulders trembled. Her breath came in shallow bursts, irregular. Like something inside was fracturing in slow motion.

Peter stepped away from the window. His expression hadn't softened, but there was something duller behind his eyes now. Not triumph. Not even vindication. Just exhaustion. His arms, which had been folded across his chest like armour, dropped to his sides, as if he no longer needed the shield, or couldn't bear its weight anymore.

As Harris guided David toward the hallway, boots echoing dully against the polished wood, David turned at the threshold.

He looked directly at Catherine. Not at the room. Not at the others. Just her.

"I didn't do it," he said. Quiet. Steady. "And I hope one day you believe that."

She didn't answer. Didn't even nod. But her gaze held his wide, glassy, unreadable.

Then Harris led him away. The sound of their steps grew fainter, absorbed by the hallway. A door opened. A pause.

And then it closed. A dull *thud* that didn't echo, because it didn't need to. It landed like a book shutting on the last page, heavy and unspoken.

It was an ending.

For now.

The silence that followed wasn't just absence. It was something active. Dense. The kind that grows in the wake of something irreversible.

Catherine stared down at the rug beneath her feet, blinking, unfocused. Her hands curled into fists on her lap, then loosened, as if she couldn't quite decide what to hold onto anymore or if there was anything left worth holding.

Peter lingered by the mantel. He watched Catherine for a long moment, his jaw shifting slightly. His expression wasn't soft, but it wasn't hard either. There was a kind of reluctant sympathy in it like a man who'd won something he didn't want.

But he didn't move toward her.

And Marion the still point in the room reached slowly for the iron poker by the hearth. She nudged the embers, coaxing a small flame from beneath the ash. It flared briefly, weak but alive. A flicker against the deepening grey of the moment.

No one spoke.

Because even though Reginald's supposed killer had just been led away in cuffs, swallowed by rain and hallway shadow...

...not one of them was truly certain they'd found him.

Chapter 25: Catherine's Desperate Search

Catherine sat motionless on the edge of the unmade bed in her dimly lit room, posture rigid despite the storm quivering in her hands. They lay in her lap, clenched together, not in prayer, but in defiance. As if holding tightly enough might keep her from unravelling.

Late afternoon light slanted through the sheer curtains in fractured bands, slicing the space with golden stripes. Dust danced in the air like falling ash. The beams lit only part of the room, the rest remained cloaked in creeping dusk. It was the kind of light that pretended to be warm but held no comfort. A gilded prison, casting its bars across the floor, the walls, and across her chest, where breath came too shallow.

The corners of the room were thick with shadow, darker than they had any right to be. Silent witnesses, they hunched like forgotten memories, full of judgment, full of things left unsaid. They watched her grief gather silently, like floodwater against a thin dam.

The emptiness beside her, where David's coat should have hung, where his scent should have lingered, was an ache made manifest. A vacuum with gravity. The room had been his sanctuary once. Now it was a shrine to absence.

She could still see him, in her mind's eye, the sharp cut of his shoulders as he was led away, the glint of metal around his wrists. There had been no outburst, no flailing. Just the weight of defeat behind his eyes, and one last look, not pleading, but *hoping*. Hoping she still saw him, the real him, beneath the wreckage.

She had. And she still did.

The clock on the mantel ticked with maddening precision. Each tick was a verdict. Each second that passed was another brick in the wall being built between them. She imagined him alone now, sitting in some grey room beneath flickering fluorescent lights, surrounded by suspicion, drowning in silence.

It wasn't just the trial looming, or the charges. It was the feeling, deep, cold, impossible to shake, that something had gone wrong. That someone had arranged the facts just so, made the truth look guilty. Catherine wasn't naïve. She knew David had lied. Lied to protect himself, lied out of fear. But lies weren't murder.

She felt it. That ancient, irrational instinct that lives beneath reason. He hadn't done this. And if she didn't act now, she might lose him to a story someone else was writing.

She stood up suddenly, the bed springs creaking beneath her like bones shifting. Her breath caught in her throat, but she forced herself to move. She grabbed the coat from the back of the chair, the soft wool heavier than usual, as though it, too, bore the weight of what she was about to do. Her fingers fumbled at the buttons. Once. Twice. Then she managed it.

The house was quiet. Not peaceful, just empty in the way places are when too much has been said and not enough resolved. The long corridor outside her door was dim, the sconces lit but flickering faintly against the panelled walls. The carpet underfoot muffled her steps, but her heartbeat thundered loud enough to compensate.

As she moved, the ancestral portraits that lined the hallway loomed above her. Their painted eyes followed her progress with a stern stillness. Each face seemed to ask: *Are you certain? Do you know what you're risking?*

She didn't flinch. Let them judge.

She passed closed doors, the guest room, the blue Parlor, the linen cupboard, each one now part of a house that felt less like a home and more like a maze. A place designed to keep its secrets in.

At the end of the east corridor, the study door stood beneath its crown of yellow and black police tape, like a wound crudely stitched. The contrast against the rich mahogany made it look obscene. Evidence markers, numbered, clinical, dotted the floor like scattered tombstones. The air smelled faintly of paper, polish, and something more sterile now. Something institutional.

A uniformed constable leaned against the wall, a paperback novel half-folded in one hand, his thumb holding his place. His eyes flicked up at her as she approached, then back to the page, polite but detached, the look of someone doing his job but not investing.

Catherine's eyes were fixed on the door. If she could just get inside. Just one more look. There had to be something they missed. Something Stowe had overlooked, or dismissed too quickly. Reginald's study had always been a fortress of details. He *liked* complexity. He *liked* layers. She just needed one of those layers to peel back.

Then, the unmistakable sound of measured, deliberate steps behind her. Not rushed. Not loud. But *certain*.

She turned.

Henshaw.

He emerged from the gloom like a Specter, as though the house itself had conjured him to keep its secrets safe. He wore his usual charcoal grey suit, pressed to perfection. Not a crease in sight. His gloves were tucked under one arm, his silver hair combed back with precision. His face, pale, lean, unreadable, was harder to gauge. But his eyes... his eyes were alert. More so than usual.

He stopped two paces from her and inclined his head.

"Mrs. Forrester," he said softly, voice low and almost reverent. "I must remind you that Inspector Stowe has expressly forbidden any unauthorized entry into the study."

Catherine didn't move. "I'm not going in," she said. "Just looking."

His expression didn't change, but something flickered in his gaze. Not suspicion, more like curiosity. Or perhaps recognition. As if he knew exactly why she was here.

"You understand," he said carefully, "that touching anything could compromise the investigation."

"I won't touch anything," she replied, voice tight. "I just need... to see it again."

There was a pause. A long one. And in that pause, the faintest creak of the house settling or shifting.

"May I offer some advice, ma'am?" Henshaw said finally.

She looked at him.

"If you're looking for the truth," he continued, "you may not find it where the Inspector expects you to. Reginald was a complex man. And complexity, in this house, rarely ends where it begins."

Catherine blinked. "What are you saying?"

He gave the faintest of smiles. "Nothing I wouldn't say to anyone seeking closure. Only that sometimes... the study isn't the only room that holds answers."

"I'm not here to cause trouble, Henshaw," she said, her voice calm but thick with urgency. "I need only a few minutes. There's something personal I left behind."

"May I ask what item that might be?" he asked, voice dipped in formality but gentled at the edges.

Catherine lowered her voice, casting a cautious glance at the constable nearby. "My diary," she murmured, as if the very word might shatter if spoken too loudly. "I was in the study yesterday afternoon. I brought it with me... I wrote some things I shouldn't have, private reflections. It's full of thoughts that aren't meant to be public."

Her eyes flicked back up to his. "If the police find it, they'll read it. Every line. Every suspicion. Not just mine, but things others have said to me in confidence. It's not evidence, it's personal. But it could be misunderstood."

There was a pause. The kind of silence that stretches just long enough to hold the weight of meaning.

Henshaw's gaze softened almost imperceptibly, the steel melting just enough to let something more human through, perhaps empathy, or recognition. "You have always been private with your thoughts," he said, a hint of memory behind his words. "I understand the value of such... confidences."

He looked toward the constable again, who hadn't moved from his post. The young officer was still reading, shoulders hunched slightly, as if determined not to interfere with things that didn't concern him.

"Very well," Henshaw said at last, inclining his head slightly. "Please, be swift."

"Thank you," Catherine whispered, her voice trembling as relief and adrenaline surged in equal measure.

Catherine stepped forward slowly, her eyes sweeping the floor just beyond the police tape. The broken cup still lay under the edge of the desk, its shattered porcelain stained faintly with old tea. A chair sat askew; one wheel turned the wrong way. A pile of papers had been swept aside, some pages half-folded, others dog-eared in haste.

It didn't look like a murder scene. It looked like a man had been interrupted mid-thought.

The study welcomed her not with warmth, but with a chill that crept beneath her collar, wrapping around her spine like a whisper. The air inside was still, too still. As if the room was holding its breath.

Her eyes locked onto the bookshelf behind the desk, Reginald's so-called "wall of truths." He kept things there. Documents. Letters. Once, a signed agreement he hadn't yet told the family about. A locked compartment behind the second row of poetry volumes.

The curtains were half-drawn, allowing narrow bands of late-day sunlight to cut across the parquet floor in pale gold slashes. Dust motes drifted lazily through the beams, undisturbed by the usual rhythm of life. Everything was as it had been left, preserved, static. A moment in time, frozen mid-collapse.

The cassette.

Reginald's ritual. Every major decision ended with a recording. His thoughts, his reasoning, his conclusions. They weren't musings, they were records. A private archive of power.

And the tape that should have followed the last conversation about the Madison deal, would be in the filing cabinet, under Madison Deal. A quick search and the tape was gone, where had it gone?

Her breath hitched, panic flickering through her chest like a struck match.

She turned slowly, gaze sweeping the corners of the room, searching for something out of place.

And there, in the corner, beside the window, the hi-fi system sat like a relic from a different age. Sleek, black, and out of place in the old-world elegance of the room. A blinking red light betrayed its status. Still powered. Still ready.

Her hands trembled as she approached. Each step felt too loud, even though the thick carpet muffled her heels. She reached out, fingers hovering over the eject button. For a second, she hesitated, afraid that pressing it might collapse everything. That she'd find nothing, or worse, *something she wasn't ready for.*

Then she pressed it.

Click.

The door opened with a mechanical sigh. A single cassette sat inside, nestled like a confession.

She lifted it gently, cradling it as though it might break. The label, handwritten in Reginald's deliberate script, made her breath catch.

Madison Deal — Final Thoughts.

It was real. And it hadn't been stored. It had been *played*. Recently.

Her mind spun.

Marion had claimed to hear voices Reginald's voice, and another. Angry. Sharp. But what if that second voice had never been in the room? What if she had heard the tape playing, and mistaken it for a confrontation?

It would explain everything. Why no one had seen David enter the study. Why he had stood outside the door, undecided, unaware that the voice inside wasn't live.

Her heart pounded wildly in her chest. The room swam slightly, as if the walls had shifted in recognition of this revelation.

And then…

A creak.

She spun around, hand clutching the tape to her chest like a relic.

Henshaw stood in the doorway. His silhouette was sharp against the gloom of the corridor behind him, but his expression was not stern.

He looked… concerned.

"Mrs. Forrester," he said gently, stepping into the room with the soundless grace he always carried. "What have you found?"

She didn't answer immediately. Her eyes met his, and for a moment, something passed between them, something unspoken, but undeniable. A shared understanding that this moment mattered.

"I found it," she whispered, holding the cassette out like an offering. "This might be the truth. If Marion heard this, and not a real argument, it means David... David might not have been there at all."

Henshaw stepped closer, eyes flicking down to the tape, then back to her. His face remained composed, but something in him eased. Not surprise, but quiet confirmation.

"Reginald never intended those recordings for anyone but himself," he said softly. "He considered them his conscience, locked away in plastic, where no one could interrupt."

She nodded. "But someone played this one. Recently."

He didn't answer right away. Then: "You must take it to Inspector Stowe. Now. Before it disappears again."

Catherine stiffened. "Again?"

Henshaw's lips twitched, almost into a smile. "This house has always been... excellent at swallowing things it doesn't want seen."

She didn't linger. With the cassette clutched tight, she rushed past him into the corridor, her footsteps echoing louder now, no longer tentative, but driven.

The hallways of the Price estate seemed to hum around her, no longer just walls and portraits, but veins of a living thing, pulsing with secrets. The rain outside deepened, battering the windows like insistent fingers.

She reached the stairwell, the world spinning around her in frantic motion. With every step downward, every flicker of candlelight across the polished banisters, she felt the tide turning. The narrative unravelling. The noose loosening around David's neck.

And just maybe, just *maybe*, the truth was about to emerge from the shadows that had kept it bound.

Because sometimes salvation came in the shape of a forgotten tape, found in the cold heart of a haunted room.

Chapter 26: Interrogation

The interrogation room had shrunk. Or so it felt.

It wasn't just the four pale walls closing in, it was the air itself, heavy and close, thickened by tension, stale sweat, and a faint, biting tang of institutional disinfectant. The overhead fluorescent light buzzed with a dull persistence, flickering just enough to be noticed, casting flickers of movement across the table that weren't there. Every now and then, it popped with a tiny surge, bathing everything in a sickly, jaundiced hue that made the skin look bruised, the eyes hollow, and the truth harder to see.

David Forrester sat hunched forward at the metal table, shoulders square but trembling slightly under the weight of exhaustion. His collar was open, tie crooked, shirt clinging damply at the back where sweat had soaked through. He looked less like a suspect and more like a man teetering on the edge of unravelling. His hands were clasped tightly in front of him, fingers intertwined and pale with pressure, as though if he let go, he might fall apart.

The walls seemed to lean in with every breath he took.

Across from him, Detective Harris sat poised with mechanical precision, back straight, pen dancing a metronome beat against his lined notepad. The pad was already littered with underlined phrases, arrows, question marks, the desperate scrawl of someone trying to force chaos into order. Harris's suit was still crisp, but his eyes were tired. The kind of tired that came not from lack of sleep but from chasing ghosts through half-truths.

"You keep saying you didn't kill Reginald Price," Harris said, his voice cutting through the stale air like a razor. "Over and over."

David's voice cracked slightly. "Because I didn't."

The fluorescent bulb above them buzzed louder, its glow casting odd, shifting shadows across David's face. His cheekbones seemed too sharp now, his eyes too sunken.

"Funny thing," Harris said, leaning forward, elbows on the metal table. "People who didn't do it, they always seem to end up alone in locked rooms with dead relatives."

David let out a short, hollow laugh. "Is that what we're calling evidence now? Coincidence dressed up as theory?"

Harris gave a small smile. No warmth in it. "I call it motive. You were spiralling. Business failing. Reginald was cutting you out. You were going to lose everything, and then, somehow, you found yourself standing outside the very room where he died."

Before David could fire back, the door clicked open behind him. That sound, simple, mechanical, landed like a judge's gavel.

Inspector Thomas Stowe entered, the weight of his presence carrying more than his footsteps. He didn't rush. He never did. His coat was folded neatly over one arm, still damp from the night. His boots tapped against the floor like punctuation marks.

He offered no greetings, no pleasantries, just a slight nod toward Harris, and a single glance at David.

Then he sat, slowly, beside the detective. Not across from David. Beside Harris. Deliberate positioning.

Authority had a seat now.

"Evening, Mr. Forrester," he said, voice low and gravelled. "We're going to go through it again. From the beginning. Clarity's a strange thing. It doesn't like speed. But it loves repetition."

David leaned back slightly, exhausted and defensive. "We've been through it already. I've told you everything I know."

"And yet," Stowe said, eyes narrowed, "you're still in this room. Which means something doesn't add up. So, we're going to start with what we know."

He raised a hand and ticked off points with fingers, one by one. Methodical. Controlled.

"You left the dining room just after nine. Everyone agrees. An hour later, Reginald Price is found dead in his study. Locked door. No forced entry. No sign of struggle. Clean scene."

Stowe leaned forward; voice low. "You were unaccounted for during the most crucial thirty minutes of that window."

David's hands twitched slightly. "I never went in."

"You walked to the study," Harris said, tone flat. "We know that. Marion saw you heading down the corridor."

David nodded quickly. "Yes. I went to the door. I stood there for a moment. And then I turned back."

"Why?" Stowe asked, his voice softer now, deceptively calm.

David's mouth twisted. "Because I didn't want to argue with him again. We'd already fought earlier. I knew if I went in there, it would be another screaming match."

"But you still went to the door," Harris said.

David's fingers curled into fists on the table. "I was going to speak to him. I wanted to... try again. Maybe make it right. But then I heard his voice. He was already angry."

"Angry," Stowe echoed, watching him closely. "So, you heard him speaking. But to whom?"

David hesitated. The moment stretched.

"I... I don't know," he admitted. "I heard Reginald. Shouting. But I didn't hear another voice clearly. It was muffled. I assumed maybe Peter had gone in."

"You assumed," Harris repeated. "But you didn't check?"

"No."

"You didn't knock?"

"No."

Stowe's tone sharpened slightly. "So, you stood outside the study door, heard raised voices, and walked away. Just like that."

David's voice rose in frustration. "Yes! Because I didn't want to make it worse."

Stowe steepled his fingers. "And what did you do next?"

"I went upstairs. I made a call."

"Ah," Harris said, pouncing again. "The infamous phone call. The client from Hong Kong."

David exhaled hard. "Yes. I've told you. A business contact. I can get the number."

"You said that two hours ago," Stowe reminded him. "And yet, no number."

David slammed his palm lightly on the table, not in defiance, but desperation. "I didn't kill him. I was angry, sure. But I wouldn't have..."

Stowe interrupted gently. "You were angry. Broke. Cornered. About to be erased from the estate. That's not nothing, David."

David dropped his head into his hands. His voice, when it came again, was barely above a whisper.

"I wanted to scream at him. I wanted to make him understand. But I didn't kill him. I swear to you, I didn't."

Stowe leaned back, watching him. Letting the silence crawl up the walls.

Finally, Harris spoke again. "Let's go back to the phone call. You said you were upstairs. What room?"

"The guest bedroom," David replied.

"Anyone see you?"

"No."

"Did the call connect?"

"Yes, it connected"

David looked up. Eyes bloodshot. "I'm not a killer. I'm just the only one left standing in the wrong hallway."

Stowe said nothing for a moment. He just studied David's face, not the eyes, but the cracks around the mouth, the tremble in his jaw. Then he stood, slowly, coat still folded over his arm.

"Let's hope your phone records says something you don't," he said.

The door burst open with sudden force, slamming against the wall with a sharp, echoing crack.

Catherine.

She didn't enter; she arrived. A force of will carved from thunder and drenched in rain. Her coat was soaked through, clinging to her like armour left out in a storm, heavy with urgency. Droplets trailed from her sleeves and hem, spattering the linoleum like scattered punctuation marks. Her boots squelched with each step, but she moved fast, head high, breath sharp.

The air shifted. Stilled.

Her hair clung to her face in wind-swept strands, cheeks flushed from the cold and the adrenaline. But it was her eyes, sharp, defiant, burning with something beyond anger, that made the room hold its breath.

In her right hand, a cassette tape, in a plastic bag. Clutched so tightly her knuckles had gone pale. In the other, a folder bulging with documents, sticky notes, tabs like torn bookmarks in someone else's story. The contents strained against the spine as if trying to spill the truth faster than she could speak it.

The room froze. Harris rose halfway to his feet, instinct rather than command. Stowe only turned his head.

The overhead lights flickered once. Even the bulbs flinched.

"You need to stop this," Catherine said. Her voice didn't waver. It didn't ask. It declared. Each word dropped like a stone into still water.

"Mrs. Forrester." Harris began, still standing.

She didn't even look at him. "Sit down, Detective."

It wasn't a suggestion. It was a command laced in shattered glass.

Harris froze, glancing at Stowe, who gave a subtle nod, not approval, just recognition. Catherine wasn't bluffing.

"You're chasing the wrong man," she continued. She marched forward and slammed the folder onto the metal table. The impact reverberated off the concrete like a slap. Papers flew free, letters, receipts, handwritten notes, statements, witness fragments all tumbling out, a mess of organized chaos.

David flinched in his seat, blinking like someone waking from a nightmare. "Catherine...?"

She didn't turn. Couldn't. Not yet.

Her gaze locked on Stowe, who now stood at his full height. Calm, unmoved, but watching her with a kind of quiet calculation. He'd seen storms before, but this one had direction.

"You've built this case on a single assumption," she said, her tone flat but simmering, "that my mother overheard Reginald arguing with David before he died. That he was angry at him. That David was in the room."

She placed the cassette on top of the folder like a final card in a game only she understood. "But that argument never happened."

Stowe raised one brow. "Explain."

Catherine pushed a damp strand of hair behind her ear, her fingers trembling for the first time. She took a breath, a deep, centring one.

"My father recorded himself. Audio memos. Business reflections. Legal notes. He called them 'voice ledgers.' He hated paperwork, but he loved the sound of his own mind. After every major deal, he'd talk it through into that hi-fi system in the study."

She gestured to the tape. "This one was labelled *Madison Deal – Final Notes.* In his handwriting. I found it still warm in the player. Someone played it the night he died. Likely right before."

Harris sat again, slower this time, his brow furrowing as the shape of things began to shift. "You're saying... Marion didn't hear a conversation?"

"She heard this," Catherine said, tapping the tape. "My father. Alone. Angry. Rehearsing what he was going to say. Working it out in his head. But it sounded like a fight. And everyone assumed it was live. It wasn't."

David inhaled sharply, his voice catching. "Then I wasn't even there. I left the table at nine, but if he was already dead by then..."

"The whole timeline falls apart," Catherine said. "And if it does, then David wasn't the only possibility. Any of us could've been near that study."

Stowe finally moved, reaching out slowly. Catherine didn't flinch. She placed the tape in his hand with care, as if it might break.

He turned it over in his fingers, running his thumb across the label. Reginald's handwriting, unmistakable. Sharp. Ordered.

"If this is true," Harris muttered, voice low, "then Marion's testimony... collapses."

"And so does the motive," Catherine said.

Stowe's jaw tightened. "Which means we're back to square one."

He stood abruptly, his chair screeching back against the floor. "Verify it," he said to Harris. "Get it transcribed. Time-stamped. Cross-reference it with the statement. If the tape clears him, I want proof. And if it's planted... I want to know who benefits."

David sat in stunned silence, eyes darting between the folder and the tape. "So, what now? I'm not a suspect... or I'm being framed?"

Stowe didn't answer. His eyes were still on the tape, as if it might, in time, speak for itself.

One hour later

The station's heavy glass doors sighed open with the weight of release, and David Forrester stepped into the blue dusk of evening.

Rain had gentled into mist. It rose from the sidewalks in thin, ghostly tendrils, catching the light of streetlamps like low fog. Neon flickered from a nearby diner, humming through the moisture-heavy air like a heartbeat in a quiet room.

David paused at the bottom step, one hand gripping the iron railing. The other dug into his coat pocket. He inhaled deeply, not for comfort, but for confirmation. The air was cold and real and outside. It filled his lungs in a way no interrogation room ever could.

His tie hung loose. His shirt was creased. But his shoulders, those finally sagged in something like relief. Not victory. Just the absence of the hunt.

Catherine stood beside him. Her coat was soaked through. Her hair still damp. But her spine was straight, and her eyes were no longer clouded by confusion. She was quiet, but not unsure.

David turned slightly toward her. "You didn't have to come."

She didn't meet his eyes. "I didn't come for you," she said, tone soft but firm. "I came for the truth."

David gave a tired smile. Not smug. Not even grateful. Just worn. "Still," he said, "you saved me."

"I gave you time," she said. "Don't waste it."

"You know, I have been sitting across from Stowe all day. I know him from somewhere, but I just can't place where it was"

Behind them, the station doors groaned once more. Inspector Stowe stepped out into the drizzle; shoulders hunched slightly against the wind. His coat flared at the bottom, his hands in his pockets. The kind of man who didn't know how to stop chasing shadows even when the rain blurred the outlines.

Chapter 27: A Day Out

The next morning dawned softer than expected.

Pale sunlight filtered through the bedroom curtains in long, golden bars, casting a quiet geometry across the floorboards. Dust motes hovered in the stillness. The kind of light that made you want to believe in new beginnings, even if only for a few hours.

Gulliford was a half-hour's drive east, a quiet harbour town curled around the skeleton of a Norman castle, its streets tight and crooked, its shop windows cluttered with charm and the ghosts of a slower era. Catherine hadn't planned on leaving the estate. Not today. Not with everything still humming beneath the surface like a wire ready to snap.

But David had been persistent.

"You need air," he said over breakfast, nudging a second cup of coffee across the table toward her. "Preferably not the kind filtered through drafty corridors and regret."

She gave him a sceptical look over the rim of her cup. "That sounds dangerously close to compassion."

He smirked. "Let's just call it survival instinct. If I have to listen to Stowe sigh one more time while rereading the same report in the library, I'll confess just to make it stop."

That earned a reluctant laugh. A real one, if only half-formed. She hadn't heard herself laugh in days. It startled her more than she expected.

"Fine," she said, setting the mug down. "Gulliford it is. But I want to be back before sunset. I don't need Stowe thinking I've absconded with the family secrets."

"He'd call in a helicopter," David muttered, standing. "Probably borrow one from the army."

They drove in silence at first, the kind that didn't feel hostile, just restful. The countryside unfurled around them in green folds, stone walls thick with ivy lining the road, trees blushing gold at the tips. A pair of pheasants darted across the path ahead, their panic absurd and endearing.

David drove, one-handed, elbow perched on the open window, his other hand loosely resting on the wheel. The breeze tugged at his hair and collar, softening the edges of him. For the first time in days, Catherine saw something near relaxation on his face, or at least the closest thing he could manage.

When the town appeared, it was like a storybook illustration: whitewashed cottages huddled along narrow lanes, slate rooftops shining with dew, the steeple of St. Anne's cutting into the sky. And there, overlooking it all, the jagged outline of Gulliford Castle, ancient and half-forgotten.

They parked beside a bookshop with a crooked awning and a hand-lettered sign in the window advertising "Scones & Sonnets. Thursdays at Noon." The air smelled of sea salt, chimney smoke, and rising bread. Somewhere nearby, a busker played a tired, wistful tune on a battered violin.

Catherine inhaled slowly, letting it fill her lungs. "It's strange," she said. "I feel like I've been holding my breath since his death."

"Then today," David said, stepping beside her with a paper bag of sugared almonds under one arm, "you exhale."

She gave him a sideways glance.

"You can pretend you're on holiday," he added. "Not a murder suspect. Not the daughter of the deceased. Just a tourist with an overactive brain."

She smirked faintly. "I've never been great at pretending."

"Then just fake it well enough for a stroll and some sugar," he said, offering her an almond. "You can be a tourist with an agenda."

She took one, chewing thoughtfully as they wandered down the high street. "I know that I didn't do it," she said suddenly. "And I know my mother, she wouldn't be able to hold herself together long enough to cover something like this up. Not for a day, let alone a week."

David slowed his pace. "Go on."

"I think *you* didn't do it. I mean, I think. I do." She glanced at him. "Well, I *mostly* do."

He raised an eyebrow. "Comforting."

She ignored him. "That just leaves Philip and Peter. And something about Peter doesn't add up. I need to talk to him. Properly. Not through these half-smiles and family-lunch performances. I want answers."

David gave her a long look. "Can't we just have a pleasant morning *without* talking about murder?"

Catherine shrugged. "We can. But murder keeps talking to me."

They passed an antiques shop cluttered with dusty brass and green glass, then a small café with fogged windows and two elderly women playing chess in the corner. A gull screeched overhead, landing with expert clumsiness near a child dropping chips on the pavement.

"Maybe this is our version of pleasant," she said after a moment. "Just enough peace to keep the questions from eating us alive."

David offered her another almond. "That's grimly poetic."

She smiled, but didn't argue.

They found the path to the castle and followed it up through wind-worn trees, boots crunching on gravel. The sea stretched out in the distance, wide, grey-blue, and full of something unspeakable. Beneath them, the town unspooled like a story, rooftops scattered like misplayed dominoes.

Catherine paused halfway up and looked down at it all. "We'll go back soon," she said. "But not before I clear my head."

David nodded, and for once, he didn't offer a quip.

They walked on in silence, the kind that didn't need filling.

Catherine paused beneath the leaning remains of the gatehouse, her breath catching as the wind picked up around them. The stone arch cast a fractured shadow over her boots, but her attention wasn't on the ruin or the sweep of rooftops below. Her eyes had locked onto something else, just beyond the trees, across the gravel car park.

A dark green car had just pulled in.

Familiar.

Too familiar.

Her jaw tightened. She took a half-step forward, squinting.

"That's Philip's," she said, her voice low and certain.

David turned, following her line of sight. He popped the last sugared almond into his mouth, chewing slowly. "Are you sure?"

She didn't blink. "I've ridden in it," she said flatly. "It's his."

They backed up quickly, ducking behind one of the outer towers where the stone had long since surrendered to weather and time. The scent of lichen and damp stone clung to the air. They crouched just enough to stay out of sight but not out of earshot.

The car door opened with a metallic thunk that rang too loudly in the still morning air.

A few seconds later, Philip stepped out. He ran a hand through his hair, glancing around, not panicked, but careful. Calculated. His fingers trembled slightly, just enough to catch the sunlight.

Then the passenger door opened.

Marion.

She climbed out slowly, one hand adjusting the scarf around her neck. Her gaze swept the lot, scanning as though she felt the need to check for witnesses. At first, she looked uncertain, but then a shift. Her expression softened, and she smiled. Not politely. Not distantly. It was warm. Familiar. Intimate.

Catherine's breath caught in her throat.

"They've been meeting," she murmured. "This isn't new."

David shifted beside her. "He always said he barely spoke to her."

"And she said she couldn't stand him," Catherine replied. "So, either they've both had remarkable character growth, or they're liars."

The pair moved slowly beneath a low-sweeping tree near the stone wall. Philip leaned in.

Then they kissed.

Not tentative. Not nervous. It had rhythm. Memory.

Catherine's stomach coiled, tight and cold. She felt the blood drain from her face.

David muttered something low and explicit under his breath. "Well. That explains some things."

Catherine stayed quiet. Her gaze was locked, eyes sharp and narrowed, like she was watching a live wire spark. Inside her, pieces were moving. Sliding into new shapes.

"They've been working together," she said finally, her voice a notch too even. "Or at the very least, they've been talking more than anyone let on."

David crossed his arms, stepping slightly forward to get a better look without being seen. "You think they're involved in the murder?"

"I think they had every reason to want Reginald out of the way," she said. "Philip's always played the harmless fool. And Marion..."

"She's a master of the quiet breakdown," David said. "Looks like grief. Smells like performance."

Catherine didn't respond to that. Her eyes were still on the car, now partially obscured as Philip and Marion strolled further down the hill, away from the vehicle, away from the ruin like a couple stealing time, not secrets.

"Maybe it wasn't about the inheritance," she said. "Maybe it was about control. Legacy. Maybe they were protecting something, or someone."

David rubbed the back of his neck. "Philip's cleverer than we gave him credit for."

"Or more desperate," Catherine added.

They waited until the pair had disappeared from view, nothing more than shrinking silhouettes on the path below. Only then did Catherine step out from behind the crumbling wall, her face unreadable. A gust of wind caught the hem of her coat, pulling it sideways like a warning.

"Come on," she said, not looking at David. "Let's walk a bit more. I need to think."

They circled the keep in silence, the gravel path crunching softly beneath their boots. Seagulls wheeled overhead; their cries jagged against the otherwise quiet morning. The sea stretched out beyond the cliff like a flat sheet of steel, calm and watchful.

David kept glancing at her, but she gave no indication of what she was thinking. Her brows were drawn tight, eyes scanning the castle ruins like they might offer answers if she stared long enough.

"They're hiding something," she said eventually, her voice quiet but certain. "I don't know if they did it. But they know who did. Or they know why."

David slowed his steps. "And you think Marion's capable of that kind of deception?"

Catherine didn't answer right away. She looked down, then out toward the sea.

"I think she's capable of protecting what she loves," she said. "Even if that means burying the truth along with the body."

David gave a low whistle. "And Philip?"

"He'd follow," she said. "Not because he's strong. But because he's scared of being left behind."

They stopped near a low stone wall, the wind rising slightly. Catherine braced her hands against the cold stone, staring at the horizon.

David stepped closer. "So, what do we do?"

She turned, slowly, the sea wind in her hair. "Now?" she said. "Now we stop trusting every face that smiles when we enter the room."

David met her eyes. "And if it's someone we've already trusted?"

Catherine looked at him, really looked, for the first time in minutes. Her voice dropped, but it didn't soften.

"Then we smile back," she said. "Until we don't have to."

Chapter 28: The Relationship

Three years ago, the Price house had looked much as it always had, stately, immaculate, untouchable.

Dinner that evening had been one of Reginald's formal affairs: polished silver, crystal glasses lined in perfect symmetry, and three courses that arrived like clockwork. The dining room shimmered under candlelight, with the chandelier above catching each flame and spinning it out across the walls in fractured gold.

Catherine was abroad that year, and Peter had begged off with some excuse about client meetings and "code deadlines." That left only Philip and Marion, seated across from Reginald at the long mahogany table, and two empty chairs that made the silence feel louder than the cutlery.

The wine had been flowing since just after dusk, a rich red from Reginald's private cellar. Philip suspected it was one of the bottles Marion had once called *the good kind reserved for guests who don't ask questions.*

Philip had laughed at that then. Now, the words echoed differently.

Reginald barely spoke through dinner, just murmured approval at the soup, asked perfunctory questions about the company's quarterly numbers, and commented once about the state of Marion's rose garden, "You should prune more aggressively this year, the whole thing's gotten unruly."

Marion said nothing to that. Just smiled that smooth, public smile of hers and kept cutting her chicken as if he hadn't said a word.

But Philip saw it.

The small twitch in her left hand. The way she pressed her knife just a bit too hard into the plate.

Later, when Reginald excused himself for a call, one he always took in the study. Marion poured them both another glass.

They sat in the lounge now, away from the polished glare of the dining room. The fire crackled low. The room smelled of wax, cedarwood, and the fading sweetness of dessert. Her shoes were off. His tie was loosened.

She looked different like that. More real.

"He was dreadful tonight," Marion said softly, swirling her wine. "Did you see the way he looked at me when I corrected him about the contractor's name? As if I'd insulted the Queen."

Philip chuckled. "You were right, though. It was Langston, not Langford."

She turned to him. "I'm always right. That's the problem."

There was something brittle in her smile, not bitterness exactly, but fatigue. The kind that settles into bones after years of diplomacy.

"He's been like this for a while," she added. "And worse behind closed doors. Not cruel, not violent. Just... dismissive. Like I'm wallpaper."

Philip watched her for a moment. "You deserve better than wallpaper."

She looked at him, truly looked and something shifted.

A slow lean. The kind born from years of proximity, unspoken affection, and all the moments that came before this one: brushing hands in hallways, knowing glances over cold coffee, the shared silences of two people who had long since stopped pretending they didn't understand each other.

Her hand grazed his.

Philip moved toward her, barely and she didn't pull away.

Their lips met, quietly, as if testing the shape of it. Not urgent. Not explosive. Just... inevitable.

When they pulled apart, neither of them said a word. The fire crackled, and in the background, Reginald's footsteps heard.

From that night on, everything changed. Not quickly. Not recklessly. But persistently.

Over the next two years, their closeness deepened. It was in the glances exchanged across formal dinners, in the quiet hours of the late afternoon when Reginald was in meetings and the rest of the house seemed suspended. They never dared call it love aloud. But love it was, measured in tea shared in the conservatory and lingering touches that dared to last just one second too long.

Philip, once always half-smiling, began to believe again, in partnership, in warmth, in a future that wasn't made in Reginald's image.

Until last week.

That's when it cracked.

Last month.

Reginald had summoned him into the study. The door closed behind them with a sound like judgment.

He didn't sit. Didn't offer Philip a drink. Just stood by the cabinet with his back to the room, staring at a decanter he didn't touch.

Then, he turned.

"Your investment plans are rubbish," he said flatly. "Thin ideas propped up by empty numbers. And don't bother defending them. I've already shredded the proposal."

Philip stood by the desk; jaw clenched. "Reginald..."

"You think I don't see what you're doing?" Reginald interrupted, his voice rising, cold and sharp. "You think carrying on with my wife gives you leverage?"

Philip's heart skipped. His hands went still at his sides.

Reginald stepped forward, eyes gleaming now. "Let me be clear. I will never approve those plans. I will drive this business into the ground and *take you with it* before I let you carve out your empire under my name."

Philip found his voice, barely. "You'd destroy your own legacy to spite me?"

"I have other investments," Reginald snapped. "And I will survive. But you? You won't. You'll be left with nothing. Not Marion. Not this company. Not a penny. You'll be ashes before you're anything close to me."

Philip said nothing.

There was nothing left to say.

Reginald turned back toward the window.

"You can see yourself out."

And Philip did.

But the echo of that threat had stayed with him. Grew inside him like rot.

Now, weeks later, as he stood by the same study door, closed again, locked from within, he wondered if Reginald had known just how far he'd pushed them all.

And if maybe, just maybe, he'd pushed one of them too far.

Chapter 29 : A Poem

The rain had eased into a steady patter against the tall windows of the police station, the kind that felt less like weather and more like background noise, constant, unrelenting, easy to forget until it stopped.

Outside, the streetlights cast long amber streaks over the puddles. A bus rumbled past, its tyres spraying arcs of water onto the curb. Inside, under the soft yellow glow of the desk lamp, Inspector Stowe leaned over his paperwork, a fresh cup of tea cooling at his elbow, the steam long since forgotten.

Opposite him, Detective Harris sprawled back in the creaky wooden chair, legs stretched out, a pen rolling between his fingers. He wasn't looking at anything in particular. Just letting the silence settle.

Eventually, Stowe reached down and opened the bottom drawer of his desk. From within, he drew out a plain cream envelope, no stamp, no return address. Unassuming, but oddly heavy for what it contained. He held it for a moment before sliding the contents, a folded piece of paper, across the desk toward Harris.

"You know that letter you found addressed to me?" Stowe said quietly.

Harris sat up straighter, the pen stilled in his fingers. "Yeah. You finally opened it?"

"I did," Stowe said, nodding. "It was a poem."

Harris blinked. "A poem?"

"A bloody good one, too," Stowe added, with an odd kind of reverence.

He unfolded the page carefully, as though it might crumble with too much pressure. The paper crackled faintly in the quiet office. Stowe cleared his throat, then began to read aloud, his Devonshire lilt giving the lines a weight they might not have had on the page.

—

To Inspector Stowe, of Devonshire's best,
A man with sharp mind and a waistcoat well-pressed.
I write with concern, not malice nor spite,
But truths lie in shadow, not always in light.

There's more to this tale than the eyes can behold,
And secrets lie heavy, like silver grown old.
So lend me your ear, kind inspector, and see
The Price family's riddled with mystery.

First, young David, with charm but no sense,
Made terrible ventures at awful expense.
His pockets now empty, his name full of doubt,
But is he the killer? I've reasons to doubt.

Then Peter, the son with a cold-blooded frown,
Has loathed his own father since school let him down.
A scholar, a thinker, yet bitter with rage
His temper could well be the crime of the age.

And though none dare speak it, I'll say it at last
Philip and dear Marion share more than the past.
A whisper, a touch, a glance in the hall
A love that's been hidden from one and from all.

Now Catherine, bold with a gleam in her eye,
Would make Poirot weep or Miss Marple sigh.
She dreams of the truth but beware her keen chase
She'll twist facts to fit if they don't suit her case.

I ask you, dear Stowe, look deeper, dig wide,
Not all is as simple as those who have lied.
The night of the murder was layered and dense
With motives and moments that still make no sense.

So, ponder my words like a storm over moor,
And knock, if you must, on each secret door.
The truth can be cruel, but justice must win,
Though devilish lies wear an innocent grin.

Yours, with concern and a heart full of fear,
A member of kin who is lurking quite near.

Stowe folded the paper again with care, pressing the crease with his forefinger.

Harris let out a slow breath. "Well. That's something."

"It is," Stowe said. "Not your average poison-pen letter. Whoever wrote this... they knew things. Things we've only just begun to uncover."

Harris rubbed his chin. "Could be a red herring. Someone messing with us. Or a guilty conscience dressed up in rhyme."

"I've read it four times already," Stowe said. "And every time, something new jumps out. This wasn't written by an outsider. This was written by someone close. Someone who's been watching. Maybe someone who's been part of it all along."

"Philip and Marion," Harris said, shaking his head. "We'd considered it, but never seriously. Not like that."

Stowe nodded slowly. "I noticed it two days ago. Subtle gestures. The way she looked at him. That wasn't grief. That was tension, personal, buried."

"Jesus," Harris muttered. "You think this... what? It's a family conspiracy?"

"I think," Stowe said, standing and walking toward the window, "that Reginald Price built his life like a fortress. And someone, maybe more than one someone, wanted to knock the walls down."

He stared out into the rain, the wet reflection of the streetlight flickering in the puddles.

"I want you to dig into Reginald's finances. Thoroughly. Not just the big accounts, not just the shell companies David tangled himself in. I want his personal accounts. Travel expenses. Donations. Private transactions. If he paid anyone off, if he kept anything hidden, I want it."

Harris blinked. "That'll take time."

"Then take it," Stowe said without turning around. "Start with his estate lawyer. Quietly. No flags. And cross-reference anything he paid to or received from Marion, Philip, Peter. Even Catherine."

"You think they all had something in the game?"

"I think someone's wearing gloves," Stowe replied. "And I want to know who."

Harris stood, picking up the poem again. He stared at it for a moment, lips pressing into a line. "If this is real, then the killer's still watching us."

Stowe turned back, face calm but tight. "Then let's give them something worth watching."

He picked up the cold cup of tea, sipped it without grimacing. "And Harris, don't underestimate poetry. It's just confession with better editing."

Harris chuckled dryly, already heading for the door. "Right. I'll look into the finances, quietly."

Stowe sat back down as the door closed. The poem lay between his hands. He tapped the paper once, twice, then slid it back into its envelope. His eyes were fixed on the edge of his desk, but his mind was elsewhere.

If someone in the Price family had sent this… it wasn't just guilt.

It was a warning.

And warnings never came without a cost.

Chapter 30: Catherine's Suspicions

Catherine sat hunched at the head of the long mahogany dining table, wrapped tightly in an oversized cardigan that had once belonged to her mother. The wool itched her arms, but the familiarity of it grounded her. Her fingers, ink-stained and darkened by graphite smudges, were curled around a mechanical pencil. Her sleeves were pushed up to her elbows, her face drawn with fatigue but lit with quiet intensity. Her hair, once pinned and perfect, now hung loose in a curtain that framed her sharp cheekbones and shadow-ringed eyes.

The table had transformed over the past few days. Once a place for inherited silverware and stiff dinner rituals, it had become a war room, a battlefield of theory and memory. Notes and documents blanketed the polished wood like fallen leaves, curling at the corners. Sheets overlapped in layers: hastily scrawled timelines, annotated interview summaries, floorplans of the estate with arrows and question marks, and old photographs creased from too many re-examinations. A cracked manila folder lay open at her elbow, stuffed with yellowing newspaper clippings, some decades old. She'd found them in the attic storage, buried under broken picture frames and a box labelled *'Estate Correspondence – Unfiled.'*

Someone had forgotten them.

But she hadn't.

The lamp beside her gave off a low, insectile buzz, its warm light pooling over the table in a soft gold circle. Beyond that halo, the room faded into shadow. Chair backs elongated into monstrous silhouettes across the floor. Picture frames loomed crookedly on the wallpapered walls, distorted by the light. The windows were tall and narrow, their panes slick with rain. Beyond the glass: nothing. Just the void of the storm-wrapped night.

The house was quiet now. Unnaturally so. Not the usual evening hush, but the dense, charged silence of a place that had witnessed too much. It sat in the rafters, in the crawlspaces, clinging to the bones of the old house like fog. The floorboards didn't creak. The radiators didn't groan. Even the clocks seemed to tick more cautiously.

Catherine's cold tea sat beside her, long forgotten, its surface filmed with a translucent skin. A slice of toast lay nearby, nibbled at the edge, the butter gone stiff and pale. Her stomach growled quietly, but the thought of food turned her throat dry. She hadn't eaten properly in days. Not since David's arrest. Not since the certainty of her life had fractured like a dropped teacup.

She whispered into the stillness: "Peter. Philip."

Just saying the names aloud gave them shape, gave them weight. They floated there in the quiet of the study like names etched in frost, delicate, incriminating, impossible to take back. The room absorbed them in silence, offering no verdict, no clarity. Only pressure.

Peter.

The sculpted, silent one. Composed right down to his fingernails. Always the crisp shirt. Always the controlled smile. But Catherine knew, had always *felt*, that the stillness was a mask. Too measured. Too rehearsed. She thought of the night before, how he sat at the end of the table as Marion spoke about her treatments, her voice brittle and brave.

Everyone else had looked away, out of respect, or discomfort, or grief. But not Peter. Peter had just watched her. Not with sadness. Not with empathy. But with calculation. Gauging something.

Not how she was dying. When.

And then the wine glass, the slight twitch of his fingers around the stem. Barely there, but real. Not nervousness. Not grief. Anticipation. He was waiting. For a moment. For someone else to move first.

Philip.

Older. Softer, at least on the surface. Once a second father, or a better one, depending on the year. He'd held her hand at her first funeral. He'd taught her how to whistle. She used to tell him things no one else knew. But over the past few years, something in him had gone... brittle. Still warm in manner, still silver-tongued, but the charm had worn thin, like an antique mirror losing its backing.

She'd noticed it more lately, the subtle recoil in his voice when Reginald entered a room. The way he never quite made eye contact when discussing money. Or how his laughter at Reginald's jokes had stopped being real and started being polite.

She remembered, two months ago, passing the study on her way upstairs. The door was half-shut. She hadn't meant to listen. But Philip's voice was unmistakable. Low, angry, ragged.

"If you won't help me," he'd snapped, "then at least get out of my way."

She remembered freezing, hand halfway to the banister. No answer came from Reginald, at least none she heard. She hadn't told anyone. Not then. Not even David.

At the time, it had sounded like frustration. Now, it sounded like motive.

Catherine rubbed at her temples with ink-smudged fingers, the scent of old paper clinging to her skin. She leaned back, the chair beneath her creaking like a groan. Her eyes flicked toward the dining room door, half-expecting Peter or Philip to step through it. But the hall remained empty, swallowed in shadow.

The wind clawed against the windows, a hiss of rain against the glass. Somewhere outside, a branch scraped slowly across the pane, an accidental, eerie rhythm.

She stood, slowly, stretching her legs. The cold floor sent a pulse of chill up through her knees. She crossed to the cabinet near the window and pulled open a drawer. From beneath a stack of receipts and yellowed correspondence, she drew out one of Reginald's leather-bound journals. Worn at the spine, his notes inside sharp and controlled.

She flipped through pages. Mergers. Meetings. Property values. Numbers and margins. Until:

Philip pressed again about the funding. Said he was desperate. I didn't say no this time; just said I needed more time. I didn't like the look in his eyes.

The handwriting had changed in that line. Less elegant. More urgent.

She snapped the journal shut.

Then, as if moved by instinct rather than thought, she turned and left the study, her steps silent on the hardwood. She found Peter exactly where she thought he might be, in the drawing room, standing at the fireplace with a drink he wasn't actually drinking.

He didn't turn around when she entered. "Can't sleep either?" he asked, voice light.

"I wasn't trying," she said.

Peter turned. His smile was faint, composed. "Well. We all have our rituals."

"I don't want to talk about rituals," she said.

Peter tilted his head. "Then what?"

"The study," she said. "You had a key."

He blinked. The smile didn't vanish, but it stalled. "What makes you say that?"

"I know you did," Catherine said, stepping closer. "And I think you let someone else use it. Or rather, you sold the right to."

Peter's glass lowered slightly. He exhaled, slow. Then, after a long pause: "Two men. Strangers. Said they needed to get something from Reginald's records. Something urgent. Said it was business, and Reginald wouldn't miss it."

Catherine stared at him. "So, you... gave them the key?"

"No," he said. "I let them borrow it. For twenty minutes. For a fee."

"You *sold* access to Reginald's private study."

Peter looked down into his glass. "I was stupid," he said. "But there you go."

"Why?" she asked, voice sharp. "You're not broke."

"No," he agreed. "But I'm tired. Tired of being the one who always does what's expected. They caught me at the right moment. The wrong moment. I don't know anymore."

Catherine swallowed. "Did Reginald ever find out?"

Peter shook his head. "If he did, he never said. Maybe he knew. Maybe that's why things got worse between us."

"And the strangers, who were they?"

Peter's face clouded. "I don't know. They used false names. Paid in cash. It felt... off, even then."

"But you still said yes."

He met her gaze then. "Yes."

Catherine stepped back, a sick feeling creeping into her chest. "You may have let someone into that room, someone who killed him."

Peter didn't flinch. "I've thought about that every night since."

The room fell silent except for the ticking of the clock and the wind scratching at the windowpanes.

"I'm telling Stowe." She said.

Peter nodded. "I expect you will."

And Catherine turned, walking back into the corridor with a new weight pressing between her shoulder blades.

This wasn't just a murder.

It was a puzzle with pieces borrowed and bought and the people she thought she knew best had been selling them off for far longer than she realized.

Her mind spun. The tape, Reginald's final argument, had cracked open a door.

But it hadn't freed David. Not really.

It had only widened the corridor of suspicion.

The illusion of clarity had collapsed, replaced by the deeper, more dangerous truth: now *anyone* could have done it. That was the cruel irony. The more she uncovered, the less she understood. Every answer peeled back another layer and beneath it, more rot.

She sat again at the long oak table, the annotated timeline spread before her like a map of a country she no longer recognized.

David left the dining table at nine.

But if Marion had heard a *recording*, not a live argument, then Reginald could have been dead already. Maybe even long before anyone noticed the study door was locked. She circled the earlier part of the evening, drawing a thick, looping ring around 8:00 PM. Her handwriting was sharper now, her thoughts more dangerous.

"WINDOW OF DEATH," she scrawled in capital letters beside the mark.

Because that's what it was.

It meant *any of them* could have done it. Every alibi frayed at the edges. The one anchor, Marion's claim that David had stayed with her at eight, wasn't enough. It was only *her* word. And she was no longer a neutral party.

David wasn't exonerated. Not yet. The tape proved something, but not innocence. It only proved that someone else could have taken the opportunity.

She looked down at the property schematics Reginald had left behind. A rough estimate. Development potential. Zoning notes.

The house, in pieces, was worth millions.

If Marion died, David, through her, as her husband, would stand to inherit a large portion of the estate. Enough to walk away from debt. Enough to start over somewhere with glass walls and nothing left to explain.

He hadn't just been a patriarch. He was the vault. The lock. The threat. And if he had learned about David's shell companies, or Philip's debts, or Marion's affair, or any number of secrets buried in this house, then he held power over more than just real estate.

He held power over *truth.*

And then there was Philip.

Philip and Marion.

Catherine had dismissed it, initially. The way he lingered by her chair. The way she glanced at him during dinner, just a second longer than needed. The comforting touch that, now in hindsight, had been far too practiced.

How long had it been going on?

Months?

Years?

Had they used their connection, their intimacy, to coordinate? Had they planned something together?

Did they kill Reginald *together*?

She gripped her pencil and circled both their names, not once, but over and over, the lead grinding into the page until it nearly tore through.

Her hand stilled. She sat back.

A gust of wind blew against the windowpane, rattling it slightly. The storm had quieted but not disappeared. It crouched over the house like a low, unseen presence.

Catherine's gaze flicked up toward the hallway.

Still empty.

The doors remained closed. The shadows didn't move.

But she *felt* something.

The house, so silent, so full of memory, was not sleeping. It listened. It always had. It remembered conversations whispered behind walls. Glances exchanged in thresholds. Keys turned. Lies told.

This house had soaked up every secret like wine into carpet.

And now it pulsed with proximity.

Not guilt. Not yet. But something close.

Someone in this house knew *exactly* what had happened.

Someone had held the key. Literally. Figuratively. Fatally.

Catherine's throat was dry. She stood, walked to the study door, well the new temporary door, and placed her palm flat against the wood.

It felt warm.

Someone's been here.

She didn't speak the words aloud. She didn't need to.

She turned slowly, her eyes sweeping the corridor once more.

No footsteps.

No voices.

But the air had shifted.

She walked back to the dining room.

She returned to the table, sat down again, and began flipping through Reginald's other journal, the one marked *Personal: 1975–1985*. If there was context, it would be buried in his patterns. The way he spoke about people. What he noticed. What he refused to write down.

As she worked, she whispered under her breath; just to herself, just to the room:

"Someone's been lying since the beginning."

And if she had to tear through every memory, every mask, and every remaining bond to find the truth?

Then so be it.

She would burn this house to the ground, metaphorically or otherwise, if it meant knowing who had killed her father.

Even if it meant destroying everything, she thought she knew. Especially then.

Chapter 31: Rattle the Cage Again

"So," Harris asked, his voice low and deliberate, "what's our next move?"

The words hung like fog, heavy, unmoving, in the quiet of the late-night station. Outside, the rain tapped against the high windows with the soft persistence of something that didn't want to be ignored.

Inspector Stowe didn't answer immediately. He sat on the edge of his desk, one hand resting on a thick manila folder, the other slowly tapping a measured rhythm against its spine. He wasn't looking at Harris. He was staring down at the poem again, the anonymous verse that had cracked open more doors than expected.

Witness statements too smooth. Timelines too clean. Emotions either too theatrical or suspiciously absent. The case hadn't stopped breathing, it had just started lying with more polish.

"We have to test the poem," Stowe said at last. "Every name it mentioned. Every implication. We put them under pressure."

"Re-interviews?" Harris asked, eyebrows lifting. "They'll see it coming."

"Good," Stowe replied. "Let them. Fear makes people sloppy. They've been controlling the pace so far. That stops now."

"Same questions?" Harris asked.

"No. Same themes," Stowe said, lifting the file. "But this time we sharpen them. We push. We press. No smiles. No soft gloves."

"Until something cracks," Harris muttered, rising and pulling on his coat. "We rattle the cage."

Stowe gave a small nod. "And this time," he said, his voice low, "we shake it until someone screams."

Harris didn't grin. He just nodded back, quiet and focused.

They moved through the station like ghosts. Fluorescent lights buzzed above, humming their tired song. A bulb flickered at the end of the corridor, washing the hallway in pulses of dimness. The place was skeletal after hours, reduced to structure and breath.

A constable slumped behind a desk, snoring softly. A sandwich wilted beside him. A fax in the next room choked out a half-page, then stalled. The station murmured with the sounds of sleep, not rest.

At Harris's desk, he paused mid-stride, narrowing his eyes. He reached for a folder buried halfway down the left stack. It was thinner than the rest, edges bent, the tab marked with Reginald Price's name.

"Wait," Harris said. "Found something earlier. Forgot it got buried."

He opened it, scanning, flipping.

"Look at this," he said, handing it to Stowe.

It was a transaction report. Sparse. Unflagged. At first glance, nothing.

Then Stowe saw the pattern.

Cash withdrawals. Large. Consistent. Always from the same account. Always in person. Over four months.

"No linked deposits," Harris said. "No matching transactions. Just money taken out. Walked out."

"How much?"

"Eighty-five thousand total," Harris said. "Spread out to look subtle. But not subtle enough."

Stowe's expression tightened. "Blackmail. Payoffs. Or hiding funds from someone in the family."

He turned the page and paused. One of the withdrawals was dated four days before Reginald's death. Fifteen thousand, taken out at 8:23 a.m., flagged as 'personal business.'

Stowe sat back down, flipping the file open fully. "Why would a man with structured investments, obsessive recordkeeping, and a legal trust suddenly start draining cash?"

"He was planning something," Harris said. "Or paying someone."

"Or both."

They worked in silence for several minutes, paper rustling, pens scratching. On the board behind them, faces stared down, Reginald in the centre, the rest of the Price family fanned out like suspects in a theatre cast.

Then Stowe reached for a separate file, one retrieved from Reginald's personal coat pocket after the body was found. It had slipped to the back of the evidence stack and only now resurfaced.

He pulled out a letter: printed, formal, dated two weeks before the murder.

Philip acted without consultation. He approached the board privately. Secured votes behind your back. There was no meeting. Only signatures. Watch your back.

Harris read over his shoulder. "Philip undermined him. Gutted him from the inside."

"With the board's help," Stowe added. "And Reginald was warned."

"He was isolated."

"Betrayed."

Stowe placed the letter flat on the desk and leaned back. The heater hissed behind them, barely keeping the chill at bay.

"I think the motive's shifting," he said quietly. "It's not just legacy. It's betrayal. Money. And something personal."

Harris stood and poured them both lukewarm coffee from the pot near the window. It tasted burned, but it was warm. He sat again.

"We should go back tomorrow. Hit them while they're off-balance."

"No," Stowe said.

Harris blinked. "No?"

"Not yet." Stowe gestured around the station. "We stay here tonight. Organize everything. Clean it up. Get it straight. If we walk in tomorrow swinging, we better know exactly where to hit."

"You want to run it all again," Harris said. "Start fresh."

"Start *clear*," Stowe corrected. "I want everything, the financials, the board correspondence, Marion's movements. And I want Catherine's notes from the timeline. If she's been keeping track, we can match it against our own."

He glanced at the whiteboard again, eyes lingering on Marion's photo.

"You still think she's clean?" Harris asked.

"No one's clean," Stowe replied. "Only quiet. The difference matters less than people think."

"Then who breaks first?"

Stowe's stare didn't move. "Whichever one forgets what they've already lied about."

Outside, the rain intensified, a steady hiss across the glass.

They worked past midnight, the station quiet except for the scribble of ink and the rustle of papers. The walls of the Price house felt far away now, distant but not silent.

Not forgotten.

And somewhere between the ledgers and the transcripts, the truth waited. Not buried.

Just *missed*.

But not for much longer.

Chapter 32: The Evidence and the Suspects

The police station simmered with late-night tension, a stew of too many hours, too little sleep, and the bitter tang of old coffee hanging in the air like fog. The occasional shrill ring of a phone answered with robotic briskness.

Boots echoed against the linoleum floors, sharp and purposeful. Doors opened and shut with practiced familiarity. A vending machine buzzed softly beside it, its contents untouched, its light flickering like a tired eye refusing to close.

Outside, rain poured with unbroken determination. It turned the parking lot into a shallow, glistening pond and pelted the windows in steady rhythms, pressing wet leaves against the glass like failed attempts at flight. Streetlights cast yellow halos into the mist beyond the windows, blurred by condensation and streaks of runoff.

Catherine Forrester stepped through the entrance like a force cutting through fog. She moved quickly but without panic, her stride sharp, shoulders braced beneath a water-heavy coat that clung to her frame. The hem was caked in mud, the fabric saturated, darkened nearly to black. Her hair was damp, her cheeks wind-flushed, but her eyes were clear. Steeled.

In her arms, she carried a large plastic-wrapped bundle, the kind used to protect fragile things. But this wasn't fragile. This was damning. Her fingers were white at the knuckles from how tightly she gripped it, as though it might vanish if she loosened her hold.

Detective Inspector Thomas Stowe looked up from his desk. The reading lamp at his elbow created a golden halo on his notes, throwing the rest of his office into deep shadow. A forgotten cup of tea had gone cold by his hand, a sheen forming on the surface. A pencil sat half off the edge of the desk, teetering in stillness, as if the sudden shift in energy had stilled even gravity.

He took one look at Catherine and straightened.

"Evening, Mrs. Forrester," Stowe said, his voice low, cautious. The way someone might greet a witness carrying fire.

Catherine stepped forward without returning the greeting. Her coat still clung to her from the storm. Her voice was quiet, but something in it pulsed, urgency beneath steel.

"I found something."

She moved to the desk and laid down the bundle with a weighty thud. Dust leapt off forgotten files. The plastic crinkled, tight, desperate, like something sealed alive.

"It was hidden," she said, not waiting for questions. "Behind the garden wall. Tucked under rotting timber and broken bricks. Someone meant it to stay there. Someone panicked."

Stowe reached for his gloves in silence, slipping them on with the kind of calm precision that always came before something ugly. A ritual he knew too well. The air changed, as if the room itself started to breathe differently.

The bundle unravelled slowly.

A dark wool jacket. Trousers. Stiff. Sodden. The fabric clung together with moisture, streaked with garden dirt and mulch. But worse, the rust-hued stains spread across the sleeve and lower torso, unmistakable. Blood. Dried, soaked through. Old, but angry.

The metallic tang wafted up through the mildew, the smell of iron and fear.

Stowe didn't flinch. But his eyes narrowed, his voice a low murmur. "Bloody hell."

He turned the jacket over. Threads along the collar were frayed. The buttons were yanked, the lining ripped with violent haste. Not age. Not wear. Panic. The tear was jagged, desperate, someone in a hurry, someone scared.

"This was worn the night Reginald died," he muttered. "I'd bet my badge on it."

The door creaked open again. Harris stepped in, soaked collar turned up, a thin file tucked under one arm. He looked down at the bundle mid-stride and froze.

"What the?"

"Evidence," Stowe said. "Catherine brought it in. Just now."

Harris came closer, brow furrowed. He crouched, examining the stains. He didn't need them explained.

"That's not a stain," he muttered. "That's a soaking. That's someone losing control."

"Someone who didn't plan to be close to the body," Catherine said, arms tight across her chest. "Someone who didn't plan to get bloody. They just needed the clothes gone."

Stowe bent forward, peering at the collars inside seam. The label had been cut, the remnants clawed away with something jagged. A knife, maybe. Deliberate.

"Whoever wore this knew it would be traced," he said. "They didn't toss it. They buried it. On estate grounds. Intentional. Hidden, but not careful enough."

"Any idea who?" Harris asked.

Catherine stepped forward again. Her voice sharpened.

"Tailored. Expensive. Male cut. Mid-length sleeves. I've seen that exact make on Peter and Philip, but the stitching, the cut, it's more Peter. He's always exact. His jackets are hemmed tight. That jacket is his taste. Not Philip's."

Stowe looked up. "You're certain?"

"I'm not guessing," she said. "I've stood beside him. I've brushed past that fabric. I've *washed* blood out of linen. I know what I'm looking at."

A long pause stretched in the room.

Then Stowe nodded once, grim. "We'll run it, full panel. blood, sweat, trace. But if you're right…"

"If I'm right," Catherine said, her eyes unwavering, "then someone in that house watched David get dragged away, knowing full well he was innocent."

"And let Marion weep," Harris added. "Pretending to comfort her."

"Not just let her," Catherine said. "*Used* it. Took advantage of it. Played grief to buy time."

Stowe removed his gloves, set them beside the jacket, and lowered himself into the chair. His eyes didn't leave the clothing.

"Peter," he murmured. "So precise. So, composed. But too clean. Too aware. That kind of man doesn't wait for chaos. He watches it, then shapes it."

Catherine nodded. "Or waits for it to erase what he couldn't."

"Philip might lash out," Harris said. "But Peter would premeditate. He'd plan the angles, and he'd know exactly how long to stand still."

Stowe closed the folder in front of him, gently placing it over the jacket like a tombstone. Then, finally, he looked at her, fully, carefully.

"You realize what this means?" he asked.

Catherine didn't flinch. "Yes."

"This isn't just evidence," he said. "This is declaration."

She exhaled, slow, controlled. Her voice steady, but her fingers trembled faintly at her sides.

"Then I'll fight."

There was silence again, a quiet beat where the rain outside seemed to pause.

Then Stowe spoke again. "There's more, isn't there."

Catherine's expression shifted, not evasive but restrained. Then she gave a slight nod. "Yes. Peter told me something. Tonight."

Stowe waited.

"He admitted," she said, "that he was paid. Twice. Two different people. They paid him for a key to the study."

Harris straightened. "He *sold access*?"

"He said he was tired of always doing the right thing," Catherine said. "That they caught him in a moment of weakness. He gave them the key for a fee. Said it was 'only twenty minutes.' But we both know what can happen in twenty minutes."

Stowe's stare darkened. "Did he say who?"

"No," she said. "Claimed they used false names. That he didn't know. But I think he did. I think he's just not ready to say."

Stowe rubbed his jaw slowly. "We'll push him."

He paused, then leaned forward.

"Catherine," he said, voice low. "You told me Reginald was withdrawing large amounts of cash. Do you know where it was going?"

Her eyes flicked down. "Not officially," she said. "But there were rumours."

"Tell me."

She met his gaze. "He had women. Over the years. Some of them, not all, had to be kept quiet. Paid off. So, they wouldn't contact Marion. Wouldn't stir anything up."

Harris blinked. "Mistresses?"

"And maybe more," Catherine said softly. "There were nights... conversations I half-heard. I always wondered if there was someone else out there. A half-sibling. Another child no one talks about."

"Christ," Harris muttered. "This family doesn't have skeletons. It *has foundations made of bone.*"

Stowe didn't speak right away.

Then: "If Reginald was paying hush money, someone might've been ready to expose him."

"Or inherit," Catherine said. "If there's another heir... and they knew they'd been hidden all this time..."

She didn't need to finish the thought.

Stowe stood slowly. His voice was quiet, but absolute.

"Tomorrow, we re-interview Peter and Philip and see where that leads us.""

"We rattle the cage," Harris said.

Stowe nodded once. "And we wait to see who starts rattling back."

Rain lashed against the window. Outside, the night closed in tighter.

Inside, the case, and the walls, were closing too.

Chapter 33: Echoes in the Storm

The Price estate stood hunched against the storm, its stone façade slick with rain, its steep gables sharp against the clouds like the back of a crouching beast. Lightning briefly illuminated the weathervane atop the eastern chimney, a twisted arrow frozen mid-spin, before thunder rolled across the hills, slow and distant, like a warning long overdue.

The gravel driveway shimmered with puddles that rippled under the steady downpour. Water ran in rivulets along the edges of the hedgerows, collecting in cold, silent pools. The old trees swayed with heavy groans, their limbs tapping the house as though trying to wake it from its sleep.

Sergeant Harris stepped from the unmarked car, his boots splashing into the ankle-deep water at the base of the driveway. His coat flared briefly in the wind before he pulled it tighter, collar turned high against the bitter wet. His face was lined with fatigue, but his eyes were alive now, sharp with purpose.

He hadn't wanted to come alone. But something about this house demanded solitude. Or sacrifice.

The front door creaked open before he reached the steps.

Catherine.

She stood framed tall a wool blanket drawn loosely around her shoulders like a shroud. Behind her, shadows danced against the wainscoted walls. The flicker of flame caught on the edges of framed portraits and gilded mirrors, distorting them as though the house itself had begun to warp.

Her eyes were tired, the whites threaded with red, her mouth set. She looked older in that moment. Not in years, but in knowledge.

"You again," she said, voice dry as dust. A small, humourless smile tugged at her lips. "The storm bringing you back, or the ghosts?"

"Neither," Harris replied. He tipped his head toward the door, water dripping from his brow. "We think we missed something."

"You always do," she murmured, stepping aside. "Peter's room is still a disaster. Feel free to contribute."

As Harris crossed the threshold, the warm air inside hit him like a sigh. It was slightly stale, tinged with polish, aging wood, and the ever-present scent of Marion's lilies. Yet beneath it, something colder lingered. A draft slipped along the floor like breath beneath a door.

Catherine's voice followed him as he passed. Softer now. Almost lost in the creaking of the old house.

"Be careful," she said. "There's something about this place. It remembers who it's keeping."

Harris paused, looked back at her, but she'd already disappeared into the shadows.

The door clicked shut behind him with a finality that felt personal.

The upper hall felt even colder than the entryway.

The walls were close, the carpeting thin. The storm outside seemed louder here, rain hammering on slate shingles above, wind moaning along the eaves like a voice caught mid-confession. The grandfather clock on the landing ticked louder than it should, each chime a metronome marking the beat of something hidden and waiting.

Peter's room remained a chaos of abandoned intention. It was a room that looked lived-in only because someone had pretended it should be.

Curtains billowed despite the windows being firmly shut. A lamp on the nightstand flickered every so often, its bulb buzzing faintly. Clothes lay strewn across a chair, a half-zipped overnight bag sat in the corner, and the wardrobe doors hung half-open like a mouth that had started to speak and thought better of it.

Harris entered with two uniformed constables at his back.

"Systematic," he said. "Every drawer. Every seam. Start with the closet."

The constables nodded and moved swiftly. one to the wardrobe, the other to the bed. Pillows tossed, sheets stripped, boxes upturned. Old receipts, cufflinks, hotel soaps. All catalogued. All bagged.

Harris moved to the desk.

It was a wreck.

A shattered pen lay among a scattering of paperclips and dried ink. A crumpled notebook sat beneath several unopened envelopes; their corners softened by time. He flipped through each item carefully, his gloved hands methodical.

Then, something caught his eye.

A photograph, dog-eared and partially folded, shoved between a sheaf of torn invoices.

Peter and Reginald.

Taken in the garden, the west side, near the sundial. Both were smiling. Peter, just a touch too wide. Reginald, just a touch too still. A line had been scored across the bottom corner, as if someone had started to tear it but stopped at the last second. The fold was deliberate, sharp, hidden something not meant to be seen again.

Then...

"Sir!"

One of the constables straightened, something gripped in one gloved hand.

Harris crossed the room quickly.

The officer held up a cassette tape, wrapped tightly in a faded T-shirt. The fabric had yellowed, and the tape's plastic case was cracked and cloudy. Dust clung to the edges. The label was smudged, but legible in block print:

THE MADISON DEAL.

Silence fell over the room. Even the storm outside seemed to pause.

Harris took the tape gently, his pulse suddenly louder in his ears. "Where?"

"Bottom drawer," the constable replied. "Buried under a stack of magazines and old bills. Locked... tucked in. Hidden."

Harris turned the tape in his hands. The plastic was cold but somehow felt heavier than it should have like it had absorbed something from the house itself.

"Why did he still have this?"

The tape. *The* tape. The one Marion had claimed to hear the night Reginald died. The one that should have explained everything. That had *already* been found.

But here it was again.

Had Peter kept a duplicate?

Or was this the original?

"Bag it," Harris said firmly. "Label it. Priority evidence. Get it to Stowe, fast."

The constable nodded and left, moving quickly.

Harris stayed behind.

He turned slowly, his eyes scanning the room again as if waiting for it to confess. The light flickered once more. The wind outside howled louder.

If Peter had the tape all along, if he had kept it, hidden it then did he make copies....

Was this guilt? A desperate attempt to retain control?

Or was it insurance?

A backup plan, in case someone came knocking too close.

He picked up the torn photo again, stared into the faces frozen in time.

Peter had answers.

And now, finally, Harris had the leverage to drag them out.

He turned toward the door, moving slowly, deliberately. The storm welcomed him again with a shriek through the hallway windows.

No more assumptions.

No more politeness.

No more pretending.

Just the truth, however ugly, however deep it had to be dug and whoever it took with it.

Chapter 34: The Second Interview with Peter

The second interview room felt even smaller than before.

The walls seemed to press inward, subtly but constantly, as if the space itself was trying to squeeze the truth from its occupant. The air was stagnant, tainted, with the scents of old sweat, cheap aftershave, and institutional disinfectant that never quite masked the rot of stress and memory. It was too quiet. No passing footsteps. Just the buzz of the overhead fluorescent light, flickering with mechanical indifference.

The room offered nothing comforting. No clock. No window. Just a cold metal table scarred by years of desperate fingers, clutched mugs, and anxious tapping. The corners of the room were shadowed, cobwebbed not with dust but with silence and implication.

Peter Price sat with his back pressed to the wall, as if instinctively trying to put as much distance between himself and the door as possible. His appearance had frayed since the last time. His blazer was wrinkled, shirt untucked at the waist, collar stained faintly with sweat. His hair, once carefully styled, now lay in loose, greasy strands that clung to his forehead. A fine tremor ran through his leg beneath the table, bouncing in short, uneven bursts. His arms were crossed, but it didn't look defensive anymore. It looked like he was trying to hold himself in place.

Gone was the smugness. The rehearsed confidence. What remained was something quiter. Something thinner.

The door opened with a click that made Peter jump.

Inspector Thomas Stowe entered first, followed by Detective Harris, who shut the door with a muted thud and remained standing. Both men carried a different weight than before, not just suspicion now, but confirmation waiting for a name. Stowe moved with a slow deliberateness, like a man setting pieces on a chessboard already halfway through the game. He didn't speak. Just sat down across from Peter, coat still on, expression unreadable.

He placed something on the table with care.

A cassette tape.

Its plastic case was cracked. The label had yellowed. But the title, written in block letters, was still perfectly legible.

THE MADISON DEAL.

The sound of it touching metal rang louder than it should have, a flat, sharp tap that made the silence ring.

Peter's eyes dropped to the tape, and his posture changed. Just slightly. Shoulders tightened. Breath shortened. His knee stopped bouncing.

Stowe didn't touch it again. He let the tape sit between them like a snake coiled and waiting.

"We're doing this again," Stowe said at last, voice low and gravelled, like it had been dragged through a storm and left to dry on cold stone.

Peter shifted in his chair. Not much, just a subtle recalibration of posture, but Stowe saw it. Heard it. A crack forming.

"I've already told you"

Stowe didn't let him finish.

"There are still too many holes," he said sharply. "And you're sitting in the middle of everyone."

Peter's jaw locked. His throat worked, but no words came for a moment. When he did speak, his voice was thinner than before. "I already told you what I know."

"Then tell us again," Stowe said, gesturing with a tilt of his head toward the tape recorder on the desk. "Because that? That was found in your room. Wrapped in a shirt. Hidden in the bottom drawer. Not someone else's drawer. *Yours.*"

Peter's gaze dropped to the tape like it might detonate on impact. The silence that followed was heavy, not with defiance, but calculation.

"I don't know how it got there," he said finally, too slowly. "Maybe someone planted it."

"Who?" Harris barked, stepping forward. His shadow fell long across the table. "Who had access? Who had a reason?"

Peter shook his head once, then again, like he could dislodge the pressure. "Anyone. The house is always open. Guests, staff. Even family. You've all been in and out."

"Convenient," Stowe muttered, leaning back. "Every suspect, all in one corridor. Must've felt like a revolving door."

Peter didn't answer. He wouldn't look at them.

"You're not new to this game, Peter," Stowe said, voice cooling. "You've always had the right words. The rehearsed answers. But we spoke to your university friends."

Peter looked up sharply.

"They remember a night," Stowe continued. "A bar. Too much whisky. You told them if your father didn't fund your venture, you'd kill him. Three separate people. Same wording."

Peter's mouth tightened. "That was years ago. I was venting. Joking."

"Were you?" Stowe said, eyes narrowing. "Because not long after, you started *selling access* to your father's study. A few grand here, a handshake there. Quiet introductions. A key passed, no questions asked."

"That's not..."

"That's not nothing," Harris snapped. "That's motive."

Peter's face reddened, his hands curling on the table.

"Catherine told us," Stowe added, voice dropping just a note. "She said you admitted to taking money. Twice. Two different people. You gave them the key."

Peter's mouth opened, then froze. For a moment, the room went still. Then he exhaled sharply, the breath shuddering from his chest.

"Yes," he said, finally. "I did."

Neither detective moved.

"I sold them the key," Peter went on. "Not for murder. They said they needed something from the records. Business. Nothing more. I thought it was harmless."

"You *thought*," Harris repeated, shaking his head.

Peter slumped forward slightly. His hands, once tight, now lay open on the table like offerings. "I was stupid. I was tired of begging for scraps. They offered, and I took it. But I didn't kill him. I wouldn't."

"Why not?" Stowe asked quietly. "You hated him. You were being strung along for years."

"Mother was getting me my trust money without Father knowing"

Peter's head snapped up. "I was getting it. Finally. Enough to start over. A proper investment. My company. A flat of my own. No more dependence. No more humiliation."

He leaned forward, voice raw. "Why would I ruin that? Why would I jeopardize *everything* for one last fight with a man who was finally stepping out of the way?"

"Maybe because you thought he wouldn't," Stowe said. "Maybe he found out about the key. Maybe he was going to stop the payment. Or report you. Or worse."

"I didn't kill him," Peter said, louder now. "I hated him, yes. Sometimes I *wished* he'd vanish. But I'm not a killer."

Stowe's gaze didn't move. "Hate is a fuse, Peter. Sometimes it burns quiet. Sometimes it explodes."

The silence that followed was different now, less tense, more resigned. Harris stepped back to the wall, flipping open his notepad. The pen scratched as he wrote.

Peter sagged in his chair, the energy bleeding out of him like air from a punctured tire. "What happens now?"

Stowe stood slowly, retrieving the tape from the table with gloved hands. "Now we verify everything. The label. The handwriting. The fingerprints. The date it was last played. And we wait for forensics to finish with the suit we found."

Peter blinked. "What suit?"

Stowe paused at the threshold. His voice was calm. Measured.

"You'll read about it soon enough."

He stepped out, the door clicking shut behind him like a final period at the end of a sentence. Harris followed a beat later, casting a last glance back at Peter, now alone, head bowed, breath shallow.

Outside, the storm wailed against the windows of the station. Rain streaked the glass like claw marks.

And in the heart of the Price estate, where secrets once whispered now screamed, something shifted. Something that had hidden too long.

The walls were closing in.

And no one, not even the careful ones, would stay clean.

Chapter 35: The Breaking Point

Stowe and Harris re-entered the room, coffees in hand.

Harris stepped closer, his boots scuffing faintly against the concrete floor. His voice, though calm, carried a weight that seemed to lower the temperature in the room.

"You knew about Philip's plan, the one your father blocked. The one that would have torn the company apart and rebuilt it around him."

Peter's lips parted, but for a long moment, no sound emerged. His eyes flicked between the two detectives. His chest rose and fell with shallow, uneven breaths. Behind the facade of indignation and fatigue, the truth was breaking through, one crack at a time.

Stowe moved with quiet precision. He opened the slim file in front of him and began spreading its contents across the table like a dealer laying down a losing hand. Each item landed with finality: photographs of a business proposal torn in two, water-stained at the edges. Bank letters detailing accounts, urgent loan deals, and flagged transactions. A printed email from a silent partner.

"Philip was going to restructure," Stowe said, his voice low but sharp as glass. "And Reginald knew it. He was never going to sign off on that deal. He knew it would change the company forever. Philip stood to lose everything. Unless…"

Peter's voice cracked. "Unless he wasn't there to stop it."

Silence crept into the room like a tide, thickening the air.

Harris stepped in, tightening the noose. "And you what? You gave Philip the key to the study. A year ago. No questions asked?"

Peter's hands were clenched in his lap, knuckles white. He nodded, barely perceptible. "I was desperate," he muttered. "I thought he just needed access to some files. Or a contract. Or something stupid."

"Did you ask?" Stowe demanded.

Peter shook his head, eyes down.

Stowe slammed his palm against the table. The metal groaned under the blow, and the sound exploded in the tight space like a gunshot.

Peter jumped, shoulders jerking. The tremor in his hands became impossible to hide.

"But you didn't care to ask," Stowe growled.

"I was drowning in debt!" Peter shouted suddenly, his voice cracking open. "I was selling off cufflinks to keep the drinks flowing. And no one, no one, in that house gave a damn. My father looked through me. Catherine avoided me. Philip... he offered help. He said it was just temporary. I believed him."

"You could've come clean," Harris said, his tone softer now. "But you didn't. You let it happen. You let him twist it."

Peter turned away, shame painting shadows on his face. "I didn't know he was going to die," he said. "Even when I hated him... I didn't want him dead."

The silence that followed wasn't accusatory. It was worse. It was understanding.

Stowe stared at him for a moment, the sharpness of his expression giving way to something cooler, more calculating. "You said you heard Philip say something. Two nights before the murder."

Peter nodded slowly, as if reliving the moment.

"I couldn't sleep," he murmured. "The wind was rattling the windows. I went downstairs; thought I'd read in the conservatory. I heard someone pacing near the study. I didn't see him at first, just the voice. Low. Focused."

"What did he say?" Stowe asked, leaning forward.

Peter's throat worked. "He said, 'Once it's done, we can move forward. The old man's in the way.'"

"And then?" Harris prompted.

"He turned," Peter continued. "Saw me. Froze. Didn't say anything else. Just looked at me... like he was measuring something."

"Did you confront him?" Stowe asked.

Peter shook his head. "No. I... I was scared. And ashamed. I didn't think he meant it. Not really. Not until it was too late."

Stowe began gathering the documents again, sliding them back into the folder with deliberate care.

"You're going to make a statement," he said, his voice calm but ironclad.

Peter looked up, eyes bloodshot and rimmed with guilt. "If I'd told you earlier… would that have saved him?"

Stowe paused, then softened, just a hair. The line at the edge of his mouth twitched.

"We'll never know," he said. "But you can still help us finish this."

A beat passed.

Then Harris stepped forward and opened the door. The hallway beyond glowed faintly under the sterile flicker of overhead lights.

Peter didn't move at first. His eyes drifted to the cassette tape still on the table. His reflection warped in the plastic. The weight of too many secrets, too many choices, reflected back at him.

"He trusted us to protect the family," Peter said quietly. "All of us failed."

He stood up slowly and walked out, his footsteps dragging like a man leaving pieces of himself behind with every step.

When the door shut behind him, Harris exhaled and turned to Stowe. "That's something, at least."

"It's more than we had this morning," Stowe replied. He reached for the file, tapped the edge against the table until it squared perfectly.

Harris crossed his arms, watching the door. "Do you think he did it?"

Stowe didn't answer right away. He looked down at the folder, then at the now-empty seat where Peter had sat. "I did," he said quietly. "But if what he said is true, about the trust money, why would he risk it? He had everything lined up. A payout. A fresh start. Doesn't make sense to light a match with all that fuel in hand."

He leaned back, exhaling slowly. "Anyway… the blood and sweat report will sort all that out."

Outside, the rain pelted the windows like knuckles on glass.

Inside, the final pieces of the puzzle had started to shift.

And in a flat across town, unaware his name had just been drawn, Philip Marsh was pouring himself a scotch, not knowing that before the night was done, everything he had buried was about to rise.

Chapter 36: Interviewing Philip

The interrogation room buzzed faintly with the low, electric hum of fluorescent lights, a cold, sterile sound that pressed in at the edges. It was the kind of hum you didn't notice at first, but after five minutes under that unforgiving glare, it began to crawl under your skin. The walls were blank, painted in the same institutional grey that made time stretch and truth contract. There was no clock, yet time was loud here. Every breath, every shift of posture, every drop of sweat seemed to announce itself.

The air smelled faintly of bleach and something metallic, old air filtered too many times. Clean, but never fresh.

Philip Marsh sat in the centre of it all, a man marooned at sea in a room with no tide. His usual poise had slipped, not dramatically, but unmistakably. His grey suit, tailored to precision in better days, now looked too stiff in some places, too loose in others, as though even the fabric had grown uncertain. His shirt collar had wilted, the knot in his tie slightly off-centre. A detail he once would have adjusted without thinking now went unnoticed.

His posture betrayed him: spine too straight, shoulders too forced, fingers white-knuckled on the table's edge. Hands that once flipped through investor reports with grace and authority now clenched like he was waiting for the earth to tilt beneath him. Sweat gathered in the fine lines above his brow and along his temples, the sheen catching under the harsh light.

Across from him sat Inspector Thomas Stowe, unmoving, grounded like stone. He didn't blink often, didn't shift in his seat. His broad frame cast a subtle shadow across the table, his presence more than physical. It was psychological, unshakeable. To his right stood Detective Harris, arms folded, leaning against the far wall. His eyes were sharp, tracking every micro-movement Philip made. There was something different in Harris today, less irritation, more calculation. The room had teeth now. And it was starting to bite.

For a long moment, the only sound was breathing, shallow, uneven, echoing faintly off metal and plaster.

Then Stowe's voice cut through the silence, smooth but cold.
"Philip."

A pause. A slight turn of his head.

"Tell me again," Stowe said, tone even but edged with steel. "You had no knowledge that Reginald Price would end up dead that night?"

Philip's mouth moved slightly before sound followed. The delay was brief, no more than a heartbeat, but it echoed louder than his reply.

"No," he said at last, voice flat, polished. "Of course not."

Harris stepped forward, deliberate. The thud of his boots on the tiled floor broke the silence in steady beats, like a slow drumroll of judgment.

"And yet," he said, eyes fixed on Philip, "somehow, everything you wanted to fall into your lap. Reginald, out of the way. The company, under your direction. Marion, closer than she's ever been."

Philip's jaw worked. His blink was just a little too slow.

"I wasn't plotting a takeover," he said. "I was trying to prevent a collapse."

"Funny," Stowe murmured, reaching down to slide a document across the table toward him. "Because this? This looks a lot like a takeover."

The proposal landed between them, crisp paper, neatly bound. The signature on the first page sat alone at the bottom, stark in its singularity.

Philip's.

"No board approval," Stowe continued, tapping the signature with a finger. "No second vote. No oversight. Just you, acting without resistance. Because Reginald wouldn't budge. And you couldn't afford to wait."

"He wouldn't listen," Philip snapped, his voice rising with the heat of pressure. "We were days from insolvency. I *had* to act. Someone had to."

"And you were also days," Stowe replied, leaning in, "from personal bankruptcy. That deal didn't just save the company. It saved *you*. Your debt, your image, your precious seat at the table."

Philip sat back sharply, breathing through his nose, like a man trying not to break under interrogation. But the cracks were beginning to show. His hands, once resting lightly on the table, were now clasped tightly in his lap.

Harris stepped forward again, laying down another folder, thinner, more surgical.

He flipped it open. "This," he said, "is a transcript. The Madison Deal recording. Reginald's voice, angry, deliberate. It matches Marion's statement, word for word. The same lines she said she heard the night he died."

Philip's eyes tracked down the page, frowning as he skimmed it. His brow furrowed, and he reached out, slowly, like the paper might bite.

"That was found in Peter's room," Harris added. "But it wasn't a conversation. It was a *recording*. Someone played it loud enough for Marion to hear and assume Reginald was arguing with someone, likely David. It bought someone time. And it bought *you* cover."

Philip opened his mouth, hesitated. His gaze lingered on the text.

"You think someone..." he began slowly, "played it deliberately? To fake an argument?"

"We don't think," Stowe said coldly. "We *know*. The only question left is *who*."

Philip leaned back again. His arms folded, defensive. "Peter's not clever enough to pull something like that off."

It came out too quickly. Too confident.

Harris arched a brow. "No," he said. "But someone else is. Someone strategic. Someone who stood to gain."

Philip's nostrils flared. "I wasn't the only one with motive."

Stowe didn't deny it. But he didn't let up either. He leaned forward, eyes hard.

"But you were the one Reginald was *blocking*. You were the one pushing the deal behind his back. You were the one seen outside the study days before the murder, muttering about 'getting the old man out of the way.'"

Philip's face lost a shade of colour. "Who said that?"

Stowe didn't blink. "Peter did. Under oath."

Philip's eyes darted toward the one-way glass. He could see his reflection now, faint but visible. His face, pale and drawn. His mouth slightly open, like he might ask for water or mercy.

But neither came.

"I didn't kill Reginald," he said finally. But it was quiet. Thin. Less denial, more admission of lesser guilt. "But I *did* want him gone. That's the truth."

Harris tilted his head. "And wanting him gone wasn't enough to take the next step?"

Philip's jaw clenched. "You really think I'm capable of murder?"

Stowe began collecting the pages on the table, smoothing them into a clean stack. His hands moved slowly, deliberately. But his voice was firm.

"I think people do what they have to when they're drowning," he said. "And you? You were already underwater. And desperate men make desperate moves."

Philip's hands twitched in his lap. The tremor was slight, but visible.

Stowe stood, tucking the transcript beneath his arm. Harris mirrored him, closing the thin folder with a flick.

He stared at them.

Then at his hands.

They were still trembling.

"I didn't do it," he said.

The words dropped like a pebble into still water, quiet, but rippling outward with a weight he couldn't gather back. Not now. Not with them watching.

Across from him, Stowe didn't blink. He didn't even shift in his seat. The inspector just stared the kind of stare that didn't stop at the surface. The kind that tried to read beneath skin, beneath the masks people wore when they knew the truth was sharp enough to cut.

The silence between them wasn't empty. It wasn't passive. It pressed in from the edges of the room, dragging the oxygen down with it.

Stowe spoke finally, and his voice was almost too soft to match the weight of the room. "Tell us about Marion."

Philip's composure, already wearing thin, cracked just slightly. His eyes closed. His shoulders slumped, like he'd been hit, not hard but deep. And when he opened his mouth, it wasn't certainty that came out.

"We weren't... having an affair," he said. The words were slow, like they had to fight their way out. "Not while Reginald was alive."

Stowe didn't move. He didn't question. Didn't nod. Just listened, the kind of silence that didn't reassure, didn't forgive. Just waited for more.

Philip's voice picked up, more rushed now. Like he knew silence would bury him faster than confession.

"We were close, too close, maybe. She confided in me. About the cancer. About Reginald. About everything. It was emotional. But not physical. Not until after."

Still, Stowe didn't react. Instead, he calmly reached into the folder beside him and pulled out a single photograph. Without a word, he laid it on the table.

Face-up.

Philip stared. It was him and Marion, in the courtyard, two weeks before Reginald died. Her hand on his chest. Their lips pressed together. The intimacy unmistakable. Not recent grief. Not polite affection.

It was love. Or something like it.

Philip's breath caught in his throat. His eyes stayed fixed on the image as if it might dissolve if he looked hard enough.

"She's terminal," he said finally, voice smaller than before. "We found each other in the dark. Is that a crime now?"

"No," Stowe replied, his voice even. "But secrets grow legs. And in cases like this, secrets become motive."

The overhead light buzzed slightly above them, its dull hum growing louder as the room quieted.

Philip looked down at his hands, shaking now, knotted in his lap like they were trying to hold the truth together.

"You think I killed my oldest friend," he said, almost to himself. "To take over a crumbling business. And be with a dying woman."

He looked up. Something flickered behind his eyes, pain, maybe. Regret. Or just the kind of guilt that wasn't about the crime, but everything around it.

"We think," Harris cut in, stepping forward, "that desperation doesn't always feel like desperation. Not until you've already justified what comes after."

Philip snorted once, not laughter, exactly, but something bitter. "I didn't kill him."

"Then help us find who did," Stowe said, finally leaning in. His voice remained firm but lost its edge. "Walk us through the night. Start to finish."

Philip hesitated. Then he nodded.

"I went to the study," he began. "Around eight. I knocked once. Maybe twice. He didn't answer, but I could hear him. He was ranting. I thought he was on the phone."

"You entered?" Harris asked, voice clipped.

"Yes," Philip nodded. "The door wasn't locked. He was pacing. Shouting. But not at anyone. It was… like a rehearsal. A monologue. He was furious. Rambling about betrayal. About how I was ruining everything. Weak. A parasite."

"Did you argue?" Stowe asked.

"Barely," Philip said. "I told him he was stuck in the past. That the company needed change. He called me a coward. Said I'd never build anything without his money. That I'd never be more than a footnote."

He paused, exhaled.

"I wanted to shout back. But I didn't. I left before I could."

"Where did you go?" Harris asked.

"The drawing room. I poured a drink. Sat alone for ten, maybe fifteen minutes. Then I came back down to dinner like nothing happened."

"No witnesses to that time alone?" Stowe pressed.

Philip shook his head. "None. But I wasn't hiding."

"That's the problem," Harris said. "No one was hiding. But the window of opportunity still opened, and someone stepped through."

Stowe leaned back again. "If what you're saying is true, we'll find it. If it's not…"

"I know," Philip said. "You'll find that too."

His voice was steady, but his face was pale.

Then silence again. Long enough for a shift in the air.

Just as Stowe and Harris began to move, Philip spoke again.

"Wait."

They both turned.

Philip's voice had dropped, quieter, more brittle.

"Marion didn't do this either."

Stowe narrowed his eyes slightly. "If you're protecting her…"

"I'm not," Philip cut in. "Not anymore. But there's someone else. Someone who's been slipping between cracks since this began. Watching. Listening."

"Who?" Stowe asked.

Philip hesitated. His jaw flexed once.

"Peter," he said.

Stowe's gaze sharpened.

"He was always nearby," Philip said. "He'd show up just after things went wrong. Or just before. He knew things people hadn't said aloud. He always played the fool, charming, harmless. But that man knows where every skeleton is buried."

Harris scribbled the name down again. "You have proof?"

Philip shook his head. "Only instinct. But you know what they say about instinct, don't you?"

Stowe didn't respond right away. His face was unreadable. Then, finally, he gave a slow, deliberate nod.

"Noted."

Stowe narrowed his eyes slightly. "If you're protecting someone, now's the time to talk."

"I'm not protecting," Philip said.

A long pause.

His eyes darkened.

"Before we come calling again."

The door hissed closed behind them, the latch clicking into place with unnerving finality.

Philip remained at the table, shoulders slumped, hands now still. The silence rushed back in around him like a tide returning to shore.

Then, a beat passed. He lifted his head, voice barely audible.

"You were right."

The door hadn't latched completely. Stowe turned back. "About what?"

Philip's gaze didn't move from the table.

"About Marion and me. We'd been seeing each other for some time."

Stowe said nothing. Just watched.

Philip gave a tight, tired laugh. "But she's not a fool. She made me sign a contract. Said if we were ever more than what we were, I'd never be allowed to own this house. Never benefit from it. Not directly. Not through her. Not through inheritance. Not through sale."

He looked up, face raw and unguarded now.

"So, when Reginald died, you know what I got?" His voice dropped. "Half a dying company... and a dying girlfriend."

A silence followed, not heavy, but hollow. Like the inside of a bell, just after it's rung.

On the table, the photograph of the kiss sat like a frozen confession. Not of murder, but of everything that never had a chance to last.

Outside the room, the storm had shifted again, no longer rage, but the quiet tension that comes before everything breaks.

Chapter 37: The Final Puzzle Piece

The police station had settled into a haunted kind of silence, the kind that creeps in only after midnight, when even time seems to hesitate. The familiar bustle of ringing phones and murmured conversations had vanished, leaving behind a stillness so profound it seemed to press against the walls. The faint hum of the overhead fluorescent lights buzzed with a nervous energy, flickering slightly in the corners like tired sentinels unable to rest.

Long shadows stretched across the tiled floor, angular and warped, reaching up the walls as if trying to claw their way into the evidence room. The distant creak of a chair and the soft clack of a filing cabinet closing somewhere down the hallway echoed like footsteps from the past, reminders that the building, like the case, wasn't finished speaking.

Inspector Thomas Stowe stood at the window; arms folded tightly across his chest. He hadn't moved in several minutes. Rain had begun to bead softly on the pane, blurring the sodium-lit street outside. His reflection stared back at him, drawn features, tired eyes, the faint sheen of sweat along his hairline from hours without pause. The collar of his shirt was unbuttoned, tie loosened, the coat draped across his shoulders like armour worn too long.

Behind him, the incident board remained lit, a monument to obsession. The red string ran like veins across the cork, pulsing with meaning. At its centre, Reginald Price, stern and unmoving, even in death. Around him: Catherine, Peter, Philip, Marion. The suspects now felt less like people and more like archetypes, caught in orbit around a single violent moment that refused to settle into clarity.

Detective Harris sat nearby, perched uneasily on the corner of a desk. His coat was thrown over a chair, his sleeves rolled up, and the coffee cup by his elbow had gone untouched for hours, the liquid inside cold, the ring beneath it permanent. His notepad lay open on one knee, but the pen in his hand hadn't recorded anything meaningful in the last hour. Instead, it traced looping spirals, unconscious and tired.

Stowe spoke without turning, his voice unexpectedly soft, too soft for the room they were in, too soft for what they were circling.

"What about Catherine?"

Harris looked up sharply, the name slicing through the lull like a sudden gust of wind rattling a loose windowpane.

"Catherine?" he repeated, uncertain. "What about her?"

Stowe finally turned from the window. The overhead light cut a sharp angle across his face, showing the hollows beneath his eyes, the wear in the lines around his mouth. He looked exhausted. But his gaze was still sharp, calculating. Alive.

"She gets half the estate, after Marion dies" he said. "Control of the west wing. A portion of the trust. A clean path to financial independence. Enough to vanish, if she wanted."

Harris frowned. "We've already been through this. She's been helping us since day one. She brought us the tape. She found the jacket. She's the one who's been feeding us breadcrumbs."

"Yes," Stowe said slowly. "And she's been helpful. Almost... *too* helpful."

The silence that followed landed hard.

Harris stared. "You think she staged it?"

"I think," Stowe said, stepping toward the board, "she's the only one who hasn't cracked. Peter slipped. Philip confessed to more than he realized. Even Marion's grieving armour fractured. But Catherine?" He stopped in front of her photograph and tapped it with one finger, once, then again. "She hasn't flinched. Not once. Not in the interviews. Not when her husband was arrested. Not even when she stood in the same room with the evidence."

Harris crossed his arms, watching Stowe. "She's composed. Controlled. That doesn't make her a suspect. Some people go cold when they grieve. Doesn't mean they're hiding something."

"I know," Stowe replied. "But this isn't just grief. It's *precision*. Everything she says is measured. She speaks like someone who's already edited the story twice before telling it."

He walked slowly, pacing between the desk and the board. His movements were tight. Restless.

"She knew Reginald's habits. She knew his routines, his study hours, the times he was unreachable. She knew how to pull the pieces together and how to leave just enough undone for us to follow."

Harris hesitated, then reached into the file he'd left on the table. "There's something else," he said. "I didn't think it mattered at first."

Stowe turned to him. "What?"

Harris opened the folder and pulled out a copy of the board minutes, stapled and neatly annotated. He laid them flat.

"This is from a closed meeting. A month before Reginald's death. Catherine was formally *removed* from the business side of the estate. No shares. No voice in board decisions. She kept her name on the will, for the portion of the trust, but he stripped her from the company entirely."

Stowe stepped forward, reading.

"'Catherine Price deemed emotionally volatile in matters of finance,'" Harris read aloud. "That's Reginald's language. Says she lacked 'discipline and long-term thinking.'"

Stowe let out a breath through his nose. "So, she was cut off. Publicly sidelined. But still left enough to look like she hadn't been punished."

"Exactly," Harris said. "From the outside, it looks like she was taken care of. But underneath? She was humiliated. Silenced. He wanted her out."

Stowe looked at Catherine's photo again, his expression unreadable now.

"If she knew that," he said slowly, "and if she thought Reginald planned to do the same to David…"

"She had motive," Harris finished. "More than we thought."

Stowe nodded. "And opportunity. She was never out of sight. But she was never fully in the spotlight either."

"She floated just close enough to be seen as useful," Harris said. "Helpful. But always at the edge. Always watching."

"She gave us everything *after* it was useful to her," Stowe murmured. "The jacket. The tape. The timeline. And each time, we let her frame it."

A long pause stretched between them.

Harris rubbed the back of his neck. "She cried for David. At the station. That wasn't fake."

"No," Stowe said. "I don't think she faked anything. That's what makes her dangerous. Love and guilt aren't opposites, Harris. Sometimes they walk hand in hand."

He moved back to the table and picked up the plastic evidence bag, the suit, still stained, still damp from the rain-soaked garden where it had been buried. The sleeve had stiffened now, dried blood curling the fabric into something unnatural.

"If the prints match hers," Harris said quietly, "we've got her."

Stowe nodded, slowly. "If."

"And if they don't?" Harris asked.

Stowe stared at the jacket, fingers resting against the plastic like he was listening for something.

"Well, it should match someone in this house, if not, we go back to square one," he said. "Or worse…"

He glanced up at the board.

"We admit the crime was smarter than we were."

Harris folded his arms. "Or we admit we stared at the picture the whole time… and never turned it the right way up."

Stowe didn't respond. He just stared at the evidence board again, at the strings, the pins, the photos, the fragments of a story almost finished. His gaze stopped on Catherine's picture again.

There was something about her face. It wasn't smug. It wasn't blank.

It was *confident*.

Controlled.

He felt it, like pressure building before a storm. The quiet hum in the bones before the sky split. A sense of something inevitable.

The case was close.

But that meant so was the truth.

And the truth, when it came, would take *someone* down with it.

Chapter 38: The Third Floor

The third floor of the Price estate always had a hush to it, a kind of stillness that didn't belong to the rest of the house.

The wallpaper there was slightly more faded, the carpet more muted underfoot. Dust gathered faster along the bannisters. Few ever came up. Even fewer asked what was kept behind the heavy oak door at the end of the corridor.

That door, smooth and unmarked, had remained shut for years.

Until now.

Stowe had mentioned it during a late-night conversation with Marion a few days before. A slip of a comment over tea in the conservatory: *"If there's anything you've kept locked away, now's the time."*

Marion had nodded slowly. "There's a room upstairs. Third floor. Reginald used to keep… paperwork. He said it was better kept separate."

When Harris reached the door the next morning, it was just after 8 a.m. Rain lashed at the window at the end of the hall, casting streaks of grey light across the dust-furred carpet. The door's keyhole looked unused, a slight film of grime settled into its brass. No key had been found, not in Reginald's desk, not in the safe, not in the housekeeper's archive.

"Locked?" Stowe had asked over the phone.

"Locked," Harris had confirmed. "But nothing I can't handle."

Now, crouched at the base of the door with a tension bar and pick, Harris worked quietly. Within twenty seconds, the soft *click* of tumblers. He stood, pushed gently, and the door creaked open.

He had expected boxes. Piles of disorganized folders. A mess that would take weeks and a whole task force to catalogue.

But what met him was the opposite.

The room was pristine.

A narrow chamber, with floor-to-ceiling shelves along one wall and a single desk pushed against the window on the far side. The curtains were drawn halfway, letting in enough light to show the room had not been touched in months, maybe years.

And on one shelf, one single shelf, sat just ten files.

Ten.

Each file thick, neatly labelled. Ten stories, perhaps. Ten secrets.

Harris stepped forward slowly, heart beating harder now, fingertips tingling in anticipation.

His eyes scanned the spines until one word caught the light.

WILL.

He pulled it down, gently, and set it on the desk.

Inside was a single stapled packet. Reginald's handwriting along the top in sharp blue ink: *Revised Testament, Private.*

Harris flipped through it slowly.

It was short. Deliberate.

The house, Marion's. The west wing, the garden, the staff, the furnishings.

His portion of the company, Marion's too, with clear succession language.

To Peter, a vintage watch. To David a painting from the study. To Catherine a modest trust "to be used for educational or charitable aims."

That was it.

No grand gesture. No sprawling empire split between heirs.

It was Marion's. All of it.

He reached for another file. This one marked **GERALDINE.**

Harris didn't recognize the name immediately. But something about it felt familiar.

Inside: a trust agreement.

Pages of it. Dense legalese. At first, it seemed generous, a seven-figure setup, established more than a decade ago. Payout scheduled on her 30th birthday. Monthly accrual. Investment growth. The works.

But then, deeper in, amendments. Quiet, creeping withdrawals.

Five years ago. Three years ago. Last year.

By the final page, the balance read nearly zero.

Harris stared at the number for a long moment. Then at the signature.

Reginald Price.

Taken. Piece by piece. Without notification. Without permission.

The trust had been cannibalized.

The girl, woman now, had been promised a future that no longer existed.

And worse, it had been hidden.

Not in plain sight. Not in public records. In this locked room, where only Reginald's hand had the final say.

Just as Harris was about to close the drawer, his eyes caught another label, dull gold ink fading on dark paper. It sat lower than the others, slightly out of line with the neat top row.

INVESTMENTS

Not corporate. Not dated. Just one word.

He hesitated, fingers hovering just above the spine. Then he pulled the file free. It was heavier than the others. Worn, as if opened and closed more times than the rest combined.

Back at the desk, Harris opened the cover.

At first, he expected balance sheets, property reports, something related to Reginald's business affairs.

But what he found instead were envelopes. Receipts. Signed letters in neat, cold cursive. Most startling were the slips of paper with names and handwritten notes beside them. Payments. Amounts. And reasons.

Helen – £10,000 – "Not to speak to Marion."

That was the first.

Then came more.

Linda – £7,500 – "Abortion, March 2019 – no contact, no name."

Camille – £4,000 – "Flat deposit – silence implied."

The entries went on. Some typed, some scrawled, all cold and direct. Each a name, a number, a reason.

Each a life Reginald had paid to disappear, or at least to stay quiet.

Harris's stomach turned. He flipped further, found a neatly stapled summary sheet at the back.

"Ongoing monthly disbursements to cover discretion."

There were notes of legal threats avoided, private clinics paid off, gag orders that hadn't been filed through formal legal channels but were "understood." One entry simply read:

Belinda – Grooming underway. Potential long-term partner. Not yet aware of pre-nuptial clause. Monitor closely.

Harris stood in the middle of the room, the folder still open in his hands, blood ringing faintly in his ears. The rain outside had picked up again, hammering the third-floor windows in a rhythmic whisper of shame.

He didn't close the file. He took it with him.

Downstairs, he found Stowe waiting near the study, thumbing slowly through a pile of old correspondence. The light was low, the fire behind him giving his face an amber hue that made the lines on it look deeper.

Harris dropped the folder on the table with a flat *thud*.

Stowe looked up.

"What's this?"

"Something uglier than I thought," Harris said. "You were right. That room's not storage. It's strategy."

Stowe flipped open the file. The first few pages were enough. His jaw tightened, eyes narrowing.

"Jesus," he muttered. "Helen. Linda. Camille. All quiet deals."

"And look here." Harris tapped a line with his knuckle. "Belinda. Monitored. He was grooming her. Called it that, in writing. Had a plan for after Marion. If he could've lived another month, we'd be dragging this whole circus into court."

Stowe scanned the rest, then closed the folder slowly, one hand resting flat on the cover.

"They weren't lovers to him," he said. "They were exits. Backdoors. Escape routes."

"And leverage," Harris added. "Against his own wife. Against his own family. Anyone who pushed him too far."

Stowe stood, the firelight catching in his eyes. He didn't speak for a long moment.

Finally: "Put it in the report. Everything."

"Even Geraldine's trust?"

Stowe nodded. "Especially that."

They both looked down at the folder one more time.

Ten thousand pounds here. A broken silence there.

Reginald hadn't been hiding secrets.

He'd been filing them.

Chapter 39: The Funeral

The chapel was old stone and silence.

Grey walls arched high overhead, fluted columns vanishing into shadow. Rain tapped lightly on the roof, steady and polite, the kind of English weather that suited a funeral. Quietly wet. Unapologetically grey.

The coffin rested at the front, draped in a deep navy cloth. No flowers, Reginald had hated them. "Wasted money," he'd once said. "Give people something they can use." The air smelled faintly of polish and wet wool, mingled with something metallic, grief, perhaps, or the absence of it.

The pews were full.

David sat near the front, eyes bloodshot, jaw tight, hands clasped like they might hold him together. Marion beside him, dressed in elegant black, her face still and composed, as unreadable as ever.

Philip had taken a seat at the end of the second row, hands folded neatly in his lap, his eyes drifting often toward the casket but never settling. Peter hovered behind him, suit slightly wrinkled, watching the room more than the service.

And Catherine stood.

Black coat. Clean lines. Hair pulled back. She walked to the lectern with calm steps, the only sound the faint echo of her heels on stone.

She cleared her throat once, eyes sweeping the rows, pausing only briefly on Stowe and Harris at the back, quiet observers in dark coats.

Then she began.

"My father was... terrible."

A murmur passed through the pews. Someone coughed. Someone else stiffened.

Catherine didn't flinch.

"He was rude. Often dismissive. He knew how to make people feel small, and he rarely apologized for it. He believed in winning, and he didn't care much about how that looked from the outside."

She paused. Her voice softened slightly.

"But he provided. He built something. He brought us up with the expectation that we would succeed, no matter what. He didn't give us gentleness, but he gave us strength."

She turned her eyes to the casket. "And now, we're left to sort through everything he built. The good and the bad. The lessons, and the consequences."

She stepped down. No tears. Just a nod.

Philip stood slowly next.

"Reginald and I," he said, adjusting his cufflinks, "were friends. For a long time. Before all of this." He gestured vaguely, to the chapel, the coffin, the mourners.

"We argued. Sometimes viciously. But we also built something together. This company. This legacy. And for all his flaws, Reginald was brilliant. He didn't suffer fools. He taught me to be sharp. To expect resistance. And to hold the line."

His voice cracked slightly, but he covered it with a cough.

"We had good times. I will remember those."

When he sat, the hush that followed was broken not by family, but by someone from the back.

A woman in her early thirties stepped forward slowly, coat still damp, hair sleek from the rain. Belinda. One of the many unfamiliar faces loitering near the chapel doors. Beautiful in a curated way. Her heels clicked softly on the stone.

She approached Stowe, who stood near the aisle, hands folded, expression unreadable.

"Inspector," she said quietly, leaning close. "He promised me the estate."

Stowe raised an eyebrow. "Reginald?"

She nodded. "He said we were going to live there together. I was moving in next month. Did you find a will? Something naming me?"

Before Stowe could answer, another woman, older, sharper, appeared beside her.

Geraldine.

She wore black, but not mourning black. Her lipstick was perfect, her eyes alert.

"I'm Reginald's daughter," she said. "From before he married Marion. He told me there was a trust. Over a million. Set to release next month. He said everything was sorted. That I just needed to contact his solicitor. Can you tell me how to get it?"

Stowe didn't blink. He turned to them both, his voice low but firm.

"The will we have is simple. Most of the estate is left to Marion. Small gifts to the others. No mention of you, Belinda."

He looked to Geraldine. "As for the trust, it existed. But it was emptied. Reginald accessed the funds six months ago."

Geraldine's mouth opened. Then shut. "He *took* it?"

"Used it elsewhere," Stowe said, not unkindly. "We're still tracing the details."

Belinda looked stunned. "So, I get nothing?"

Stowe didn't answer. Didn't need to.

Behind them, the funeral wound down. The organ hummed its slow, closing chords. Mourners began to rise, heads bowed, coats gathered. Marion remained seated; her hands folded. David hadn't moved. Peter stared hard at the stone floor.

And outside the chapel, the rain started again, not heavy, but insistent.

The kind of rain that washes secrets just far enough to be seen, but never far enough to forget.

Chapter 40: The Calm Before

The mist clung to the hedgerows like breath on glass, heavy and unmoving, veiling the landscape in an eerie, silver shroud. As Inspector Thomas Stowe pulled into the narrow gravel drive leading to his cottage, the tyres crunched through shallow puddles that glinted in the pale, indifferent moonlight. The night had a quiet weight to it, not quite still, not quite moving. Just… waiting.

His hands remained on the steering wheel after the engine stopped. The dashboard light dimmed and clicked off, leaving him in darkness broken only by the reflection of low-hanging branches and the occasional scatter of wind-blown leaves across the windscreen. The tap of cooling metal echoed faintly around him, rhythmic and hollow. Somewhere in the distance, the wind howled through the fields, a long, plaintive sound that made the landscape feel uninhabited, like a place between worlds.

Inside the car, Stowe exhaled through his nose, tired but alert. Beneath the fatigue was something more dangerous: unease. The case, so tangled, so elusive for so long, now felt poised on the edge of revelation. But the clarity hadn't brought peace. If anything, it brought suspicion deeper than any before.

He stepped out slowly, boots splashing in a shallow puddle. His coat flared behind him in the breeze, damp from the station, and he drew it tighter with one hand as he climbed the short stone steps to the front door.

When he stepped inside, the warmth hit him like a memory he hadn't known he missed.

The familiar scent of Debbie's cooking hung in the air, onions softened in butter, rosemary crushed between fingers, garlic still clinging faintly to the wooden chopping board. The fire in the hearth cracked and popped, casting golden flickers across the walls and floorboards. Shadows leapt and danced across the familiar furniture like restless ghosts.

Debbie looked up from her armchair as the door closed behind him. Her crossword lay half-finished on the coffee table, pen resting between two clues. Her glasses had slipped to the end of her nose, and she peered over them with that gentle, sharp look he'd known for years.

"You look like you walked through the storm," she said softly, watching him peel off his coat.

"Felt like it," Stowe muttered, hanging the dripping wool on the hook beside the door. Water tapped onto the mat below, slow and steady, like a second-hand clock. His shoulders slumped as the cold fell away, inch by inch.

Debbie rose and stretched, arms arching above her head until her spine gave a soft, satisfying crack. Without a word, she turned and disappeared into the kitchen. A moment later, the gentle hum of the microwave started up, followed by the familiar clink of ceramic on stone. The warmth of the house wrapped around him like a hand on his back, steady, familiar, anchoring.

He lingered by the hearth a moment longer, eyes unfocused, breath slow. Then, finally, he eased into the worn leather armchair, his chair, the one that had shaped itself to him after years of sitting with unsolvable puzzles and unanswered questions. The cushions sighed beneath him.

When Debbie returned, she handed him a mug of strong tea, no sugar, just heat and weight and a reheated plate of shepherd's pie. The scent of it pulled him back to the present like a rope.

"Thanks," he said, voice rough. He picked up the fork, let it hover, then took a bite.

She settled beside him, knees tucked under a thick grey blanket, one hand resting on her cup, the other curled beneath her chin. She didn't look at him, but he felt her attention anyway. Like always.

"Still chasing shadows?" she asked after a minute.

Stowe chewed slowly, swallowed, and set the plate aside. His eyes flicked toward the fire, orange light dancing across his face.

"It's not the crime that's bothering me anymore," he said. "It's how... *convenient* it all is. Everything lining up just right. Each clue obvious enough to feel real. Each piece sitting where we're supposed to find it. It doesn't feel organic. It feels... orchestrated."

Debbie's brow furrowed slightly. "You think Catherine planted the jacket?"

He didn't answer immediately. Instead, he sipped his tea and let the silence stretch.

"She had access," he said finally. "Opportunity. And she's sharper than she lets on. Calm under pressure. Every word, every move, measured. She didn't stumble once."

Debbie leaned her head back. "But that doesn't make her guilty."

"No," he agreed. "But if she didn't *plant* it... she knew where it was. And she let us find it."

A pause. Then she asked gently, "And what if she's not covering for herself? What if she's protecting someone else?"

He turned toward her, brows drawing together. "David?"

"Maybe," she said. "Or Marion. Or both. Not forgetting Peter and Philip that family's tied together like rope knots. Pull one wrong, and the whole thing tightens."

Stowe exhaled through his nose, a low, frustrated sound. "I've been turning that around in my head all night. I keep thinking about the tape, the clothes, the sequence of events. Everything points in just one direction, but it's *too neat*. Someone's guiding the story. And I think I know who."

Debbie's eyes narrowed slightly, curious. "Who?"

He didn't answer right away. He just looked down into his tea, the steam rising slowly, as if hesitant to leave.

"I think it's someone we trusted to help," he said quietly. "Someone who never raised their voice. Never got angry. Just... stayed in the background and let us build their version of the truth."

"Catherine," she said, almost breathless.

Stowe nodded once. "She's at the centre of every turn. She finds the tape. She delivers the jacket. She gives us leads that push blame toward Peter, toward Philip, toward anyone but her. But she never inserts herself too far. Never justifies. Never protests too loudly. She knows exactly when to speak, and when silence is more convincing."

Debbie looked away; her lips pressed into a thin line.

"But what if she's doing it because she has to?" she said. "Because someone else asked her to. Or needed her to."

"I've considered that," Stowe said. "But if she's protecting someone... she's also *framing* someone else. That's not just loyalty. That's strategy."

The room was quiet for a long moment, just the soft pop of the fire filling the air.

Finally, he added, "And Harris found something else."

Debbie looked over, attentive.

"Board minutes. A meeting a month before Reginald's death. Catherine was formally cut out of the business. No shares. No say. Reginald called her reckless. Unstable. She was allowed to keep the trust, but the company? He shut her out completely."

"So, he betrayed her."

"He erased her," Stowe said. "And she found out. We don't know when. But if she saw that in writing, and if she thought he was planning to do the same to David... she wouldn't let that happen again."

Debbie said nothing for a while. Then, slowly, she reached out and took his hand.

"You're close," she said. "Closer than you think. You always are. Even when it doesn't feel like it."

He gave her a faint, grateful smile, but it didn't reach his eyes.

"The prints come back tomorrow," he said. "Whoever wore that jacket was in the garden the night Reginald died. Close enough to do it. Close enough to bury the evidence before the rest of the house even knew what had happened."

"If they match?" she asked.

"Then we end this," he said. "Formally. Finally."

"And if they don't?"

He stared into the fire for a long time before answering.

"Then someone played us all," he said. "And they played us perfectly."

Outside, the wind shifted again. The trees whispered through the hedges. Branches scratched softly at the windows like fingers testing the glass. In the distance, an owl called, low and long, and the fire crackled in response, as if answering.

Inside, the warmth remained. But the stillness had changed. It wasn't peace anymore.

It was the hush before the truth arrived.

Stowe could feel it, not in the case notes, not in the photographs, but in his bones. The pressure in the air. The way every silence tonight lasted a beat too long, every flicker of flame moved like breath.

The answer was coming.

And this time, it wouldn't knock. It would tear the door off its hinges.

He closed his eyes, fingers tightening around the mug. One more night. One more silent hour.

And then?

The reckoning.

Chapter 41: The Author

The conservatory was unusually still.

Even the breeze outside seemed to pause before it passed the windows, as though giving space to the quiet inside. The mid-morning sun cast soft shapes of shadow across the tiled floor, filtered through the lattice of old ivy that clung to the glass walls. A teapot sat untouched on the table, steam long since faded, the china cups delicate but empty.

Marion sat in the high-backed wicker chair with a blanket folded neatly over her knees, her posture straight, hands folded gently in her lap. She wore grey today. not quite mourning, not quite peace and her hair had been pinned into a careful twist, strands of silver catching the light like thread pulled through cloth.

Inspector Stowe stood by the door for a moment before stepping in, his footsteps careful on the tile.

She didn't look up at first. Just let her gaze wander the vines outside. Then she spoke low, smooth.

"I thought you'd come by."

"I meant to earlier," Stowe said. "Too many loose ends." He reached up and scratched the side of his jaw. "But I didn't want to leave this one hanging."

Marion finally turned to look at him. Her expression was tired, but clear. As if sleep had become more difficult but not impossible.

"I wanted to thank you," Stowe said, voice quieter now. "For the poem."

Something flickered across her face, not quite surprise. Closer to acceptance.

"It was very helpful," he continued. "But what I still don't understand is... why include the affair with Philip? You didn't need to tell us that."

Marion's fingers tightened slightly around each other. Then she drew a slow breath.

"I knew Philip couldn't have done it," she said simply. "Not murder. Not that kind of violence. He isn't capable of that."

Stowe didn't interrupt. He just waited, letting her speak in her own time.

"I wrote it," she continued, "because you already knew most of it. I could see it in the way you looked at me during David's arrest. You weren't just reading people. You were waiting for someone to admit what you already suspected."

A silence followed, soft but thick with understanding.

"And I..." she paused, then smiled faintly, "I thought maybe it would be easier to hear it in rhyme."

Stowe almost smiled back. "Not your first time with verse, I take it."

Marion tilted her head slightly. "Before all this, I used to write. Mostly for myself. Poems, little essays. It's what I did before I became Reginald's wife. And then... I stopped."

"Why the poem, though?" he asked. "Why not a note? A letter?"

"Because poetry slips through the cracks," she said. "People dismiss it as emotional, even fanciful. But it tells the truth, only softer. I wanted you to have our secrets. All of them. Or at least the ones I thought might help you find whoever killed him."

Stowe moved toward the armchair across from her and sat slowly. His shoulders were heavy under his coat, but his voice stayed light.

"You gave us a roadmap," he said. "One clue after another. Some of it was buried. Some of it was just waiting to be seen differently."

"I couldn't say it all out loud," she said, looking back toward the vines. "Not then. Not to them. There were things they weren't ready to hear and maybe I wasn't ready to say. I hope you understand."

Stowe nodded. "I do."

They sat in the quiet for a moment longer.

Outside, a blackbird hopped across the stone path near the garden beds, scattering bits of old leaves as it pecked.

Marion's voice came again, softer.

"Reginald wasn't a cruel man. But he kept things... controlled. And I learned, over the years, that secrets are sometimes the only power you have left when you've been told what you're allowed to be."

Stowe leaned forward slightly. "Do you regret it? Not telling the family?"

She shook her head. "They know now. And maybe they'll understand in time. But I wrote the poem for *you*. Because catching a killer isn't just about footprints or fibres. It's about knowing the rooms people walk through when no one's looking."

Stowe studied her for a long moment.

Then, finally, he said, "You were more help than you'll ever know."

Marion smiled, thin but honest. "I knew you'd listen."

He rose, carefully, almost reluctantly.

At the door, he paused and looked back. "You didn't sign it."

Marion looked down at her hands, then up at him with a glint of something almost playful in her eyes.

"Well," she said. "A poem's just a ghost of the truth. Best to let it haunt quietly."

Chapter 42: The Final Accusation

The drawing room of the Price estate, once a haven of old-world charm and refinement, now bristled with the kind of tension that made even the dust in the corners seem alert. The fire still burned in the hearth, casting long, shifting shadows on the worn panelling, but its warmth felt thin, distant. A performance, like everything else in this room. A small black envelope sat on the mantlepiece ready to reveal its secrets.

The thick Persian rug muffled every footstep but couldn't mute the dread crawling across the floor. The heavy velvet curtains swayed ever so slightly, although no windows were open. A strange, electric stillness filled the air, as if the house itself were holding its breath.

Inspector Thomas Stowe stood near the centre of the room, not speaking yet, but *present*, in the way only someone about to change everything could be. He was flanked by Detective Harris, who clutched a manila folder under one arm and an evidence bag in the other. The light from the fire glinted off the plastic, catching threads of crimson through the folds of fabric inside.

The family was assembled, but not unified. Not anymore. They sat or stood in scattered, anxious postures; each person isolated by suspicion.

Catherine sat closest to the fire, but the heat did not seem to reach her. She was perched on the edge of the armchair, spine straight, jaw locked, one hand gripping the armrest like it anchored her to reality. Her eyes were on Stowe, watching, waiting, calculating.

Peter stood across the room, caught mid-movement, a glass of scotch in one hand, a crystal decanter still tilted in the other. His expression was that of someone interrupted by a thought they didn't want to finish.

Marion was curled tightly into herself in the corner near the piano, wrapped in a thick shawl that dwarfed her frame. Her pale hands were clasped in her lap, unmoving, her eyes wide and distant, like she was watching something only she could see.

Philip lingered near the window, silhouetted against the streaks of rain snaking down the glass. Arms folded. One foot tapping rhythmically. He had the tense stillness of someone who knew a reckoning was coming but refused to flinch.

Stowe finally spoke, his voice gravelled, deliberate.

"The lab results have returned," he said. "And they complete the picture."

The fire cracked once, sharp and sudden, as though reacting.

A hush fell over the room, a hush that wasn't merely silence, but anticipation wound tight as piano wire.

Harris stepped forward and placed the clear plastic bag on the coffee table. Inside, folded carefully and tagged, was the bloodstained suit, the one found buried near the hedge, hidden and almost forgotten.

"Fingerprints," Stowe continued. "Lifted from the inside of the study window. Sweat residues in the collar lining. Carpet fibres from the west hall embedded in the cuffs."

He turned toward David Forrester.

David flinched.

Stowe's voice dropped, deadly calm. "It was your suit, Mr. Forrester."

David's face drained of colour. "That... That's not possible."

Catherine's lips parted. Her voice came out in a whisper. "What...?"

David turned, searching her face. "That's wrong. I didn't, I didn't even *go in*. I didn't know...I was only gone ten minutes."

Peter's voice cut through the din, sharper than intended. "You were gone for longer than that."

David wheeled on him. "Barely fifteen minutes!"

"Fifteen minutes is a long time to kill a man," Peter said, voice low.

David stepped forward; eyes wide. "You really think I staged that? That I *killed* him and set up a fake locked room? Are you hearing yourselves?"

Harris opened the folder. His voice was flat. "David Forrester. Financial collapse. Business assets frozen. Two private investors pursuing legal action. Three unsecured debts. Bankruptcy proceedings imminent."

David turned to Catherine, desperation in his voice. "You *know* me. You know I would never…"

She didn't answer right away.

Her eyes stayed on him, but her expression was unreadable. After a long beat, she spoke, softly, but with a strange detachment.

"I want to believe you," she said.

Silence fell again.

Marion whispered into the stillness; her voice barely audible: "It doesn't make sense."

Philip took a step away from the window, expression grim. "Because it was never supposed to make sense. Theatrics. The tape. The locked door. It's all too complicated. Overdone. Someone wanted this to look clever. Wanted us chasing shadows."

Catherine stood.

Her movements were slow, almost ritualistic. She stepped forward, her voice low but certain. "Because it *was* meant to."

Every eye turned to her.

Peter spoke, confused. "What are you saying?"

She looked around at all of them, her family, her ghosts and then down at the suit, still sealed in plastic.

"This was staged," she said. "Every piece of it. The tape. The suit. The hidden bundle. Every clue designed to push the investigation… just far enough."

Stowe's voice was quiet now. "By whom?"

Catherine met his gaze directly. "Someone who knew how to manipulate timing. How to direct suspicion. Someone who understood where each of us would be… and how we'd react."

Stowe's jaw tightened. "Are you making an accusation?"

"I'm saying," Catherine said, stepping past the table, "that whoever planted the suit knew it would be found. Knew it would point to David. And knew that I would be the one to discover it."

David exhaled, shaking. "Then who…?"

Chapter 43: The Key

A year ago....

It had rained the morning Peter left the boardroom, though he barely noticed it at the time. He remembered the scuffed marble tiles outside the meeting hall more vividly than anything said inside, the way the water pooled in the grooves like veins. The sky had been a slate-grey bruise and so had his ego.

He'd stood there, coat unbuttoned, tie pulled loose, blinking down at the wet pavement as if it might offer him a better strategy than anything he'd just presented.

They'd laughed at him.

Reginald hadn't, of course. Reginald didn't laugh. He dismissed. He silenced with a glance. But the others the senior partners, the ancient heads of the table who hadn't made a new decision in a decade they'd ridiculed him. Scoffed at his pitch for digitization. Said it was "premature," "unrealistic," "a phase."

That was the word that stuck. *Phase.* As though innovation was something that passed like a flu.

Peter had clenched his fists until his palms ached.

He didn't even call anyone. He just drove. Back to the house. Back to the only place that had ever felt more like a test than a home.

The gravel at the Price estate crunched under his wheels with a satisfying bite. The sky above had begun to break, clouds splitting like bruises fading. As he stood by the iron gate, watching the old house loom like a disappointed parent, the idea struck him, fully formed.

If they wanted to make him the joke, then fine.

Let the real punchline be carved out *from within.*

The first call was clumsy. The second, smoother. By the third, he had his pitch. A quiet offer to rival firms who wanted eyes inside the old man's empire. Thirty minutes. No questions. No cameras. Just a glimpse at the ledgers, contracts, confidential partnerships. A stroll through the kingdom Reginald Price had built one sealed cabinet at a time.

And Peter? Peter would be the helpful son with access. Who'd been told "stay out" one too many times.

It wasn't difficult. Reginald was gone most weekdays. And Peter, for all his quiet resentment, remembered everything. Including where ten-year-old Catherine had once retrieved a secret key.

The third wooden panel in the west bookcase in the library. The one that didn't sit flush. He'd seen her, years ago, eyes darting like a pickpocket's, fingers sliding into the slot just deep enough to fish out brass.

That afternoon, he followed the memory like a map, his pulse steady, his face numb. And there it was: the key. Still tucked behind the false spine of a forgotten volume on maritime law.

The first man arrived a week later.

Suited, silent, and smug. A faint accent, maybe German or Swiss and a folded envelope full of clean notes. He said very little, nodded once when Peter handed him the key.

Peter had already opened the cabinets, pulled the files forward for easy reach. Nothing taken, nothing moved too much. Just enough for eyes to scan. For secrets to settle.

"You've got thirty minutes," Peter said. "No longer. Lock from the inside when you're in. I'll keep watch."

The man disappeared into the study.

For the first ten minutes, Peter paced in the front hall. The rest he spent near the library window, pretending to read. His heart beat a little too loud, but nothing happened. The man left just before the half-hour, nodded once more, and drove away into the dusk like nothing had passed between them.

Peter had stood in the hallway long after he left, staring at the study door, wondering what he'd just done.

The second man was Philip, this was easy, open up the filing cabinets and let him look inside. This was the easiest money he had ever made.

The Third man didn't introduce himself.

He came a month later. Paid in cash, twice what the first man had. Peter gave him the key but this one didn't meet Peter at the gate. Didn't wait in the drawing room. By the time Peter heard footsteps on the landing, the man was already at the top of the stairs.

Peter hurried after him, calling, "Hey, wait, I need to... "

But by the time he reached the study door, it was shut. Locked. From the *outside*.

That wasn't supposed to happen.

He knocked once. No answer.

Twice. Nothing.

"Sir?" he called, voice low, nervous.

Still nothing.

He leaned in. No sound on the other side. No movement. No shuffle of pages. Just silence.

Peter stepped back, heart racing. He tried the handle again. Still locked. That same cool click unmistakable.

Panic began to crawl up his throat. If Reginald came home early

He waited an hour. Pacing. Sweating. But no one came out. And when he checked again still locked.

Eventually, he had no choice. He called a locksmith. Lied. Said the door had jammed.

The man was quick, competent. Opened the lock without any damage.

But the room was empty.

No sign of the man. No money taken. No files touched. The cabinets were still sealed. No prints, no stray items.

And the key, the key he had given him was gone.

Peter stared at the open door in disbelief, then whispered aloud to no one, "Where the hell did you go?"

It cost him all the money the man had given him to repair the lock.

And more than that to stop hearing the *click* in his head every night afterward.

He never called another contact. Not because he'd grown a conscience.

But because he knew, somewhere deep in his gut, that the second man had gotten exactly what he came for.

And that whatever it was, it had never belonged to Peter in the first place.

Chapter 44: The Final Reveal

"It was staged," Catherine said, her voice low, deliberate. "A performance. A misdirection designed to trap us in this room, turning on each other."

The words settled into the silence like ash, soft at first, but suffocating.

Inspector Stowe shifted slightly, the first crack in his otherwise immovable posture. Detective Harris blinked as though he hadn't heard correctly, his brows beginning to knit.

Catherine moved into the centre of the room, her boots soundless on the thick rug, her frame calm but coiled. The fire behind her flickered higher for a moment, casting her face in sharp relief, the set of her jaw, the glint in her eyes. Every movement, every word now had the weight of finality.

"This wasn't about inheritance," she continued. "Or a crumbling business. It was never about David. Or Peter. Or even Philip."

Her gaze travelled across each of them, lingering for a heartbeat.

"It was about control. About crafting a narrative, step by step, suspect by suspect. Someone with knowledge of our habits. Our weaknesses. Someone who understood how we'd react. How we'd splinter." She went to the mantlepiece and picked up the black envelope.

She turned slowly.

And faced Stowe.

"Susan."

The name shattered the silence like a stone through glass.

"She was bright," Catherine continued, "Brilliant. Her first job was something she talked about constantly. Secretary to a respected man. She'd finally stepped into the world, and it felt like her whole life was just beginning."

David shifted uncomfortably in his seat. Philip lowered his gaze. Peter sat frozen; hands clasped between his knees. Marion blinked slowly, like waking into a nightmare she'd hoped was only a dream.

"She was proud. Hopeful. She felt seen. Until she was seen by the wrong man."

She paused, letting the stillness stretch, tension crackling beneath it.

"She didn't know who he really was. Reginald Price."

Gasps echoed, soft, disbelieving. Marion let out a sharp breath. Peter's mouth opened slightly; his expression frozen in shock.

"He offered her guidance," Catherine continued. "Support. Opportunity. But he wanted more. That evening, he took her out under the pretext of mentorship. But it wasn't drinks and encouragement."

Stowe shifted. His lips pressed into a thin, bloodless line.

"She came back different," Catherine said, her voice now taut with pain. "She was quiet. Withdrawn. She smiled less. Laughed almost never. She started locking her door at night. And slowly… she disappeared."

The fire hissed, a single log cracking in protest.

"She never spoke of what happened. Not in detail. But it was enough. Enough to change her. To bury her from the inside out."

Her voice broke.

"Six months later, she took her own life."

A beat of absolute silence followed.

"Susan Stowe, your daughter."

Catherine took the small black envelope that had been on the mantlepiece all afternoon. She opened it and took out the three cards and threw them at Stowe "It was Inspector Stowe in the Study with the Dagger, I win."

"You planted the suit," Catherine said, stepping forward. "You led the investigation from the start. You controlled the pace. The narrative. You took us by the hand and guided us from suspect to suspect. First Peter, then David. Philip. Me."

Harris took a half-step back, his shock obvious now. "Tom…?"

"You framed David. You used your last case to get rid of two 'terrible' people" Catherine continued. "You had access to the study. To the grounds. You had the tape. All to move suspicion."

"You were careful," she said. "But not perfect. You kept moving. Kept pressing us to confess to things that didn't add up."

She turned to the others now. "And none of us saw it. Because we trusted him."

Peter's hand trembled. The glass in his grip slipped, fell to the floor and shattered, the sound oddly delicate. No one reacted.

Catherine turned back. "I'm sorry about Susan," she said softly. "But grief doesn't justify revenge."

Stowe's chest rose and fell slowly. Then he closed his eyes.

The silence stretched, long, terrible.

And then, at last, he spoke.

"He destroyed her," Stowe said, his voice low and cracked. "She thought he was family. She trusted him with her future. With her *life*. And he let her drown."

He opened his eyes again.

The exhaustion was gone.

Only cold remained.

"Reginald ruined lives behind closed doors for decades," he said. "He was never going to stop. Just shift victims. Another deal. Another name. Another Susan."

"And so, you became the executioner?" Harris asked, incredulous. "That was your answer?"

"I watched her disappear," Stowe replied. "Every day. A little more. And when she was gone, all I could see was him."

Marion covered her mouth.

Philip looked down at the floor, unable to meet anyone's eyes.

Catherine stepped closer, not afraid, not angry. Just resolute.

"You didn't just take his life," she said. "You tried to ruin ours. You broke this family apart to justify your grief."

Stowe finally turned to Harris, his expression empty of defence, stripped of rank and pride.

"Do it," he said simply.

Harris didn't move at first. His hand hovered near the cuffs at his belt. Then, slowly, methodically, he stepped forward.

His voice was thick. "Inspector Thomas Stowe, I'm placing you under arrest for the murder of Reginald Price."

Stowe raised his wrists without resistance.

The click of the handcuffs was deafening.

Outside, the first light of morning spilled through the mist, soft, hesitant. Frost glittered on the stone terrace, melting slowly under the blush of the sun.

Inside, the house was finally quiet.

No accusations. No suspicions. Just silence.

And the sharp, strange weight of truth finally spoken aloud.

Catherine sat down slowly, her limbs trembling. Peter poured himself another drink, this time with both hands. Marion reached out for Philip's hand, and, for the first time in days, he took it.

They were wounded.

But for the first time since Reginald's death, the question that had haunted them who?, had an answer.

And with it, came something none of them had dared to believe in:

Relief.

Freedom.

The truth.

And now, at last, the chance to begin again.

Chapter 45: Catherine Explains

The silence stretched, brittle and breathless, coiling through the room like smoke that refused to dissipate. Not a cough, not a shuffle, not even the creak of a chair interrupted the stillness. A single log shifted in the hearth with a muted crack, the flickering flames casting pale gold against the faces gathered in the drawing room. Once a place of laughter, warmth, and polite conversation, it now felt like a mausoleum, its walls weighed down with accusation and consequence.

Peter sat stiffly at the edge of the sofa, his fingers gripping his knees, knuckles white. He looked like he wanted to speak but couldn't trust his voice. David had turned toward the window, his hands cradling his forehead, shoulders hunched in disbelief. Philip leaned against the mantel, unmoving, as if afraid one false move would collapse the fragile tension in the room. Marion, pale and trembling, sat upright in her chair, her eyes blank as porcelain. Philip stepped beside her, placing a gentle hand on her shoulder. She didn't react.

Catherine stood alone. She was no longer the grieving daughter, the dutiful wife, or the polite hostess. Now, she was something else entirely, an avenger with calm clarity, a woman who had turned her pain into purpose.

"What I really wanted to understand," she said, and her voice, though soft, drew everyone's attention like a flame in the dark, "was why."

She took a slow breath, grounding herself. "Why would the killer go to such careful, deliberate lengths to make it look like one of us?"

She turned, speaking now to the room as a whole. Her words carried the cadence of logic, but her tone held sorrow.

"We were all here. Together. Neatly positioned at the dinner table like characters in a parlour game. A locked room. A timed recording. A sealed window. It was perfect.

Too perfect."

She took a step forward, her voice firmer now. "What if the whole point... was to make it look like only one of us could have done it?"

Gasps stirred, small murmurs rippling through the room. Philip raised an eyebrow. Peter finally glanced over his shoulder, and David looked up, his expression shifting from confusion to horror.

"That's when I started looking outside the circle," Catherine continued. "Outside the house. Outside the narrative we were being told."

"What really happened," Catherine said, "started before dinner. Before the soup, the wine, the polite smiles. Before anyone realised, we were pieces in someone else's game."

She gestured toward the side window.

"Stowe knew that dinner was at 7, He knew that Reginald always went to his study, and we would all be at the dinner table. He entered through window, it was open and unlocked. He had been here before. He knew the layout. He even had a key that Peter had provided."

She turned to Peter. "You gave it to him once. Remember?"

Peter swallowed. "Yes... I mean, I gave it to someone"

Catherine nodded gently. "You didn't. But he did."

She resumed her slow pacing, as if marking steps in a courtroom.

"He slipped in unnoticed. While we were pouring drinks and setting places, he was already here. Preparing the scene."

She turned toward the study door.

"When my father entered, he was alone. As always. Philip went in to talk to him but left shortly afterwards and Stowe was waiting. It was quick. Efficient. Cold."

Marion let out a faint cry. Philip placed both hands on her shoulders.

Catherine's voice did not waver.

"He then went over to lock the door to make sure he was not disturbed."

"He staged it. He was in a suit like David's, same cut, same colour. Doused it in enough blood to implicate but not to soak. He had two cassettes, he had made a longer tape, one hour of silence, then after that Reginald talking about the Madison deal, he put it into the hi-fi and pressed play. That is why no one heard Reginald until nine. The second cassette he kept that at home ready to deploy at a later date he settled on putting it in Peters room a day or two later to implicate him"

Peter looked angry "You mean he was deciding who to pick on next."

"Stowe shut and locked the remaining windows, leaving open the window he had arrived through"

"He changed back into his own clothes, putting the bloody clothes in a bag. He was wearing gloves throughout; the mistake he made was not getting rid of the footprints. He walked calmly out of the estate. Then drove calmly to the station."

She stopped and turned.

"By the time the body was discovered, he was already the man in charge. The trusted inspector. The investigator. The only person who couldn't possibly be guilty."

David whispered, "He framed me?"

Catherine nodded. "He had motive. Means. Knowledge. And vengeance."

"And when he came back to the scene, he waited for his moment. Just one. Enough to lock the window from the inside."

A collective intake of breath.

Then later he knew the truth about the key would come out, that you could lock the door from the outside.

"That was the final illusion. Locked windows. The murder contained. No killer but us."

The fire flickered. The truth settled. And something like peace began to take its place.

Chapter 46: David's Investments

Four Years Ago
The view from the rooftop bar in Madrid glimmered, all red-tiled roofs and domed churches under the soft gold haze of sunset. Glasses clinked around them, laughter threaded the air, and the gentle hum of a jazz trio carried on the breeze.

David Price wore a navy suit, sleeves rolled, collar loosened just enough to suggest relaxation, but not carelessness. He leaned back in his chair with practiced ease, one arm draped along the backrest, wine glass twirling gently in his fingers.

Across from him sat Alan Greaves. Sixty, quiet, observant. The kind of man who'd done his time behind a desk, watched markets rise and fall like tides, and had the kind of smile that never reached his eyes. A teacher of economics, recently retired from the university, or so he said. He was polite. He listened more than he spoke.

He was also watching David very, very closely.

David flashed that signature grin, the one that had launched more than one startup pitch and saved more than one boardroom meeting from collapse.

"Alan," he said smoothly, "thank you again for putting your faith in the Spanish Villa project. Truly. For such a small investment, the upside is phenomenal."

Alan nodded slowly, hands resting on his drink. "And the risk?"

David waved a hand, dismissive. "Always risk, sure. But the groundwork's done. The permits are secured. And the region's on the cusp of a tourism boom. You've got timing on your side. I wouldn't be surprised if we see returns in 18 months. Two years, tops."

Alan sipped his drink. "You're sure?"

David leaned in, warmth in his tone. "I'd stake my own name on it. You'll be glad you got in when you did."

Two Years Ago

Rain tapped against the high windows of David's London office, not hard, but persistent. The kind that seeped into the corners of everything. The kind that stayed.

David sat at his desk, one hand cradling his phone, the other absently tapping a pen against a half-finished expense report. His jaw was tight, the veneer thinner than usual.

On the line, the voice hadn't changed much. Just slower now. Tired.

"David," Alan said, "I wanted to ask about the villas. It's been a couple years. I've got... well, I've got retirement coming in a year or so. Thirty years of work, and I thought, maybe now's the time to enjoy something for once. Sun. Sea. Something to show for it."

David closed his eyes.

The script was ready. He'd said it before. Variations of it. Dozens of times.

"I'm really sorry, Alan," he began, voice calm, rehearsed. "The market turned. Permits were revoked. Legal trouble with a local contractor..."

"But you said..."

"I said we had strong indicators," David cut in gently. "And we did. But these things shift fast. As I mentioned at the time, it's always best to diversify."

A pause.

Alan's voice came quieter. "So... what am I getting back?"

David inhaled. Exhaled.

"Nothing," he said, softly. "I'm so sorry."

Silence.

Not angry silence. Not yet. Just... flat. Like the other side of the line had gone grey.

Then: *click*.

The call ended.

David stared at the phone for a long time, before he put it down.

He didn't know that Alan wasn't Alan at all.

Chapter 47: Filling in the Details

The study had been cleared of most of the crime scene paraphernalia. The dust had settled, literally and figuratively, but the air still felt off. Thick with something unfinished.

Catherine stood by the fireplace, one hand resting on the mantle, the other gripping a half-drained glass of brandy. The fire had long burned low, little more than embers now but the room still held its heat, too close, like secrets pressing against the walls.

David sat opposite her in the worn leather armchair, his coat still on, hair damp from the rain. He didn't move, didn't speak. He just waited, the knot in his chest tightening with every second she didn't look directly at him.

Finally, she turned. Her eyes were sharper than usual, but not cruel. Not angry. Just... focused.

"Do you want to know what really happened?" she asked.

David gave the faintest nod. "I'd like to believe something still makes sense."

She set her glass down with a soft clink.

"Well," she said, "start with this: Stowe's main aim wasn't to find the truth. It was to *tie down* the investigation. Box it in. Make sure it looked like one of us, you, me, Peter, Philip, Marion, had done it. And then make sure *you* went down for it."

David blinked. "Me?"

"Yes," she said. "He was in charge. He controlled the narrative. The reports, the tests, the chain of evidence. He could swap prints. Alter sweat traces. Steer the investigation wherever he wanted. We weren't suspects, David. We were props. His little theatre."

David leaned forward slowly; his voice tight. "But why? Why me?"

"Because," Catherine said, "You had lost a lot of his retirement money, in your investment scheme, remember you said you had seen him before, that is where. He had to land it on someone who made sense. Someone with motive, with no airtight alibi, someone emotionally volatile. You were perfect. Financial pressure, proximity, the locked room angle."

She started pacing, slowly, like walking helped her keep the facts in order.

"He took the carving knife from the kitchen *after* the murder," she said. "A day later. It was the same type he had at home. I checked. He bought a full set weeks ago. He knew the model, the exact shape, weight, the serrated edge."

David frowned. "How would he know what knives we had?"

"Because" she said, stopping to face him, "he had a friend. A friend who paid Peter for access to the study weeks before the murder, he took the Madison tape. While he was here, poking around under the guise of interest in Reginald's estate, he checked out the kitchen too."

David's face twisted. "Peter sold access?"

Catherine gave a short, bitter nod. "Three times. That's how Stowe knew about the back hallway, the study lock, and, most importantly, how the door could be locked from the outside."

She crossed to the window, drew the curtain back a little, let the storm-light trickle in.

"Stowe was the one who kept hammering the *locked room* detail. The windows sealed; the door locked from inside. Everyone bought it, because it felt unshakable. But then, like a magician revealing the trick, *he* discovered the crucial fact: the door could be locked externally with a master key."

She turned back.

"So suddenly, the impossible crime wasn't so impossible. And guess what? That didn't expand the suspect list. It narrowed it, to *us*. Because if the room was locked from the outside, someone *inside the house* had to be guilty."

David's voice was quieter now. "So how did he try to pin it on me?"

"Well, he did not know where we would all be, so he played the tape knowing how it might be useful to change the time of the murder. Did you decide on the time to make the phone call to Hong Kong or did they?"

"They did, just after nine they said" The realisation was now just becoming apparent in David's mind.

"Stowe again, got you, via his friend to call Hong Kong after nine meaning you would be outside the study just before that"

Catherine came closer, folding her arms.

"First, he used what you *didn't* hide, being outside the study before Reginald died. That gave him the seed of suspicion. Then, he tried to erase the one thing that might've helped you."

"The tape," David said softly.

"Yes," Catherine said. "The cassette. The recording Reginald made of himself, ranting about the Madison deal. Marion heard that and assumed it was a live argument, with *you*. But it was never live. It was pre-recorded."

David swallowed. "But I never even knew it existed."

"You weren't supposed to," she said. "And you never would have, if the constable had done his job properly. If Henshaw hadn't slipped me a whisper, I wouldn't have found it either. Stowe was planning to come back and collect it the next morning. He *knew* what it was and where it was. That was his second mistake."

David stared at her, brow furrowed. "Second?"

She nodded grimly. "The first was underestimating me, or was it the footprint?"

He almost smiled. Almost.

"And then, when that didn't work" she went on, "he got clever. He made sure *I* 'discovered' the bloody suit in the garden. Planted deep. Close enough to be credible but hidden enough to be 'accidental.' This time, he wouldn't risk the evidence walking away. Blood, sweat, fingerprints, all neatly staged."

"Modified," David whispered.

Catherine nodded. "Adjusted. Enough to tip suspicion. Enough to bury you."

She crossed the room again, picked up the brandy glass, but didn't drink from it.

"He used us, David. The whole lot of us. He built a crime around performance, evidence placed where it would lead, not where it belonged. And he got away with it for days because we were so busy tearing each other apart."

"Luckly for you I was one step ahead of him, as you know if you play a game with me, I always win."

Chapter 48: Prison

The cell was small, but not silent.

The humming buzz of the corridor lights never fully stopped. The distant clang of a gate, the low murmur of guards passing, the occasional shout from another block, it all formed a kind of rhythm. A grim metronome ticking off the slow march of hours.

Stowe sat on the edge of the narrow cot, his elbows resting on his knees, fingers laced, head bowed.

There was no window. Just a slit of light from the corridor and the dull cream walls that never seemed to warm, no matter how long the day stretched. A metal sink. A metal toilet. A shelf with a single paperback.

He hadn't touched the book.

Instead, he thought.

Sometimes you can't catch the bad guys.

He'd known that before, of course. Years on the force had taught him that much. The ones with connections, charm, or cleverness, they slipped through. They smiled in the courtroom, nodded at the cameras. Walked out with clean shoes and ruined lives trailing behind them like shadows.

Stowe had always thought justice was about patience. About method. He'd built cases like clockwork: tight, deliberate, every piece ticking into place.

But sometimes, even when everything lined up, the testimonies, the motive, the opportunity, it still wasn't *enough*. Not for the courts. Not for the law.

He leaned back against the cold wall, staring at the ceiling, where a faint crack split the plaster like a scar.

Reginald Price.

It always came back to him. Even now.

There'd been whispers for years and not just the ones about business. Whispers from women who had sat across from him in closed rooms, knuckles white around teacups. One night, he'd told them, as if that erased the damage. As if trauma had an expiry date.

Some stories didn't reach evidence folders. They came in fragments. In the way a woman hesitated before saying his name. In the pauses. In the tears she swallowed rather than showed.

And still, Reginald stood. Tied ties, threw parties, gave interviews about *family legacy*.

He treated people like things, Stowe thought. *And women like warnings.*

And David, God, David.

There was no law against bad advice. No legal clause that punished arrogance. But David had ruined lives with a smile. Dozens, maybe more. Sold dreams like raffle tickets and told people to be patient. Diversify. Hope.

And when they lost everything, he offered them tea. Sympathy. Silence.

Stowe had spoken to a man once, pensioner, widowed, skin pale from chemo, who'd invested with David. Trusted him. Lost his house. The man had cried in Stowe's office. Not for the money. But for the shame of being *so stupid.*

And what did David do?

Smoothed his tie, shrugged, and said it wasn't personal.

Stowe rubbed his temple.

How do you stop men like that when the law won't help you?

He'd asked himself that a thousand times before it all began. Before he'd crossed that line blurred as it was between, justice and vengeance.

You don't stop them with procedures.

Not with forms. Not with patience.

You stop them with pressure. With fear. With the kind of cold logic they respect.

Control the evidence. Steer the case. Nudge the pieces.

Stab them in the back, it was what they deserved.

Chapter 49: A Month Later

The Price Mansion looked different now.

It still had the same looming silhouette against the spring sky, all sharp eaves and proud windows, but the tension that once gripped its hallways had softened. The ivy on the south wall was blooming again, full and unapologetic. The garden had been trimmed back into order. Even the gravel in the drive had been raked smooth, like someone had taken time, real time, to make it feel like a home again, not a mausoleum.

Philip stood at the threshold of the drawing room, leaning against the doorframe with a glass of wine in one hand and a subtle smile in the corner of his mouth. He wore a soft cashmere jumper instead of his usual blazer, and for once, his face wasn't pinched by stress or guilt. There was ease there. Quiet, hard-earned ease.

Marion sat by the fire, wrapped in a pale shawl, her silver hair pinned with care. Her illness was still a shadow in the room, but not the only one. Not the heaviest. She laughed at something Peter said, a soft, clear laugh that cracked open the room like sunshine.

Catherine watched them from the far end of the long dining table, one hand around a wineglass, the other resting casually on David's knee beneath the table. He leaned in as she murmured something, grinned, and shook his head, then returned to helping Peter pass a bowl of roasted vegetables.

The table was full, not just with food, but with warmth. Glazed carrots, herbed chicken, bowls of buttery potatoes, and a tart so fragrant it nearly glowed under the chandelier. Dishes clinked. Silverware scraped. Conversation bubbled, comfortable, spontaneous, overlapping.

Philip cleared his throat. "I will say this," he announced, "Marion's Sunday roasts are officially superior to mine. Though I maintain the duck in '84 was a highlight."

"You set the kitchen on fire," Catherine replied dryly, without missing a beat.

"Creatively," Philip said. "Controlled chaos."

Marion gave him a sideways look and smiled. "I am with him for charm, not for culinary skill."

Peter snorted. "Well, good thing you didn't pick *me* to cook."

"Speak for yourself," Catherine said, raising her glass teasingly. "Peter's managed to launch a whole software company and *still* not burn down a single building. Impressive restraint."

Peter gave a mock bow from his seat. "My legacy shall be one of stable code and un-scorched kitchens."

Laughter rippled around the table.

David poured more wine into Catherine's glass, then leaned toward Peter. "And your data collection program is taking off?"

Peter nodded. "Couple big clients lined up. And we just secured funding for the next round. I mean... who knew investors like revenue and quiet founders?"

"That's not what I heard about you at university," Philip said, grinning.

"I've matured," Peter replied. "Tragically."

They all laughed again.

There was something gentle in the room now, not innocence, exactly, but forgiveness. Shared history acknowledged and, for the moment, not weaponized.

Philip caught Catherine's gaze across the table. They exchanged a small nod, a silent agreement. A few months ago, this dinner would have been unthinkable. Now it felt necessary.

Catherine stood slowly, glass in hand.

The room settled. Voices hushed.

"I've never been good at speeches," she said. "But I want to say something before dessert because... well, this is the first time in a long time that this house has felt like a place people *wanted* to be. Not out of obligation. Not out of guilt. But because we *chose* to come back. To stay. To try again."

She looked at each of them, Marion, graceful and watching with quiet pride; Peter, fiddling with a napkin, smiling shyly; Philip, his arm lightly resting behind Marion's chair, eyes bright; David, solid and grounded beside her.

"I want to raise a glass," she said, lifting hers slightly, "to Reginald."

There was a pause. Not heavy. Just still.

"To the man who built this place, who made mistakes, yes, but also held this family together in his own, complicated way. And to the fact that we're still here, together. Trying to do it better."

Glasses clinked. Muted, respectful.

"To Reginald," they echoed.

"To the past," Catherine added, "and to the next chapter."

Chapter 50: The Price of Truth

Rain streaked the kitchen window in wavering, watery lines, each droplet trailing like the fading echo of a confession. Outside, the garden lay still under a grey morning sky, the storm finally passed but its breath still clung to the earth. Every blade of grass, every stone along the path shimmered with moisture, catching what little light broke through the clouds. The trees, skeletal now in the late season, trembled faintly in the wind, their branches clicking softly like the ticking of a distant clock.

The light that bled into the kitchen was the pale, tired sort, the colour of breath on glass. It cast long, distorted shadows across the chipped linoleum floor, turning chair legs and table corners into reaching limbs.

David Forrester sat hunched at the old wooden table, shoulders slouched like they'd never known how to sit tall. His hands were wrapped around a mug of coffee long gone tepid; the ceramic no longer warm enough to comfort. His fingers curled around it anyway, as if sheer grip might keep something, his thoughts, his future, himself, from slipping.

Beside him sat an unopened newspaper, still folded, headlines creased in silence.

His eyes were red-rimmed, skin sallow. Days of stress had left their fingerprints beneath his eyes and around the tight line of his mouth. And though he stared into the mug, he wasn't really seeing it. He was somewhere else entirely, back inside the locked cell, or in the hall where his brother-in-law had called him a coward, or in his father-in-law's study, imagining how close he'd come to being buried with suspicion.

He exhaled, the sound flat and low, like air forced from a cracked lung.

"I'm ruined," he said, voice barely above a whisper.

The words dropped into the room like a pebble into water, quiet, but undeniable. The stillness around them rippled.

"No money. No clients. No business. No bloody hope."

He gave a short laugh. Dry. Lifeless. The sound of a man attempting humour and finding none left in the tank.

"But hey," he added with a hollow grin, "thanks for getting me out of prison. Twice. Real highlight of the year."

Across the table, Catherine Forrester raised an eyebrow, her posture a study in composed contradiction. She sat upright, spine straight but shoulders soft, one bare foot tucked beneath her knee, cardigan hanging loose over a thin blouse. Her hair was long and flowing.

She sipped her tea, the steam drifting lazily past her face. Her eyes, sharp as ever, held him steady, not with judgment, but something harder to define. Patience. Compassion. A kind of dry loyalty that had weathered the storm and remained, like a lighthouse that never moved, even if you did.

"Well," she said after a beat, "it's a good thing I still love you, isn't it?"

David blinked.

He looked up slowly, as if uncertain whether she'd just spoken a line or thrown him a lifeline.

"That..." he said, his voice rough, "is unexpected."

Catherine didn't reply. Instead, she stood, crossing the kitchen with the easy grace of someone who had lived long enough in grief to wear it like a second skin. Her bare feet made soft sounds against the worn tile. She moved with purpose, not to distract herself, but because that's what people do when they still believe in the structure of mornings, in the small rituals that hold lives together.

She filled the kettle, its ancient whistle wheezing softly as it heated. Then she retrieved two mugs, the chipped blue one she always used, and his favourite green, still with a faint line of paint across the rim where he'd once dropped it in the sink.

"You've always had a gift," she said as the water began to bubble, "for walking into fires with your eyes wide open. Business partners. Investment schemes. Most family holidays."

David huffed. It might've been a laugh, if he had more in him.

"You forgot my taste in shoes."

"And wives," she said, glancing at him, tone light but not cruel.

He managed a small, crooked smile. "Very true."

The kettle clicked off with a tired rattle. She poured water into the mugs, the steam rising in soft coils, blurring her face for a moment. In that fog, she looked almost ghostlike, part memory, part presence.

She slid his cup across the table. The ceramic thunked gently against the wood.

He wrapped his fingers around it again, like the heat could thaw him.

"I wanted to hate you," she said, settling into the chair again. "When the business crumbled. When I thought... maybe you really had killed him. I wanted to scream. To leave. But I couldn't."

He swallowed hard. "Why not?"

She shrugged, staring into her tea. "Because beneath all the mess... you're still you. You were reckless. Selfish. But not a killer. And I knew that."

He looked down.

Silence stretched between them. Not awkward, just honest. The kind of silence that only comes when the worst has been said and you're still there, still breathing.

"I think I'm going to lose the flat," he said after a while.

Catherine nodded. "Then we'll move."

He looked at her again, searching.

"And us?"

She looked back without blinking. "That depends."

"On what?"

"On whether you're done running."

He didn't answer right away. But he didn't look away, either.

A bird chirped outside. Just once. The first real sound of the new day. The sky was beginning to lighten, clouds still thick, but not unbroken. Somewhere beneath the grey, the world was still turning.

David took a sip of his coffee.

Still lukewarm.

Still bitter.

But drinkable.

He set it down gently.

And said, "I think I'm ready to stop."

Catherine leaned back in her chair, finally letting her shoulders relax. Her mug cradled in both hands.

"Good," she said.

Outside, the garden waited. Damp. Quiet. But whole.

Inside, they stayed seated at the table. No arguments. No illusions.

Just the quiet, fragile peace that follows truth.

And the long, slow work of learning how to live with it.

"But now," she continued, turning toward him with quiet finality, "you finally get the chance to invest in something that might actually matter."

David tilted his head, brow furrowing. "You?"

Catherine didn't answer immediately. Instead, she moved with calm purpose back to the kitchen table, set a steaming mug in front of him, and then, with a firm, satisfying thump, placed a thick leather-bound notebook between them. Its edges were slightly worn, the corners dog-eared from use. A black elastic strap looped across its middle like a secret waiting to be broken open.

"No," she said simply. "*Us*."

The word landed with more weight than he expected.

David glanced at the cover. Handwritten across the worn leather in thick black marker, scrawled in her familiar all-caps script, were the words:

THE PRICE OF TRUTH

He stared at it.

Then back at her.

His voice dropped, unsure if this was a joke, a fever dream, or both. "You're serious?"

She met his gaze, eyes gleaming with a spark that had been missing since long before the investigation began. "Dead serious."

He blinked slowly. "As in... this is a real plan?"

She gave a half-smile. "As serious as a coroner's report."

David leaned forward, resting his elbows on the table. "You do remember when our lives nearly fell apart solving just *one* murder?"

Catherine didn't flinch. "Which makes us exactly the kind of people others will trust."

There was a beat of silence.

He rubbed both hands over his face and let out something between a groan and a laugh. "You've completely lost it."

She grinned now, fully, unapologetically, and flipped the notebook open with a practiced hand. Inside: page after page of handwritten notes, bullet-pointed ideas, timelines, sketches of a logo, even an estimated startup budget. The writing was neat but aggressive, the kind of penmanship that suggested it had been jotted down at 3 a.m. while adrenaline still pumped through her veins.

"I mean, look at this," she said, sliding the book toward him. "Contact lists. Potential cases. Cold leads from the last three years.

"At first I thought we could be called Forrester and Forrester"

David squinted. "We sound like a bank."

"Well, we won't *be* one," she said dryly. "But we might actually make money. Eventually."

He flipped through a few more pages, eyes widening at the level of detail. Each section was more meticulous than the last, not just clients, but case types, skill assessments, legal loopholes. A surprising number of post-its were dedicated to how much they'd need to pay a decent accountant. And in the margins: tiny doodles of a magnifying glass and what looked suspiciously like Peter behind bars.

"You're actually suggesting I partner with you," he said slowly, "in an *actual* detective agency?"

"I am."

He exhaled and shook his head. "You're terrifying."

"Which makes me *excellent* at extracting confessions."

He laughed despite himself. "And what do I bring to this terrifying venture?"

She leaned forward slightly. "You're charming. Disarming. Good with people. You know how to ask questions without sounding like you're asking questions."

"Thanks," he said dryly. "I sound like a waiter."

"You've also survived this mess without killing anyone. That's more than I expected from half the people in this family."

David turned another page. "You've thought this through."

She nodded, more solemn now. "I've thought everything through."

Her voice dipped lower, quieter, not secretive, just sincere.

"This family destroyed enough lives, David. My father. And nearly you. If I can use what I've learned, what we've learned, to stop that from happening again? Even once? It's worth it."

The air between them shifted. The moment turned. Not dramatic, just meaningful.

He looked up from the notebook, properly meeting her eyes. They weren't cold now or cutting. Just clear. Focused. Her pain had become purpose.

"You're not just doing this for fun," he said.

"No." She folded her arms on the table and rested her chin atop them. "I'm doing it for Susan. For the people who don't get justice because the cases are too complicated to solve"

Her voice softened further.

"And maybe," she added, "a little bit for me."

David leaned back slowly in his chair. The silence between them wasn't empty now, it was full of something new. Possibility. Perhaps even hope.

He glanced down at the notebook again.

"And I'm the sidekick?"

"You're the *equal partner*. With slightly less wardrobe input."

He gave her a long look. "I wore one paisley tie."

"And it haunts me."

He laughed again, louder this time, and raised his mug. "To madness."

She raised hers too, and the soft clink of ceramic-on-ceramic echoed through the kitchen like a vow.

"To justice," she replied.

The moment lingered, warm and unspoken.

The rain had started again, a gentle tap against the windowpanes. But inside the kitchen, the kettle hummed softly on the counter. The air was warm, the light low and amber. The chaos had passed, not erased, not forgotten, but distilled into something they could use.

Something they could carry forward.

David took a sip of coffee and made a face. "Still cold."

Catherine smiled, pushing back her chair and standing up with a stretch. "Good."

He raised an eyebrow. "Good?"

"You'll need to get used to it," she said, flipping to the next page of the notebook. "We've got work to do."

She tapped her pen against the top of the list.

Client #1: Murder in the Peamont Mansion – Cold Case Reopening

"Time to prove we're not just lucky."

David grinned, finally. "Let's do it."

And just like that, the Forrester name, once tethered to scandal, suspicion, and tragedy, took on a new form.

Not legacy.

Not burden.

Purpose.

Outside, the clouds began to thin, the rain softening to mist.

Inside, at the kitchen table, a new story was beginning.

One case at a time.

The Price of Truth had just begun.

Chapter 51: Beyond the Grave

Two months ago.

The house was quiet in the late evenings. That was the only time Reginald truly felt like it belonged to him.

Not during breakfast, when Marion filled the kitchen with her clipped commentary about news articles she didn't read. Not during the day, when Peter lurked in corners pretending to be more than he was. And not at dinner, when Catherine sharpened her voice like a blade and David tried to pass off charm as competence.

No, nightfall was his.

Reginald Price sat in the high-backed leather chair in the study, a half-finished glass of whisky in his hand. The light from the desk lamp was low, casting sharp angles across the wood grain. Outside, the branches tapped gently against the windows. Wind. Or maybe the trees reminding him that even roots had something to say.

He swirled the amber liquid in his glass and exhaled through his nose.

This job is too bloody stressful.

It wasn't the numbers. It had never been the numbers. The ledgers lined up just fine, at least when he pushed them hard enough.

No, it was the people.

The people I've surrounded myself with are a bloody liability.

Peter — posturing little mimic. Always dressed the part, always eager to please, but with no original thought between his ears. He was a reflection, not a person. A mirror for praise, nothing more.

Philip — smug and slippery. The kind of man who thought being well-spoken was the same thing as being right. Reginald had trusted him once, briefly. Then he'd seen the ambition in Philip's eyes, not raw enough to be threatening, but dishonest enough to be dangerous.

David — charming, aimless David. A boy with no brakes. Always pitching, always reaching, never finishing. He gave advice like he was handing out confetti and left others to sweep up the mess.

Marion — once clever, once beautiful, once essential. Now? Distant. Scheming. Cold in all the ways a woman could wound a man. And carrying on with Philip. He wasn't stupid. He'd seen the glances, the ghost of a smile that lingered too long. No loyalty left there. No decency.

Even Catherine — she had the spark. The brains. But none of the discipline. Always pushing, always questioning. She'd never been content to follow, and she had no idea how to lead. Not in business, at least. Her loyalty was emotional, not strategic. That made her dangerous in a different way.

They've all failed me.

And yet the pressure never eased. Every day it mounted — decisions, deals, projections, image. Always image.

The only way to cope was to retreat. Into distraction. Into beauty.

Women — young, eager, uncomplicated. They didn't argue about board meetings or asset allocation. They didn't throw shade with their eyes at dinner. They listened. They agreed.

They cost him, yes. And now they were *demanding*, money to keep their mouths shut, to stay out of Marion's line of sight. A few thousand here, ten thousand there. But manageable. For now.

Belinda was different, though. Sweet. Young, early thirties, if that. She wasn't clever yet. That was a blessing. He could mould her. Shape her into something elegant. Reliable. Someone who'd be grateful. Someone who wouldn't question the books or the late nights or the silence.

Yes, he thought, *she could be taught.*

The idea had been crystallizing for weeks now. He'd already begun laying the groundwork. It was good, very good, that he'd made Marion sign those papers all those years ago. Back before anyone asked questions about prenups. Before the courts sniffed around for fairness. He'd locked everything down when he married her. The estate. The assets. The house (that was only in his name anyway).

The kids were grown. The company could survive a few waves. And Marion? Marion could be dismissed. With dignity, of course, he wasn't a monster but dismissed all the same.

Cleanly.

It was nearly midnight when the doorbell rang, barely audible over the sighing wind. Reginald moved with purpose, crossing the marble hall and opening the side entrance. There was no chance anyone would see.

Johnny, his solicitor, waited on the step, collar turned up against the cold, a battered briefcase in his hand. The man's eyes were quick, darting up and down the length of the drive as he entered.

They didn't shake hands. Johnny just nodded and followed Reginald into the study.

The meeting was efficient. Johnny laid out the paperwork, Marion would be out of the mansion in a couple of months, passing the relevant sheets across the desk. The Will, everything going to Belinda. Reginald read every word, slowly, with a frown of concentration. He signed with a sharp, steady hand.

"Everything's done?" Reginald asked, not looking up from the final page.

Johnny nodded, snapping his briefcase shut. "I'm off to South Africa in the morning, for two months or more. I have your signature; all copies are secured with my clerk. It's airtight."

Reginald nodded once. "Thank you, Johnny. Have a well-deserved break."

Johnny allowed himself a thin smile, the smile of a man who'd seen too many secrets and was grateful to be leaving them behind. He glanced around the shadowed study. "No one knows about these documents, Mr. Price. I kept your business quiet, as always."

"Good," Reginald said. "You know how it is. Too many eyes. Too many questions."

Johnny was gone within five minutes, melting back into the night, his car slipping quietly down the gravel drive.

No one else in the family knew about Johnny. Reginald kept his affairs and his solicitor to himself. He'd always believed in keeping his leverage invisible, even now, with everything about to change.

Tomorrow, Johnny's plane would land in Cape Town. By then, Reginald thought, his affairs would be set for good.

He poured himself another whisky. Outside, the rain started to fall in earnest. The house, and everything in it, felt more his than ever.

This time, they'll learn who really built all this. And who gets to keep it.

He sat in the quiet for a long while, watching the fire burn low.

About the Author

Alan Moody has always loved a good murder mystery. For him, it's not just about solving the puzzle of whodunit, but also exploring the emotional depth and tangled relationships that lie beneath the surface.

He lives with his wife, their mad dog, Tinker and Silver the cat, in a semi-rural village in Kent, where the quiet surroundings offer the perfect setting for plotting fictional crimes. By day, Alan is a teacher; by night (and early mornings), he escapes into the world of mystery writing.

The Price of Murder is his debut novel, introducing Catherine Forrester — a sharp, determined investigator and the kind of strong female lead Alan has always admired.

If you enjoyed this book, please consider leaving a positive review on Amazon. Reviews make a real difference and help authors like Alan continue sharing stories.

He is currently working on his second book, **Murder in the Sun**, which is set for release in July.

Printed in Dunstable, United Kingdom